Outstanding praise for Tom Dolby and *The Trouble Boy*

The *San Francisco Chronicle* bestseller!
A Main Selection of the InsightOut Book Club!
#1 Amazon.com Gay & Lesbian Bestseller!
#1 InsightOut Book Club bestseller!

"Hip and sexy . . . Dolby's writing is smooth and his flashy scene-setting spot-on . . . [the novel] could win Dolby a solid following."　　—*Publishers Weekly*

"Tom Dolby's debut is an entertaining tableau of the lives and loves of struggling freelancer-cum-aspiring screenwriter Toby Griffin and his own vicious (or vacuous) circle . . . they'll keep you laughing all the way to Sunday brunch."
　　—*Genre*

"The directness of Dolby's observations have a way of nestling up to the reader . . . Toby's modest little corner of the center of the world is so accessible, it's not long before the pages begin to zip along, block by block, like a 5 AM cab ride home through the Village."　　—*The San Francisco Chronicle*

"Tom Dolby has concocted a tart, frothy, and tantalizing novel, one that has the snap, wit, seduction and vitality of a new *Bright Lights, Big City*. Uproariously funny and unexpectedly poignant, *The Trouble Boy* is as juicy and delicious as a Manhattan with a twist."
　　—Melissa de la Cruz, author of *Cat's Meow*

"Tom Dolby's debut novel *The Trouble Boy* is an alternately fun, sexy and serious chronicle of life lived on the guest lists of downtown New York . . . Career woes, substance abuse, sexually transmitted diseases, family matters, and social situations provide this gay male version of Bridget Jones or Carrie Bradshaw with enough drama to fill at least one book (but we're hoping for more). Dolby deftly handles his subject matter, keeping the pages turning and the intrigue stirring."　　—*Next Magazine* (New York)

"It's always great fun to watch a character like Toby wrestle with his demons, because you're never quite sure who's going to win."
　　—Bart Yates, award-winning author of *Leave Myself Behind*

"An accurate depiction of gay-boy life in the Big Apple . . . the lesson of the book is that nothing good happens in life until you start living for the present."　　—*Out.com*

"A racy romp of fabulosity, fierceness, scandal, and enlightenment."
　　—Michael Musto, *The Village Voice*

Please turn the page for more extraordinary reviews for Tom Dolby . . .

More outstanding praise for Tom Dolby and *The Trouble Boy*

"Like Tom Wolfe's everlasting satire *Bonfire of the Vanities*, Dolby's novel weaves a tale of someone whose moral compass is called into question in the aftermath of an accident—only *this* book features some hot boy-on-boy action."
— *Instinct*

"*The Trouble Boy* is a gripping debut novel that roars along at a cracking pace, delivering thrills and shocks, as well as poignant moments . . . Smart, sexy, and page-turningly good. . . ."
— *Bay Windows* (Boston)

"Tom Dolby may have accomplished something very smart here—a book about veneer composed entirely of that veneer, but exposing, in its final moments, a sweetly beating heart."
— *MetroWeekly* (Washington, DC)

"Breakout novelist Tom Dolby emerges as the new It Boy of gay literature."
— *The Dallas Voice*

"Dolby's debut novel—about being gay and 22, yearning for love but settling (for now) for sex, and striving for literary and monetary success in the shark pool of contemporary Manhattan—is both frothy and solid, a dandy fusion of hugely entertaining satire and seductively humane sentimentality."
— *In Newsweekly* (New England)

"Debuts rarely go this well. Tom Dolby's *The Trouble Boy* is a rare example of mature, seamless writing on the first time out. Not too much needless action, not too many quirky plot twists that don't ever happen to anyone in real life. Just a solid, if flawed, leading man, and a well-written story."
— *OutSmart Magazine* (Houston)

"It turns out that hip urban flashiness, when narrated by a slightly bumbling, less-than-glamorous, unlucky hero, is surprisingly fresh and fun."
— *SFGate.com*

"Exhilarating . . . picture a male version of Carrie Bradshaw from *Sex and the City* . . . Tom Dolby does an excellent job depicting the nightlife of a young, handsome, up-and-coming twentysomething, who happens to be gay. His biting and harsh, yet realistic depiction of Toby is commendable . . . Readers, gay or straight, will relate to Toby's journey."
— *The Nob Hill Gazette*, (San Francisco)

THE TROUBLE BOY

a novel

Tom Dolby

KENSINGTON BOOKS
www.kensingtonbooks.com

KENSINGTON BOOKS are published by

Kensington Publishing Corp.
850 Third Avenue
New York, NY 10022

All Kensington titles, imprints, and distributed lines are available at special quantity discounts for bulk purchases for sales promotions, premiums, fund-raising, educational, or institutional use.

Special book excerpts or customized printings can also be created to fit specific needs. For details, write or phone the office of the Kensington special sales manager: Kensington Publishing Corp., 850 Third Avenue, New York, NY 10022, attn: Special Sales Department; phone 1-800-221-2647.

Kensington and the K logo are Reg. U.S. Pat. & TM Off.

ISBN: 0-7582-0617-8

First Hardcover Printing: March 2004
First Trade Paperback Printing: February 2005
10 9 8 7 6 5 4 3 2

Printed in the United States of America

for my mother and father

The world is our salvation and our danger.
       —Arthur Rimbaud, "Youth"

"I've got too many problems. Really, I'm not the person to get involved with. I'm trouble."

"Honey, trouble is my middle name."
       —Woody Allen and Marshall Brickman, *Manhattan*

ACKNOWLEDGMENTS

My extreme gratitude to everyone who has supported me on the first novelist's journey.

Thanks to my agent, Jandy Nelson at Manus & Associates, for her enthusiasm and encouragement, and to my editor, John Scognamiglio, for his vision and patient guidance.

To my first readers: Sarah Kate Levy, who was always willing, from start to finish, to offer notes on a new draft; John Morgan, who provided invaluable editing advice; and Tom Williams, for his insight and perspective.

To my younger brother, David, for his love and understanding.

To all my friends, but especially Laird Adamson, Kevin Arnovitz, Antonia Clark, Katie Davis, Melissa de la Cruz, Alexander Dodge, Stewart Foehl, Tina and Marisa Frank, Dave Friedman, Tina Hay, Mike Karsh, John L'Ecuyer, Marcia and Bill Levy, Joel Michaely, Abdi Nazemian, Pete Nowalk, Charles Ogilvie, Marissa Shipman, Jesse Slansky, Jay Victor, Ed Vincent, and Mary Clare Williams.

To my writing mentors through the years: John Crowley, Patricia Jones, Shelly Lowenkopf, Gina Nahai, John Rechy, Caroline Rody, and Sarah Tames.

Finally, I would like to give loving thanks to the RTB: Juliano Corbetta, Joe Daniszewski, Ken Henderson, Evan Jacobs, Giovanni Lepori, Nir Liberboim, Ryan Pedlow, Adam Plotkin, Ilya Seglin, Ken Sena, Doug Stambaugh, and Andrea Valeri. You make New York the city that it is for me.

1

Two weeks after I moved to New York, I met Jamie Weissman at one of those parties where people don't talk to anyone they don't know already. The living room of the Chelsea apartment was packed with girls in headbands and guys with banker butt, a condition that afflicts first-year investment analysts who spend too much time at their desks and too little time at the gym. We were in the gayest neighborhood on earth, but it wasn't that kind of party.

I knew I had worn the wrong thing when my plaid clam-diggers, perfect for the early September heat, were met with sneers from a group standing in the hallway. Most people were wearing khakis and I looked like I was ready for the beach.

In the kitchen, I poured myself several fingers of vodka and mixed in some off-brand cranberry juice. A guy in a pink Polo shirt and glasses with tortoise shell frames came up to me.

"Ever get the feeling you're at the wrong party?"

I looked down at him quizzically. His curly chestnut hair was receding, more like a thirty-year-old's than someone who was probably twenty-two, twenty-three tops.

"Oh, never mind," he continued. "Sometimes I just say whatever comes into my head. I'm sort of A.D.D. that way. I take Ritalin for it."

I never understood people who bragged about the meds they were on. I had been taking sixty milligrams of Paxil every day for the past four years to combat my depression, but I didn't go around telling people about it.

"Hey, can you pour me some of that?" he asked.

I poured him some vodka, and he dropped in a few ice cubes.

"You want a mixer?" I held up a bottle of tonic water. I thought it was obnoxious when people drank booze straight to show off.

"Naw, it's a taste I acquired at prep school. Gets you drunk faster."

"Where'd you go?" I asked. I had gone to a small boarding school in Connecticut, the kind whose glossy catalogs were featured in *The Preppy Handbook.*

"Oh, it was in Jersey. I was a day student. Actually, most people were day students. But we played all the other prep schools." He sipped his drink. "You're not part of this Princeton crowd, are you? 'Cause I've never seen you before."

"I went to Yale," I admitted.

"Ecch, New Haven."

New Haven was a place where your car would be broken into if you left change on the dashboard, but I still hated snobbery about my college town.

We gulped our drinks.

"This is so weird," he said, "hanging out with so many 924 people. It's like work."

"Sorry?"

"Oh, God." He laughed and wiped a drop of sweat from his bony forehead. "Okay, like the digits on a phone, 429 is G-A-Y, so that backwards is 924, get it?"

"You're gay?" I should have guessed by the pink shirt; no real men wore preppy pink anymore.

"Yeah. Aren't you? 'Cause if you aren't, then I've just made a big fucking idiot of myself."

It could be fun, posing as straight. Should I hold out a little longer?

"No, I am," I finally said. It must have been my pants that gave me away. "I just didn't expect to meet anyone—"

"Neither did I! When we got here, I was like, fifteen minutes, that's it! And then we get into this conversation with this guy, and before I know it, I've had four vodkas, and I'm like, shit, where did the night go? Come sit with us, we're in the bedroom. You can smoke there." He offered his hand. "I'm Jamie Weissman."

"Toby Griffin," I said, shaking his hand in an odd gesture of formality. I followed him through the living room into the bedroom.

I had spent the past four years in New Haven at that venerable university that promised light and truth to those who passed through its portals. What I had found instead was beer and boys. After a sexless four years at boarding school, I was ready to sleep with every available gay undergrad in the tristate area. It was at a Lesbian, Gay, Bisexual, and Transgender Co-op dance (a mouthful, to be sure—they figured if you could say it, you were really gay) that I got drunk on cheap rum punch and allowed myself to be seduced by Kent Simmons, a sophomore whose room in Davenport College was plastered with advertisements from fashion magazines. I learned from Kent the technique I would use for the next four years: attract, anesthetize, and go in for the kill. It served him well that night, and resulted in a six-week relationship, the first of many during my college years. I had never been able to break that six-week barrier; like divine intervention, something always came between me and the object of my affection.

Now that I was in New York, I was desperate to meet new people. Though a number of friends from college had landed in the city, I didn't want random play dates, scattered through the city like birdseed. I wanted a package deal, a take-it-all-or-leave-it, one-phone-call-means-dinner-for-six. So when a distant acquaintance had invited me to his housewarming bash, I accepted the invitation, though I hated showing up at parties alone.

The bedroom of the apartment was filled with smoke.

"Here, sit on this side," Jamie said, moving over on the couch.

"Why?"

"It's my good side. I'm deaf in my right ear. I had meningitis when I was a baby."

I sat down on his good side and lit a cigarette.

Jamie introduced me to his friend David. "We work at Pelham Robertson together. Investment banking. What do you do?"

"I'm a freelance writer," I said. My last professional piece had been published over a year ago, when I interned at *Flix,* an indie film magazine. Currently, I was gainfully unemployed. That it was already September and I didn't have a job made me feel like a loser.

"Who do you write for?" Jamie asked.

"Lots of places." I named a few publications that I had written for in previous summers. I knew, though, that freelancing wasn't going to keep me in vodka cranberries; a steady editorial position was in order.

"Are you looking for something permanent?" David asked. He had a slight Minnesota accent that reminded me of the hockey players from my high school.

"I know a site that's hiring," Jamie offered. "CityStyle.com. I think they're looking for a nightlife editor."

Even though I was getting career leads from a couple of investment bankers, I made a mental note to check out the site. The summer before last, while reporting for *Downtown File,* a glossy monthly, I had become quite adept at balancing a notebook, a drink, and a cigarette all at once. Unfortunately, *Downtown File* had folded after its publisher was arrested for dealing coke out of his loft.

Jamie launched into a story about his parents, two dermatologists who lived in Upper Montclair. ("The nice part of Jersey," he explained. "Near where *The Sopranos* is filmed.")

"My parents, they don't understand 429 people. They always refer to it as that 'disgusting lifestyle.' I don't think I'll ever be able to tell them."

He spoke to me urgently, as if I were a long-lost soul mate he had recently rediscovered.

"This crowd is depressing," David said. "Let's get going."

Jamie invited me to join them for a drink at G, a bar off Seventh Avenue. Before we left, I stopped by the bathroom to check my acne. Everything seemed under control. I always looked better after I'd had a few drinks.

I opened the bathroom door to find two jocks talking in the hall. "Can you believe Jamie Weissman is a fag?" one asked the other.

I stared the two down, disgusted, before leaving the party.

Once we were on the street, Jamie looked ridiculously thin, like a rat that had been drenched in water, as he tried to keep pace with the buff David. I later learned that no matter how many protein shakes, late night food deliveries, or sessions he had with his trainer, Jamie was never able to gain any weight. It was like a reverse thyroid condition, one many guys would kill for, though it made Jamie miserable.

David, however, had definite potential. A hulking giant of a guy, he looked like someone who could take care of me. And an investment banker! Finance types had always bored me, but somehow the idea they could be gay had never crossed my mind. It made the prospect of number-crunching just a little more appealing. David, I was sure, was smart and sensitive. I would cook him dinner each night and he would entertain me with tales of adventure in high finance. I would iron his shirts—well, I would send them out to be ironed—and make sure a fresh latte and the paper were waiting for him in the morning. . . .

We arrived at G. A lounge with pulsing disco remixes and sullen boys stirring their frozen Cosmopolitans, it was worlds away from the party around the corner.

"Hey, sexy boys!" shouted a young guy sitting on a leather banquette. He had a South American accent and was a dead ringer for Ricky Martin, if Ricky Martin were twenty and wore deconstructed jeans and Prada sneakers. He gave Jamie a peck on the cheek and David a kiss on the lips. "I was waiting for like two hours at the Big Cup!"

"You wouldn't have liked the party anyway," David said.

"I have to keep you out of trouble, you know!" Ricky Martin bounced up and down on the tips of his sneakers.

"There wasn't any trouble for us to get into," Jamie said. "But we did meet Toby." He motioned to me. "Toby, this is David's boyfriend Alejandro."

I offered my hand, but Alejandro pulled me closer and kissed me on both cheeks. "I'm from Argentina," he said. "That's how we like to do it there." He looked me over. "Oooh, I love your pants!"

Though my future wedding plans with David were ruined, I was still charmed by this little South American pixie, who explained to me that he was studying menswear design at Parsons. The four of us ordered drinks and sat down, Jamie once again arranging himself so I was on his good side.

"I had this boyfriend senior year," Jamie said, leaning in towards me. "We met online, and it turned out he was the head of our debate team. Totally closeted. So was I. We used to meet in these random places to have sex—classrooms and whatnot—to keep the secret from our roommates. Now he's working for a Republican congressman in D.C."

"Are you still seeing each other?" I asked.

"He dumped me for a freshman who joined the squad."

I wasn't sure what to say. It was pathetic. "I'm sorry," I offered.

"No, it was okay. I outed him the next day by writing anonymous emails to a few of his friends."

"Oh, my God," I said. This guy was the Joe McCarthy of Princeton. "How long had you been dating?"

"Quite a while, actually. Almost six weeks." He sipped his martini. "How about you? Are you single?"

I nodded.

"This is so cool! You're like the first person I've met in New York who really has my background, you know?" He grinned at me, a little drunk, as if certain I would say the same thing.

"I guess so." I wasn't interested in playing into his class-conscious act.

"So, do you want to go somewhere?" he asked me.

It was this easy, sometimes. But I didn't think I wanted to do anything with Jamie. He wasn't attractive enough to be a one-night stand, and he was too spastic to be a boyfriend. Though I hadn't been with anyone in over a month, I thought Jamie could be a friend. Experience had always shown me the best way to meet cute guys was to get to know their less cute friends.

"I should be getting home," I said.

He looked disappointed, but not surprised.

Jamie gave me his home, work, and cell numbers, along with his email. After considering it for a moment, I decided to risk it and give him my home number. He walked me out to the street and I hailed a cab. We hugged.

"Wow, it was really amazing meeting you," he said. "I hope we can, you know, get together soon." I was sure I saw the beginning of tears in his eyes.

"I'm sure," I said, though I wasn't. As I got into the cab, he stood there on the street watching me, forlorn, as if among New York's entire twentysomething population, I was his only hope for a healthy relationship.

The next day, I checked out the CityStyle site. It was a hip online guide, the perfect next step in my career as a writer. I found the job listing for the position of nightlife editor and put together a package of clips, including several pieces from years past uncovering what I thought were major cultural trends, phenomena like drag kings and Japanese anime-inspired fashion.

At the end of the week, I was sitting in the office of Sonia Chang, editrix-in-chief of CityStyle.com. She wore a slim pants suit with a designer tank top and blue contact lenses that made her eyes appear unnaturally bright. She had on just enough eyeliner to look like she had stepped out of a Gucci ad. I had to admit, I was afraid of her.

"So you're just out of college," she said, her gaze cutting right through me. "What makes you think you're right for this job?"

As she tapped her pen on the desk, my heart started racing.

"I've done my fair share of nightlife reporting." There, that was good: confident, direct.

"But are you really in with the whole scene? I mean, the writers we have working for us live and breathe what they do. Fashion, food, nightlife, that's their thing. I need to know what qualifies you above the other people I've got lined up here. Some of them have been doing this stuff for years."

"I've been going out in the city since I was seventeen. Half the doormen in the city know me by name. Hell, I've even slept with some of them," I said. I had actually only had a one-night stand with a club kid who occasionally promoted at Kurfew, but the doorman line seemed like it would get Sonia's attention.

"That's good. But you've got to be objective, you know. That's the most important thing." She lowered her voice. "We get a dozen press releases a day touting the hottest spot in town from these PR idiots, and they don't know shit." She waved her hand at the garbage heap of editorial samples that filled her office—gift bags, beauty products, party invitations, bulging press kits. "Like I'm going to let some bitch in a little black dress with a cell phone plastered to her ear tell me what's cool."

She paused to take a sip of her iced coffee. I smiled, and I was sure I caught the glimmer of a smile in her look back at me.

"I know editorial is pretty wary of the whole dot-com thing these days. Company doesn't make it through its next round of financing and, *poof!* everyone's laid off. I need to know that's not a problem for you, that you can roll with the punches. I tell everyone, if you're looking for security, this is the wrong business to be in."

Sonia stood up and paced back and forth behind her desk. She was framed by an enormous poster from a book called *The Illustrated Couple in America* that featured a nude man and woman, both covered in tattoos. I was having trouble focusing on what she was saying. Was the man's penis really tattooed or was that just a shadow?

"So what do you think?" Sonia said. "Oh, the poster gets everyone."

I blushed. But wasn't every writer a voyeur?

"You're not afraid to look," she continued. "That's good if you're going to be writing about nightlife."

"What exactly is your revenue model for the site?" I asked. I could have a head for business, if I wanted to.

"We've got several potential buyers lined up. Large media conglomerates. We just need to make it through our next round of financing and then we're golden. Most of our competition has already been wiped out. And we have some very high-profile investors that we can pull out as ammunition if we need to." She paused to fix a strap on her Jimmy Choo heels. "Anyway, you would receive stock options, along with a benefits package. I would also need you to sign a confidentiality and noncompete agreement. If I pick you, I don't want you moonlighting for *Time Out* or *Paper.*"

"What about on other topics?" Though the CityStyle offer was decent, I would still be able to use some supplementary income.

She pulled out a burgundy MAC lipstick and started applying it with the help of a small mirror. "Other topics are fine," she said, looking at me out of the corner of her eye. "Just nothing on nightlife, fashion, restaurants—you know, nothing on what we do."

She put down the lipstick and mirror. "But frankly, if I pick you for this job, you're not going to have the time or the energy."

After the interview, I headed back to the small one-bedroom on East Seventh Street that I was subletting from a German woman who had moved in down the block with her rocker boyfriend. It was a third-floor walkup, with enough room for a bed, my computer, and Gus, my overweight orange and white tabby. When I moved in, the walls of my apartment had been painted a sickly eggshell white that had seen too many years of dust, pets, cigarette smoke, and rough sex. My sublettor had given me permission to paint the living room an art gallery white and the bedroom a matte midnight blue.

That week, the entire apartment was covered in drop cloths, so every time the phone rang, I would bound over to it across the slippery plastic, leaping over sticky paint trays and cans, and check my caller ID. At least twice a day, it read "Pelham Robertson," and at least twice a day, I let it go to voice mail. It was creepy the way Jamie kept calling and not leaving a message. I was grateful to him for suggesting the CityStyle job, but I was worried about how I was expected to return the favor. More specifically, I didn't know what to say if he propositioned me again. I always had trouble saying no.

On Monday afternoon, I picked up the phone when it rang.

I heard someone crunching on what sounded like candy. "Hi," he finally said.

"Why do you keep calling me and not leaving a message?"

"You're never home."

"You didn't answer the question."

"Look, I wanted to get you in person, okay? We're going to B Bar tomorrow night. Do you want to meet up?"

"I could do that," I said. I hated coming off like an asshole, but Jamie seemed to encourage that kind of behavior, like a person wearing the proverbial "kick me" sign. He was a cautionary tale about the perils of appearing too eager.

"David and Alejandro and a few other people will be there," he said, as if to sweeten the deal. "We'll be sitting in a booth in the back room."

My call waiting beeped. "I have to go," I said.

It was Sonia from CityStyle.

"I hope you're still available," she said. I heard her take a slurp of her iced coffee.

I said I was. I couldn't have been any more available.

"Good," she said. "I probably shouldn't tell you this, but the other chick—you know, one of those types who has her own Web site and posts everything she's ever written on it?—didn't show, and the guy with all the experience turned out to be pushing fifty. So, Toby—"

"Yeah?"

"Don't disappoint me."

I knew working at CityStyle wasn't what my parents had in mind when they said they would support my living in New York. Since writing and editing were not the most lucrative of careers, they had agreed to cover my rent for a year. If I could sustain myself after that, I could stay in the city. If not, I would have to move back to San Francisco, live with my parents, and join my dad's firm or find other suitable work. After living under their roof for the first fourteen years of my life, I knew that moving to San Francisco would be an enormous step backwards. I had to make it in New York.

My ultimate goal was to finish one of the four screenplays I had in progress, but that was an avocation far too dark and embarrassing to admit to anyone. These days, everyone was working on a screenplay. I had briefly considered getting into the film industry full-time—my major had been film studies—but I didn't want to spend my time reading other people's screenplays. I wanted to write my own. And I wanted them to be New York stories, not Hollywood fantasies.

My mother and father had viewed my goal of screenwriting

as if I had announced that I wanted to become a professional potter or sell organic vegetables in Union Square. My mother was a fashion designer who owned a small couture house in San Francisco that catered to the society crowd, and her dresses were sold at Saks and Bendel's in New York. My father owned a venture capital firm that specialized in biotechnology.

My mother's first boutique had been written up in the *New York Times* when she was twenty-five; my father had made his first million just one year out of business school, after he had invested in a few choice tech stocks. Since both of my parents had prospered in their twenties, I had always been expected to as well. Their success had ingrained in me a fear of growing old too quickly, a fear of not putting my mark on the world at an early age. I wanted them to be proud of me, to respect me for the path I was choosing. Instead, I feared that they considered me a dilettante. I recognized that they were hard acts to follow, but acknowledging that didn't make it any easier knowing that I might never reach their level of success.

It wasn't that they were infallible, either. Though my parents had enough money, it was never as much as people thought. My father had been floating the couture house for years with the revenue from his own company. My mother refused to expand her offerings to include ready-to-wear, fragrances, or a bridge collection, and so she was both blessed and cursed with a brand that was worth more than its bottom line. A certain kind of woman would kill to own an Isabella Griffin original, but selling dresses one by one would never put us among the ranks of the Very Rich. My mother once said that if she were paid every time her dresses appeared in *Vogue* or *W,* she'd be running a New York-based fashion house by now and we'd be living on Fifth Avenue. Sometimes I wished that had happened.

CityStyle rented its small suite of offices from Ariana Richards Public Relations, a firm that had experienced a meteoric rise in the past few years. The ARPR loft was located on the fifth floor of a former sewing machine factory in Chelsea; the space had a bank of windows that looked out on a sea of fire escapes and faded advertisements from the early 1900s. We were the new sweatshop workers, the remaining dot-commers who had come to the city in hopes of a few press clips and a steady paycheck.

Though we shared the same vantage point, the employees of ARPR had different goals than we did. They lived in a world of movie premieres, nightclub openings, and dinners held in honor of bold-faced names who had been flown in for the occasion. Their leader, Ariana Richards, arrived at the office no earlier than eleven each morning, fresh from her personal trainer and blow-out, though she demanded that her employees show up promptly at nine. Our workday didn't start until ten, but under the steely gaze of Sunny Diebenstahl, Ariana's Teutonic office manager, we always felt late.

Though the offices made our operation look slick, the truth was that we were second-class citizens. Visitors to the CityStyle offices were directed by Ariana's receptionist with a weary "They're back there," and a wave of her manicured nails. Since Ariana didn't allow us any signage of our own, the writers, photographers, and illustrators who passed through our offices often assumed we were simply a division of the ARPR empire, a thought that would have horrified her and her legions of Manolo Blahnik-heeled minions.

When I arrived on Tuesday morning, Sonia set me up at a terminal next to Donovan Tripp, the site's restaurant editor. Though Donovan was my age and had only been working at the site for three months, he already gave off the appearance of having Made It. Next to his monitor was a Rolodex overflowing with business cards and scribbled phone numbers; his file trays were carefully organized with notes on upcoming pieces. Over his desk, he had tacked up a paraphrase of that old Woody Allen joke about the food being terrible and the portions too small. His sandy blond hair was styled with insouciance, while his tanned and freckled skin made me imagine weekends spent in the Hamptons.

There was nothing sexier than someone who was attractive *and* had it all together.

"So you're Toby Griffin," he said to me, turning away from his monitor and removing his chunky glasses.

I grinned shyly. "It's great to meet you. You did that Morning-After Hangover Food piece, right? I really liked it."

"Yeah? I thought it stank."

I reddened as he handed me a photocopied packet. "Here's the instructions for the site's publishing system. Should be self-explanatory, but let me know if you have any questions. I'm usually not this crazed, but Sonia gave me several short deadlines, so I'm swamped today."

I nodded, and started organizing my work area as I tried to avoid amorous thoughts about my co-worker. As I busied myself with learning the intricacies of the site's online publishing system, I found it difficult to concentrate. Donovan had the potential to be an occupational hazard.

Sonia gave me a dozen clubs to review in the coming week, in addition to the task of rewriting almost two hundred old reviews in light of new developments in the nightlife world. It was just the three of us in editorial, not including interns, plus a few marketing and finance people who worked in the other offices. Most of the site's writers worked from home and then emailed in their work. To the outsider, the site gave off the appearance of being a much larger operation, but such was the man-behind-the-curtain quality of Web publishing.

Later that afternoon, I was treated to my first glimpse of Lola Copacabana, one of CityStyle's nightlife reporters. I would be editing her column, "Whatever Lola Wants." I knew Lola wrote for the site, but I didn't know that, unlike the site's other writers, she would be coming in once a week to compose her piece.

"Lola doesn't have a computer at home," Donovan explained, rolling his eyes.

Lola was known around the city as a post-op transsexual nightclub performer who had come to New York from Miami eleven years ago. While in Miami, she had peddled an act in which she impersonated Marilyn Monroe, smearing herself with birthday cake during her "Happy Birthday, Mr. President" number and then shooting herself in the head with a squirt gun filled with pig's blood. A nightclub in New York had flown her up for the weekend to perform and she ended up staying in the city permanently. In order to offset her act's significant investment in dry cleaning, Lola quickly found work go-go dancing or performing nearly every night of the week.

Donovan told me it had taken Ariana's office—especially Sunny, who had strict ideas about appropriate office attire—a few weeks to become accustomed to this milky skinned, collagen-enhanced, silicone-breasted wonder of the world. When Ariana's account reps discovered that Lola in a photo with any celebrity made instant gossip column fodder, Lola became a regular fixture at ARPR events, and everyone in the office now welcomed her presence.

Today, Lola sashayed into the office wearing a yellow sundress with bamboo platform sandals and carrying a Japanese paper umbrella. Her hair was dyed jet black; combined with her outfit and pale skin, it made her look like a Japanese woodcut come to life.

I introduced myself to her when she sat down at a nearby terminal.

"Oh, hi," she said, looking at me as if I were the one who had undergone sex reassignment surgery. "I heard about you." Her voice rattled slightly, as if she were a heavy smoker; though she was more delicate and beautiful than many women, she could never shake that slight hint of testosterone. Her lips were as hornet-stung as they seemed at night, and her skin was poreless, like a Barbie doll's.

I spoke to her as if talking to a small child who was sure not to understand. "I'll be editing your work from now on. I've read most of your columns and I was wondering why you switch from first to third person." Lola's columns, while not unoriginal in their observations, were the grammatical and narrative equivalent of a train wreck.

"I use first person when I want to express my deepest self, how I really am inside. I use third person when I write about myself the way others see me."

"We may have to talk about that, because I'm not sure if it's working."

"Okay," she said, pausing to examine a nail. "Oh, I'm performing at B Bar tonight. I'll be on a platform in the back room with a few of the other girls."

"What will you be doing?" I asked.

"Absolutely nothing," she said, a blank look on her face. "It's a conceptual piece."

When I arrived at B Bar that night, there was a line stretched all the way to the Bowery. Converted from a former gas station, the combination restaurant-bar-lounge was now all about gas station chic: photographs of trucks, blue and orange trim, wood paneling. It was the perfect backdrop for this weekly parade of the beautiful and the bizarre.

"Step aside, step to the back of the line," barked the enormous black bouncer to a crowd trying to storm the velvet rope.

I approached, reaching into my bag for the stack of business cards Sonia had printed up at Kinko's. "Toby Griffin, Nightlife Editor," they read. I spoke to the doorman, a rail-thin man with a goatee and blue-tinted glasses whom I had never seen working before. After I explained that I was doing a review, he still seemed skeptical. "City what? Citysearch, did you say?"

"No, CityStyle. It's a site about nightlife, fashion—" My hands were clammy. What if I had to wait in line?

"Never heard of it. Is it a gay Web site?"

"No, it's not. I mean, we have a large gay readership, but, no, it's not exclusively gay." I remembered the Lola connection. "Lola writes for it."

"This is a gay night. Are you sure you belong here?"

"Look, it has a very gay sensibility. And I'm gay. Isn't that good enough?"

"Prove it."

Just as I contemplated grabbing a boy off the street and kissing him, the doorman laughed. "I'm just giving you shit. Go on in. But I better see that review in a couple of days." He turned to his assistant. "Write that down for me, will you? CityStylin.com."

"CityStyle.com," I said.

He laughed. "Whatever."

After grabbing a vodka cran at the front bar, I found the boys sitting in the back room as promised. The back lounge was outfitted as a ski-lodge-slash-rec-room, with the final touch being a series of Nan Goldin-esque portraits of drag queens, heroin addicts, and Filipino prostitutes lining the walls. Through the windows, the trees in the garden were decorated like a Midwestern Christmas with strands of twinkling lights, a glittering paradise for those who had once bitten the apple of knowledge, but were now content to drink apple martinis. Like an outpost of the Velvet Mafia, Rupert Everett, John Waters, and Rufus Wainwright were parked conspiratorially in a nearby booth.

"Hey," Jamie said. "We weren't sure if you'd show."

Jamie, David, and Alejandro were sitting in a brown leather banquette with another friend, Brett Perotta. A little guy, he had a body created by too many trips to the gym and too many helpings of his mother's ziti. To prove his bulk did not equal fat, he had a habit of lifting up his shirt to reveal his perfectly formed abdominals, something he did several times over the course of the evening.

Unlike Brett and Alejandro, David and Jamie were still wearing their suits from the office, ties loosened, sleeves rolled up. "We just got off work," Jamie explained.

"You worked until 10 P.M.?" I asked.

"Yeah, I-banking. The hours are insane."

"Except when you sneak in at ten in the morning," David said. "We're supposed to be there at eight. His secretary covers for him when he's late."

Jamie grinned. "Sometimes I leave my jacket there overnight, so if people come by my desk early, they think I'm in the restroom or something. I'm sorry, I have a life, you know?" He held up his drink.

I pulled out my pack of Merit Ultra Lights, and Jamie took a cigarette for himself.

"I'm trying to quit," he said.

I asked him how they'd all met.

"During orientation for work, David and I were in the same group. I didn't want anyone to know, I mean, no one knows we're, you know, 429, but David kept following me around and asking me what I was doing each weekend."

"I didn't know anyone in the city," David said.

"One day, I just told him, 'I'm going dancing at the Roxy,' to see if he would get it. That's a good way to tell if people are 429, to ask what clubs they go to, and on which nights." I had never thought of nightlife listings as a way of running a witch hunt. "Everyone's really homophobic at work. We have to be careful."

"And how did you meet everyone?" I asked Brett.

He laughed and Jamie blushed.

"We met online," Jamie admitted. "I mean, nothing ever happened. It's a good way to meet people . . . well, sometimes it is."

So Jamie was an AOL slut. I looked at him askance.

"Oh, come on, don't tell me you've never done it," he said.

"I never have," I said. I had heard about friends' adventures in the chat rooms, but it had never interested me. It seemed like such a calculating way to get someone into bed. I preferred to wake up next to someone in the morning and pretend it had all happened by magic.

On the other side of the room, Lola was standing on a platform, posed like the Venus de Milo rising from her shell. She was naked except for a translucent sheath wrapped around her lower half. Having begun her transformation at age sixteen, she had attended to every detail over the years, including having a pair of ribs removed, further highlighting her concave stomach. Her nipples stood at attention, large as silver dollars; her black hair was piled on top of her head like an expensive hat. Despite Lola's gyrations, most of the room—it was getting crowded with a mix of fashion queens and young professionals—pretended not to notice the spectacle taking place directly over its head. I pulled out my pad and made a few notes.

"That woman is such a freak," Jamie said. "She's got so much plastic in her, she's probably flame-retardant. Do you want another drink?" He motioned to my empty glass, and I nodded as he got up.

"It's so good to see you!" he said, giving my shoulders a quick grab, as if we were on a soccer team and he was motivating me for the final quarter.

I tensed up, then tried to relax.

Jamie, undeterred by my lack of enthusiasm, left to get the drinks.

Brett had gone to talk to someone across the room, so I was left with David and Alejandro. In this room full of swarming singles, they sat together like two smug suburbanites who had just come back from their honeymoon.

"You know, Jamie is really into you. He can't stop talking about you," David said.

"You two would make a cute couple," Alejandro said, as I almost gagged.

"What are you, his PR machine? Please, he's totally not my type. But don't tell him that—I don't want to hurt him."

"Of course you don't."

I squirmed as I realized Donovan was standing beside me. He had on the same light blue cotton sweater he had worn earlier that day, but now his khaki cargo pants were stained with ink, the result of too many hours at the office.

It turned out that Donovan and Jamie were friends from Princeton. The banker boys had formed a little posse over the summer, galvanized by their status as gay outcasts in the mostly straight world of finance; Donovan and Alejandro provided just the right amount of bohemian color. They were actively seeking new members, and I had arrived right in the middle of rush.

Since I had already had a few drinks, I felt more relaxed around Donovan than I had at the office. I couldn't help thinking about what it would be like to bring him home.

Donovan slid into the booth, sitting next to me. "So I'm outside, getting out of a cab, and this queen yells at me, 'Oh, my God, that man's wearing a sweater!' as if it's a hundred degrees or something. I mean, I know it's warm out, but it wasn't this morning, and I came straight from the office. Of course, that guy will probably be wearing the same sweater himself next week, since he saw I didn't have to wait in line."

"Why didn't you have to wait in line?" I asked.

"Please, I never wait. I'm press."

"I hope you didn't tell them you were doing a review."

"Don't worry about it; they know me. You'll get the hang of this soon. Before you know it, you'll be the King of New York."

"Queen," David said.

"*I* want to be the Queen of Seventh Avenue," said Alejandro, who had a habit of continually bringing the conversation back to himself. At some point, I would have to mention to him that my mother was a fashion designer.

Donovan told me about his history as a food writer, and how he had launched the first serious restaurant column for the *Daily Princetonian* by traveling into New York to review downtown restaurants.

"My parents give me shit about being a food writer with an Ivy League degree," he said. "But food is about everything: art, culture, history. People think of food writing like it's not the real thing. But it's about the journey, you know?"

Donovan was in the middle of telling me about his childhood in Kansas City when Jamie came back and interrupted everyone with a tirade about the long line for the restroom.

He looked at Donovan. "I didn't know you were coming tonight," he said as he handed me my drink and sat down at the other end of the booth.

"What's that about?" I whispered to David.

"Donovan sleeps with everyone Jamie is interested in. Jamie's afraid that he'll steal you away."

I scoffed as a tingle ran to my groin.

"Oh, my God," Jamie said, pointing. "It's the guy from *The Real World.*"

I resisted the urge to slap his arm down. "You mean the gay guy from this season?"

I never watched the show anymore, but I recognized him from a photo in *Entertainment Weekly*. His features were striking, framed by curly blond hair cut short on the sides; he wore a suit and loosened tie, and was carrying a large duffel bag by its shoulder strap. And he was headed right by our banquette.

Like a snake charmer, I willed him to talk to us.

Come to me, but don't bite my head off.

He saw us, but kept moving.

Fuck it. I would have to make the first move. Emboldened by the drinks, I said hello.

"Hey," he said, sizing up our table.

I asked him if he was coming from work. It was a stupid question, but it got him talking and before we knew it, Real World

Guy was sitting down with us. I could see that Donovan was impressed.

"We should get shots," Jamie said, and Real World Guy agreed that this was a good idea. Jamie waved to a nearby waitress to bring us tequila and limes.

I was convinced that if I was going to seduce Real World Guy, the best way would be to pretend I didn't know who he was. And he went right along with it, until he got to the part about explaining what he had been doing for the last year. "I was on this show," he said.

"Oh, really?" I said. "What show?"

"It's on MTV," he said. "You know, *The Real World.*"

"Oh, that show!" I said. "I don't watch much MTV."

"Yeah, well, I was on it," he said.

"That must get you laid a lot," Donovan said.

I glared at him.

Our shots arrived, and we downed them, licking the salt off our hands and sucking on limes. It felt like spring break in Cabo, not that I had ever done spring break in Cabo. It was goofy and unsophisticated and made us look like frat boys, but it didn't matter, because we had Real World Guy at our table.

Jamie was obviously having similar thoughts, because after he finished his shot, he turned to me and said, "Don't you just love being part of the Beautiful People?"

I told him to shut up, and hoped Real World Guy hadn't heard him. It was something you could think but weren't supposed to say, like arriving at a party and announcing, "I'm so fabulous!" Anyway, it was ridiculous: while we were all decent-looking, we weren't exactly an Abercrombie & Fitch catalog.

Real World Guy said he should really be going, so I gave him my CityStyle card. When I asked him for his number, he just said, "I'll call you," before disappearing into the crowd, his duffel bag trailing behind him.

"I can't believe you just talked to the guy from *The Real World,*" Jamie said. "That is so incredibly cool." I could tell he was jealous.

"He's never going to call me," I said.

"You never know." Jamie downed his drink. "Do you want another?" he asked, sliding out of the booth.

I gave him money. I could get used to this table service.

"I'm going to see if Brett's around," Donovan said, getting up, "though he's probably lost in hookup land."

David started giggling as soon as Jamie and Donovan were out of earshot. "Oh, my God," he said. "While you were talking with that guy, Jamie whispered to Donovan, 'Hands off, he's mine! I met him first and you're not stealing him away from me!' We call Jamie the cock-blocker."

"Why, was Donovan interested in me?" I stirred the ice around in my glass, suddenly excited again.

"I think he knows it wouldn't be a good idea, since you guys are working together."

I must have looked disappointed, because David piped up again. "Don't worry about it. Jamie said the exact same thing to me when we first met Alejandro. It didn't stop us from getting together." They smiled at each other.

I was starting to get annoyed with David and Alejandro's continual flaunting of their matrimonial bliss. "So," I said to Alejandro, "when does your visa run out?"

"I have as long as I want," Alejandro said. "My father knows people at the Argentinean embassy. Of course, I'm in school now, so it doesn't matter."

I thought about what David and Alejandro had—and what I desperately wanted. I had to make it happen.

Jamie was tapping me on the shoulder. "It's almost two."

I knew the smart thing would be to leave, but I had a good buzz going. I was on my fifth drink, plus a beer I had drunk at home.

"I'm going to stay for another drink," I said. I looked in my wallet; I had just enough for one more.

David, Alejandro, and Donovan took off. Donovan was clearly a long-term project.

I slid into the banquette so Jamie and I had more room. I flagged down the waitress and she brought me another vodka cran. At the next table, there was a guy I didn't recognize sitting with the Velvet Mafia. "That's Cameron Cole," Jamie said. "The guy next to Rufus Wainwright. He used to go to my school when his dad lived in Jersey."

"What's his connection to all those celebs?"

"He's a film producer. He runs a company that's a division of his mom's business."

Since I was drunk, I smiled as I looked at him. He caught my eye, and I looked away. I wanted to talk to him, but what would I say? I would just be another interloper with several unfinished screenplays deep in the bowels of my computer.

Jamie slid closer to me in the booth.

"I should be getting home," I said, and was met with a frustrated look from Jamie. "But give me a call tomorrow. We'll chat."

"Now I know where to reach you," he said. We exchanged cheek kisses before parting.

I stumbled out into the warm Bowery night, the cars whizzing by, and walked east to Avenue A. Maybe Real World Guy would call me tomorrow. We would go on a date and hit it off instantly, realizing we were soul mates. Since he was a bona fide C-list celebrity, we would go to movie premieres and restaurant openings, and my writing career would soar. *New York* magazine would write us up as a gay "Power Couple to Watch," and the two of us would make the *Out* 100. David Geffen would invite us to pool parties in the Hamptons and Fire Island, where he would introduce me to Barry Diller, who would sign me for a three-picture deal based entirely on the quality of my repartee. Barry, as I now called him, would also be interested in CityStyle.com, which he would purchase and take public, making our stock options worth millions. . . .

When I reached my building, there was a homeless teenager sleeping in the entryway near the mailboxes.

"Come on," I mumbled to him. "Go crash somewhere else."

He woke up with a jolt, grabbed his backpack, and tripped down the stairs, seemingly annoyed he had been roused at this hour.

"Cocksucker," he muttered.

*   *   *

I had forgotten to feed Gus the night before, so I was woken in the morning by his mewing at my bedroom door. Since all I had managed to do after getting home was to strip naked and collapse into bed without drinking water or taking a Tylenol, I was now in the throes of a painful hangover. It wasn't the I-scored-and-it-was-worth-it kind, either. It was the kind that meant panic.

It was 11:30 A.M. and I was late for my second day of work.

Donovan greeted me at the office, looking as bright-eyed as he had the night before. My stomach was still churning, my limbs fatigued. "You're lucky Sonia was out at meetings all morning," he said. "She called, and I said you were in the restroom."

"What time did you get in?"

"Nine, like I always do."

"But weren't you exhausted from last night?"

"It's my routine, it never changes. Learn to work hung over, that's my secret."

I slumped down at my desk and wished I could have Donovan's dedication. It was one thing to tie one on in college and sit through a "Films of Alfred Hitchcock" lecture or a screening of *Satyricon* the next day, but it was entirely another to suffer the wages of sin while working. At CityStyle, I was in charge of my own time, and I needed to be alert and organized in order to get everything done.

I opened up my Web browser and decided to do some research on Cameron Cole. I learned that he was twenty-six years old and had graduated from Tufts with a degree in economics. Every summer he had interned for his mother's company, Eastside Pictures. Katherine Cole's company had made its mark with strong female-driven comedies like *Working Moms* and *Relax, It's Just Therapy*. A champion of the niche genre, she had decided her gay son would be the perfect person to exploit that market, so when he graduated, she gave him his own production division that operated under her company's roof. According to a recent profile in the *Advocate,* Cameron liked to spend his time at clubs like Lotus and Bungalow 8 with friends like Alan Cumming, John Waters, and, I was surprised to learn, publicist Ariana

Richards, who represented Cameron and his company. I glanced through the open door towards Ariana's corner office. I hadn't realized I had gotten a job so close to a contact in the film business.

Cameron's production company would be the perfect place to pitch the sci-fi drama I was working on. It was a story called *Breeders* in which most of the world's population is gay, and a select ten percent of the population—the breeders—has to come out as straight. In an age of mandatory artificial insemination, heterosexual sex is prohibited, so the breeders are forced to copulate behind closed doors. I saw it as a societal commentary along the lines of *Planet of the Apes* and *Soylent Green*. When it was released, I would be lauded as a member of the gay cinematic vanguard.

I was on page forty of the screenplay, and had been for the last year and a half.

I was scrolling through more articles about Cameron when Donovan pulled me out of my media-induced daze. "Hey, you want to go to lunch?" he asked. "I'm expensing it. I have to review this new Thai place."

Thai Me Up was in Chelsea and specialized in nouvelle organic Thai cuisine. The waitstaff were hip Thai kids with eyebrow rings and dyed hair.

"This is so Sonia; I knew she would like this place," Donovan said as we both sat down. "She's such a trendoid."

He turned to a waiter. *"Mee krai pood pasa angrit dai bang mai?"* Donovan asked.

The waiter responded in Thai and fetched us menus.

I looked at Donovan, surprised.

"I learned it in college. I'm fluent in Thai."

I was impressed. I had never made it past second year Italian.

"Listen," he said, "there's something you should know."

I felt queasy again. "Yeah?"

"Jamie's crazy about you. He keeps emailing and calling me about you." Donovan waved his arms around in imitation of Jamie. " 'Oh, my God, he's so cute! He's exactly what I've been looking for! He's so WASPy and goyish!' "

" 'WASPy and goyish?' That's such a strange thing to say

about someone." Though many of my friends were Jewish, no one had ever said that about me.

"In addition to not being comfortable with being gay, Jamie secretly wishes he were a WASP," Donovan explained. "I always tease him that his ideal boyfriend would be some sort of Hitler youth. But he's willing to settle for you."

"I'm not interested in him," I said. "There's nothing I can do about that. I mean, I like him as a friend."

"I know," Donovan said. "And I think he knows it, too. Someday, though, I wish someone would just give the guy a chance."

After we ordered, Donovan gave me the lowdown on CityStyle. The guy who had founded it two years ago and served as editor-in-chief had been ousted by the site's investors several months ago after he had been discovered embezzling funds. Sonia had been brought in to refine CityStyle's editorial focus and bring in national advertisers and strategic partners. So far, she had succeeded, but many had their doubts. Donovan told me who the mysterious high-profile investors were: one was an aging pop star who hadn't had a hit in years; another was a law firm specializing in high technology. They were not insignificant parties, but they weren't exactly Madonna or Rupert Murdoch, either.

Though the site was run on a shoestring, it had a healthy public profile. It had been featured two months ago in *Rolling Stone,* and *New York* magazine had covered a recent party for its redesign. It had an estimated 70,000 readers each month, which put it right up there with the best of the other sites of its size.

"The problem," Donovan said, as he cut a piece of mint chicken, "is there's no real revenue stream. Sure, there's advertising, but everyone knows that doesn't work in the long run.

"They used to pay all expenses, for drinks, whatever. The nightlife editor took a car service everywhere, which I think was why he got fired. Now the only person who can expense stuff is me, and even I'm not supposed to order alcohol when I do a restaurant review."

"The perk of free food is good enough for me," I said. "Most of the time all I can hope for is a few lousy drink tickets."

"At least we always get VIP treatment at Ariana's clubs," he said. "That's one of our few benefits for the astronomical rent we pay. Last time we were at Mirror we sat in the booth next to P. Diddy and got free drinks all night."

Donovan told me that three years ago, Ariana had quit her job at an important boutique PR firm and, armed with their database on a Zip disk, started her own business out of a spare cubicle at her dad's office. Her last name was actually Rakowski, which she had changed to Richards. With the help of her father, a producer who had worked with everyone from Tom Cruise to Reese Witherspoon, Ariana had put together a formidable client list that was only strengthened by her seven-nights-a-week networking at the city's plushest nightclubs. Her firm was now one of the top agencies in the city, responsible for film premieres, celebrity representation, nightlife, and corporate products. She had also just scored a major coup by signing on Miles Bradshaw, a notoriously reclusive indie film director, as a client.

Her detractors claimed that while she had a mailing list to kill for, her events involved no creativity whatsoever: she simply threw all her clients together in a room and let the media lap up the carnage. A typical Ariana stunt would be a film premiere attended by her celebrity clients with an after-party at one of her clubs and a gift bag filled with designer fragrances, fashion accessories, and bottled water, all products she represented. Still, everyone attended and wrote up her events because they would be populated with a hip, young, beautiful crowd.

Concurrent with the growth of her business, Ariana herself had become a pseudo-celebrity, often photographed next to her clients as if she were the star. She had been in the headlines most recently after totalling her mother's Audi while speeding back to the city from East Hampton; while she had emerged unscathed, the luxury car was unsalvageable. The tabloids had a field day over her reckless driving: "PR Princess Learns Speed Doesn't Pay" was one headline that Donovan gleefully recited to me.

But Ariana's failures were nothing in light of her successes: she was only twenty-eight years old, and her firm was billing two million dollars a year.

"That's out of control that she's doing so well," I said, leaning back in my chair.

"I know," Donovan said. "And the bitch didn't even graduate from college. Dropped out after three semesters."

"I bet she can't even put a sentence together."

"Last month, I was at the office late, and she asked me to proof a press release she had finished. It was so poorly written that I was like, 'Did you even go to high school?' Most of the time she just has her assistants do everything."

"She's probably the kind of publicist who will read a bad review of her club and then thank you for writing it, because she didn't understand it anyway."

"I panned this restaurant she represents and she had an exotic fruit basket sent to me the next day. I feel sorry for her, though. Her dad died last year of a heart attack, and her mom is one of those crazy Scientologists."

When we got back to the office, Ariana was standing by the front reception desk. The woman she was with looked familiar, but I couldn't place her.

Donovan nudged me. "It's Jordan Gardner," he whispered.

Ariana and her companion glanced at us, then went back to their conversation.

Once we were back at our desks, Donovan reminded me who Jordan Gardner was. She had recently starred in an espionage thriller alongside a famous actor who was twenty years her senior. As the latest British import, her exotic Eurasian looks and mahogany hair with artfully streaked blond highlights had made Jordan a favorite of magazines like *Interview* and *Vanity Fair*.

"She's a hellraiser," Donovan said. "Ariana had a Fourth of July party at her house in the Hamptons and Jordan got so drunk that she decided to dance on a glass coffee table in the living room. The whole thing shattered." He shrugged. "It was on Page Six."

Just at that moment, Ariana came into our office.

"Are you Toby Griffin?" she said to me. "The nightlife guy?" She was about my height, with straightened hair and an obvious nose job.

I nodded.

"It is so good to meet you," she said, shaking my hand. I hoped she couldn't detect my hangover. "I heard you were

Isabella Griffin's son. I love her stuff. My mom wears her all the time."

"Thank you," I said. "I'm sure she'll be glad to hear it."

"Look, if you ever need anything, guest list, comps, whatever, just let me know, okay? I've got a few new clubs opening in the next month, and we could definitely use the publicity."

I thanked her. She was so unassuming. Nice, even.

"She's never like that," Donovan hissed at me. "She must be on new meds."

When I got home that evening, my Powerbook was calling to me, so I popped a frozen dinner in the oven and started writing. I was a page in—my hero had just discovered the breeders living in his basement—when my mind started to wander. I tried to remember which advertising agency Real World Guy said he was working at. I thought it was BMD—Brown Madison Davidson— or was it BMG, like the record company? That didn't sound right. Even if I did find his number, calling would make me seem like a stalker.

Real World Guy could be a Scooby Snack, or he could be something more. An evening with him was what I wanted, needed, desperately. But I knew he probably wasn't going to call. Surely he had forgotten me; once he got home, he had decided I was too ugly or boring to be wasting his time.

But I had to believe something might happen.

2

Over the next month, I became a nightlife contender: I completed fifty new club reviews by going out every night. Some places required visits of an hour or less, while others were all-night affairs, calling for extensive documentation of the ambiance, patrons, music, and décor. I tried to stick to the one-drink-per-venue rule, but sometimes the night got away from me. I brought someone along whenever possible, though many of my friends soon grew tired of my specific needs and requirements for each evening's activity. I became known as a person you could never meet at the same place twice, the nightlife equivalent of a vagrant, a wanderer. The only person who would go anywhere with me, no questions asked, was Jamie; no matter how unfashionable or bizarre the venue—a leather bar in the meatpacking district, a western club in midtown, a Russian mafia hangout in Brighton Beach—Jamie would tag along as my quasi-date. He was starting to grow on me, I had to admit. I enjoyed having an admirer.

When I wasn't with Jamie, Donovan and I were quickly becoming a reporting team: I would partake in free lunches and dinners, giving opinions on gastronomical matters, and he would accompany me to venues that required a real date and not just a companion like Jamie. Of course, it was only I who pretended Donovan and I were dating; at the end of each evening, we would bid each other goodnight with a friendly kiss on the cheek, and the illusion would be broken. I tried to convince myself our nightlife excursions would lead to something, but in the six weeks I had known him, nothing had happened. Still, he made me happy when we were together. It reminded me of being at boarding school, where I had been in love with a handful of boys, none of whom had the slightest clue about my affections but enjoyed the attention nonetheless.

Sonia liked the work I was doing, as I steadily updated the database of entries the previous editor had let fall by the wayside. She was also buoyed by the *Daily News* reporter who had come by the office several times in the past week to interview us for a series of articles on the "Dot-Com Survivors," as we were being called. Any press was good press, she said, and would put us closer to attracting the investment that would take us to the next level.

Even Ariana continued to be friendly to us, which Donovan was convinced was the work of her shrink and not what he called her "true evil self." On Ariana's invitation, Donovan and I even attended a small film premiere together, which made Jamie and the boys jealous.

One evening, just as we were about to meet everyone for dinner, I noticed my voice mail light flashing. It was Real World Guy. "Sorry I didn't call sooner," his message said. "I was really busy, and then I thought I lost your number and I couldn't remember the name of your site. Anyway, let's hang out, maybe go for a drink or something."

I started getting excited as I realized last month's fantasy might come to fruition. And even if it didn't work out, Real World Guy's attentions might make Donovan realize I wasn't such a bad catch after all.

When I jotted down Real World Guy's home number, a 718, I was quickly dragged back down to reality.

Real World Guy didn't live in Manhattan. That was so, well, real. Dating people who didn't live in Manhattan meant forty-five-minute subway rides and expensive gypsy cab tabs. For Real World Guy, though, I was willing to give dating a 718 a chance. I saved the message so I could listen to it over the next few days. I knew it was pathetic, but no one had to know.

I told Donovan about the message as we walked down Seventh Avenue, but he seemed indifferent. I hoped I would get a better reaction from everyone else. After all, what was the point of making a hot date with a quasi-celebrity if no one cared?

"He called you back?" shrieked Jamie when Donovan and I arrived for dinner at a bistro in Chelsea. "I can't believe it!"

"Congratulations!" David said. "You scored!"

Alejandro clapped his hands, and Brett toasted me. It was all a bit embarrassing, as if I were some kind of dating cripple who had miraculously gotten up and walked.

"Look, don't get too excited. I haven't scored yet," I admitted. Despite my false modesty, I had a good feeling about this one. Real World Guy might turn out to be the Real Thing.

I called him back the next day and we made a date to have dinner at Rialto, an Italian restaurant on the Lower East Side that Donovan had recommended. I was running late that evening, since I had wanted to shower and change after work, so I rolled in at ten after eight. I had worn one of my nice outfits: khakis, Polo shirt, Prada loafers I had bought two years ago on deep discount at the Barneys Warehouse Sale. I didn't want to be dressed like a slob if he showed up in work clothes. I was looking good, except for the blotchy red remains of a pimple on my chin that I had slathered with cover-up. While I was getting dressed, I had flipped on MTV. They were running a marathon of this season's episodes, and I saw him hanging out in a corner of the impossibly large living room. Compared to his gregarious housemates, he seemed shy, reserved.

He was apparently running late himself, so I gave my name to the maitre d', ordered a glass of red wine, and sat at the candle-lit bar. Ten minutes went by, then twenty, and no sign of him. Had I gotten the date wrong? Or was I being stood up? I was too embarrassed to call Donovan's cell and find out what the evening's dinner plans were, so I decided to sit and finish a second glass of wine before leaving, just on the off chance that Real World Guy showed. Since it was Thursday night, the restaurant was filling up with a colorful mix of fashionistas who were grooving to the live DJ at the bar. I felt silly sitting alone, as if I had "stood up" written all over me. I wondered if I could slip out without the maitre d' noticing.

At 8:45, Real World Guy tapped me on the shoulder.

"I am so incredibly sorry," he said, and I believed him. "I got stuck on the subway coming from my apartment, and there was no way I could call you." He gave me a peck on the cheek. He looked as cute as I had remembered him, his hair slightly mussed and his cheeks flushed with the effort of rushing from the train.

"No problem," I said. "I've been enjoying the view." I knew it was better to feign nonchalance than to confess my paranoia that he wouldn't show.

Real World Guy, I learned, lived in Queens. Being on *The Real World* might grant you fame and notoriety—or at least your own fitness video—but the $5,000 stipend the "cast" received would hardly cover the expenses of living in Manhattan for the following year. After his stint on every sixteen-year-old's favorite show, he had moved to New York and started a job at Brown Madison Davidson Advertising, working in the public service division.

"My job is to write those anti-smoking ads for cigarette companies," he explained. "They might use one of my concepts for an ad that's going to run during the Super Bowl. You can't mention cancer, death, show anyone smoking, or even show a pack of cigarettes. It's federally regulated that they have to spend a ton of money on it, but the tobacco companies don't want us to incriminate them at all, so it's a bit of a Catch-22."

I was worried he might be offended by my smoking, though I finally gave in to my craving after we finished our salads. "You're not an anti-smoking Nazi yourself, are you?" I asked, pulling out my pack. Since a large portion of the restaurant's clientele was European, the owners often waived Manhattan's stringent anti-smoking laws.

"Oh, no, I don't care," he said. "Actually, I'll have one myself. I usually don't smoke unless I'm drinking, but, well, I guess I am." He pointed to the bottle of wine we had put a sizable dent in and grinned as we both lit up.

"I read some of your reviews on that Web site. Pretty cool stuff," he said. "I hate all those fag bars though." I had just done a roundup of gay bars in the East Village and Chelsea.

"What do you mean?"

"I just hate the whole scene, the muscle guys, the prissy little queens, the posing. You can get AIDS by hanging out in places like that."

"Oh, come on!" I said. "Don't be ridiculous." I realized I would be banished to the seventh circle of date hell if I continued, so I changed tack. "Look, I know what you mean. A lot of people hate all that stuff. Not everyone is into the superficiality of it all."

"No, they love it. They love their fucking ghetto-ized lifestyle. They wouldn't have it any other way. I like places that are mixed. I don't even go to B Bar that much."

"Where do you go?" I asked, bracing myself with a sip of wine.

"Anywhere but those places. Sports bars. Hotel bars. Anywhere." I supposed hotel bars of the Ian Schrager type were okay, but sports bars? Ugh.

The waiter brought our entrees and we ordered another bottle of wine.

"Have you read *The Rise and Fall of Gay Culture*?" I asked. "It discusses a lot of what you're talking about—the cloned look, the whole bit."

"No," he said. "I don't read much."

We finished our meal in silence, which wasn't so bad, since he was better to look at than listen to.

I decided this would be a one-nighter, and I might as well carry it to its logical conclusion. I believed in having one-night stands if I never wanted to see the other person again. If I thought it had potential to be long term, I waited—usually.

"Do you want to get a drink somewhere around here?" I asked once we were out on the sidewalk. I was already pretty buzzed, but I was afraid it might be in bad taste to ask him back to my apartment right away.

"I want to smoke up. I've got some killer buds back at my place."

Killer buds? I felt like I was back at boarding school. "We could do that," I said. "Um, how far away is Queens?"

"Twenty dollar ride, no biggie," he said, hailing a cab.

When we got out in Queens, I offered to pay half and was annoyed when he accepted. It was his fault we had to cross a major body of water to get to his apartment.

He led me down a few steps to the basement of a row house. Inside, the lights were blindingly bright. His walls were completely bare and both rooms were furnished solely with futons, milk crates, and stacks of old magazines. It was nothing like the living arrangement I had imagined, one that, funnily enough, looked similar to what I had seen just hours ago on TV.

He sat down at the kitchen table—one of his few nods to domesticity—and started packing his bong. He had five lighters lined up on the kitchen table, and he grabbed one and fired up the bong, sucking in slowly as the water gurgled. He offered me a hit, and I accepted, mainly because it was the polite thing to do. I hated smoking pot, but it was the only thing on offer, save for a flat bottle of tonic water in his fridge. After I exhaled, I went over to the kitchen alcove and looked for a glass. There were a few plastic cups of the football game souvenir variety, so I filled one of those. His tap water tasted like there was rust in the pipes.

After he finished the bowl, he walked over to the futon, where I was patiently waiting. Pot always made me paranoid, and I suddenly thought he was going to ask me to leave or hit me or something. Instead, he kissed me slowly, and we fell down onto the futon together. He tasted like marijuana, but I didn't care. His body was built, with muscles a lover could hold onto.

We took a break from kissing, and the paranoia started creeping up on me again. I felt exposed, kissing him in this halogen-lit room, as if all of Queens were watching us through his front windows.

"Do you want to, uh, go in the bedroom or something?" I asked.

In the half hour it seemed to take him to answer, a feeling of profound foolishness washed over me, burning my cheeks.

What was I doing here?

I took deep breaths to keep the feeling at bay.

I reminded myself that he had asked me here. And it was his fault I had turned into a hyperventilating mess.

I was relieved when we dove into the cool of the bedroom.

The sheets on the second futon smelled like they hadn't been washed in weeks. He methodically took off his shirt and pants, and I took off mine as we both lay down on the bed. His body was practically hairless; he had a few light wisps on his chest. We kissed for a moment longer, as his erection poked out of the flap on his boxer shorts, begging for attention. I started kissing his stomach, slowly going lower, and then pulled down his shorts. This was going to be the best blow job of my life, I decided. Even if I never saw him again, Real World Guy would always remember me for this.

After about two minutes, his body started shuddering, and so I stopped.

"No," he said, "keep going."

I slipped off my shorts, and went back to work, splayed out on his futon, hoping he would notice me, my bare ass, anything. In less than a minute, he started to come, and I removed my mouth just in time, jerking him off onto his stomach. I wanted him to remember this, but I wasn't about to swallow.

"Thanks," he said. "That was really great."

I flopped over onto my back. He just lay there, not doing anything. This was ridiculous.

"Do you think you could . . ." I started.

"Blow you? Oh, I never do that. I mean, if you want to jerk off or whatever, that's fine, I don't mind."

"You never blow anyone?"

"I mean, I've done it before, but I just don't like it."

Though I was annoyed at his arrogance, it ultimately didn't matter. I knew I wouldn't be able to come, not with someone I had just met. The antidepressants I had been taking since age eighteen made it impossible to have a normal sex life. In order to have an orgasm, I had to be completely sober, and with someone I was comfortable with, or at least had slept with several times. And I had to find the person completely attractive. While Real World Guy satisfied the third condition, there was no way I would be able to do anything after five glasses of wine, not to mention a hit from his bong. And I knew Real World Guy wouldn't be into giving me pleasure for pleasure's sake; a boy like that wanted *results*.

Still, I wished he would pay attention to me, instead of acting like I was an inconvenience.

"That's okay," I said. "Never mind."

He went into the other room to smoke another bowl. When he came back, he put his boxer shorts on and crawled into bed.

"Do you mind if I spend the night?" I asked. Though I wasn't relishing the thought of staying over, finding a cab at this hour in Queens didn't seem promising either.

He said it would be fine, and started arranging the sheets in some semblance of order. "You wanna know something funny?" he said when he was finished.

"Sure," I said, though I was exhausted. The paranoia was gone, but my temples were throbbing and I wanted to forget about the night.

"Before I went on the show, I had really bad acne. They put me on Accutane six months before filming started and it sucked that shit right up. Never had a pimple again."

"Is my acne that bad?" I asked. I knew it wasn't. It was just one of those annoying things that never went away.

"Oh, no," he said. "I was just saying." He turned around, his back facing me. I tried to spoon him, my legs curled in against his, my stomach touching the warmth of his back.

"So, listen," he said, "the only way I can sleep is back to back, you know?"

I turned on my side, my back towards him, and rocked myself to sleep. I felt like a child again, on the nights when my stomach would be growling even though I had eaten a full meal. There was an emptiness gnawing at my gut, and it had nothing to do with food.

I woke at 7 A.M. and quietly slid back into my clothes. As I walked to the subway, I thought about the evening. There was a kind of draw—a lose-lose situation—when both parties in a one-night stand didn't want to see each other again. Real World Guy had been the first person I had slept with since moving to New York, but it was an empty victory.

I wondered if I would have felt some sense of completion, of closure, if I had been able to have an orgasm. I knew jerking off

boys and forgoing my own pleasure was not what it was supposed to be about, though I rarely experienced anything else.
Unlike those who had discovered a loss of libido on antidepressants, my libido was as strong as ever, which made the situation
worse. I felt like an injured athlete who could only cheer his
team on from the sidelines.

It wasn't that I had a problem relieving myself when I was
alone; in fact, I was content to do it almost every evening. With
the help of some furtively viewed net porn or even just a memory
from the gym or the showers at boarding school, I could get myself off in five minutes. The fantasy would never judge me for
taking too long, for not being hairless or buff, for having a zit on
my chin. When I was with other people, something inside me
shut off. But I was afraid to switch to other drugs, or to stop the
medication entirely, afraid of the depths of depression that could
result, catapulting me into the darkness I had first experienced at
eighteen. I couldn't afford to be unstable in my first year in New
York. Yet this morning, unsatisfied, having just had Real World
Guy, and yet not having had him at all, I knew something needed
to change.

And what was the business about the acne? Was that why he
didn't like me, because I didn't have flawless skin? He had called
me, I reminded myself. He was the one who had wanted to set
up a date.

Maybe he was just an asshole, plain and simple.

I transferred to the number 6 train at Fifty-ninth Street. At
Grand Central, a boy with shoulder-length wavy blond hair
boarded and sat across from me. He pulled out a manuscript and
started reading, pencil in hand. I wanted to ask him about it, but
I couldn't get up the courage. He was wearing a white oxford
cloth shirt and khakis, so he must have been headed for work,
though it was barely 8 A.M. He didn't look uptight the way
someone like Jamie would in such an outfit. He looked fresh and
pure, as if he had stepped out of an Ivory Soap commercial.

He noticed me watching him, so I averted my eyes. At
Twenty-third Street, he stuffed the manuscript in his bag and got
off the train.

After showering, changing, and fortifying myself with a large coffee, I arrived at the office right at ten. Donovan greeted me as he happily clacked away at his keyboard.

I checked my email and started working, annoyed that he hadn't asked me about the date. At quarter to eleven, he turned toward me. "I totally forgot about last night. How was it?"

"It was good," I lied.

"Are you going to see him again?"

"No, probably not," I said, as I fiddled with a paper clip. "Oh, fuck it, it was terrible. He's a total idiot. I've had dates with eighteen-year-olds that were better. And the sex—" I paused, not knowing how much I wanted to reveal. "Let's just say he was totally into himself."

"At least you can say you scored," Donovan said, shrugging.

"Who scored?" Sonia asked, standing in the doorway.

"Toby slept with the gay guy from *The Real World,*" Donovan said before I could tell him to shut up.

"How was it? Was it fabulous? Tell me it was fabulous!"

"It totally sucked," I said.

"This would make a great piece for our new column, 'Star-Fucker,' " she said. "You know, real life celebrity encounters. Lola is going to write about doing Mick Jagger, but she won't have it ready until next week. You can launch the series if you want."

I wasn't sure I wanted to go down that path. A girl I knew from college was a sex columnist for another Web site, and it had all but ruined her personal life. All she could attract were freaks and exhibitionists, and she was reviled by half of the twentysomething population of New York, most of whom were jealous they didn't have the sex life or the journalistic success she had. But she was laughing all the way to the bank: Miramax had just bought the rights to turn her columns into a feature film.

"I can't write about this," I told Sonia. "I mean, what about the drugs and everything? I'm sure the story would get back to him somehow."

"Pseudonyms, baby," she said. "Just say he was a 'twenty-something reality TV star.' There are so many of them out there." She wagged her finger at me. "Remember what they say about good writing."

"What do they say about good writing?"

"I don't remember exactly what they say, but it's something like 'Good writing comes from the darkest truths.' "

I wasn't sure I was ready to whore out my personal life for the enjoyment of CityStyle's readers. Writing about nightclubs was one thing; writing about my cock was another.

3

Though I always claimed he was, Kent Simmons wasn't the first guy I ever slept with. I had never told anyone about my actual first experience, because it happened to another person, another Toby Griffin.

When that Toby Griffin moved into his freshman dorm room, one of his roommates, Jim Huntsville, was, in the words of their college's dean, "in the process of flamboyantly coming out." This meant he had attended the introductory Gay and Lesbian Co-op meeting, wore a pink triangle pin on his backpack, and told anyone who would listen that he was bisexual.

Toby wasn't ready to take such a stance, and so he watched and observed, attending that same meeting, staying silent but taking everything in. One of the coordinators at the meeting thought they should celebrate National Coming Out Day by each carrying a pink balloon to class. Toby imagined people bursting those balloons in protest, the pink rubber shards falling along the flagstones of Cross Campus like fetuses, shriveled and pathetic.

Toby had heard Jim describe himself as trailer trash, which discouraged snickering when he told stories about driving his pickup truck on the dirt roads of Wyoming and working construction at a dude ranch. The only male influence in his household was his mother's on-again, off-again boyfriend. Jim was attending Yale on a combination of scholarship money and student loans. But none of that mattered.

Here it was now: Yale, the great gay mecca of the western world.

* * *

Toby knew what he wanted, but it was the getting there that was the hard part, not the act itself, but the before, the approach, like a trip more stressful to pack for than to take. On his tenth day in New Haven, two days into classes, Toby found himself with Jim, drinking watery beer at Naples, the local student pub and pizzeria. With each new pitcher, Toby's resolve became greater. In the twilight of beer haze, in the hopsy, nicotine-tinged world, it made sense: Jim would be his first boyfriend. Living arrangements, after all, had already been settled.

That evening, they were back in the common room, and their other two roommates, Steve Wallace and Colin Lydell, had gone to bed. Jim was lying on the couch, drunk, and smoking a cigarette, which was against dorm policy.

Toby, who was equally intoxicated, asked Jim about what it was like to be gay in Wyoming.

"I slept with a few guys there," Jim said. "But I wouldn't say I was gay."

Toby sat on the edge of the couch and leaned over Jim. "I think you're cute," he said. "Can I kiss you?"

Jim gave a half-nod that said, *I don't care what you do.*

Toby placed his lips against Jim's, thrusting his tongue in Jim's mouth.

"Easy there," Jim said, pulling away. "You gotta go a little slower. Haven't ya ever kissed a girl before?"

Toby said he hadn't. He tried again. His body was shaking.

"Don't be so nervous," Jim said.

They proceeded in the dim Ikea light, removing articles of clothing, folding out the futon couch and transforming it into a bed. Toby lay back on it, clad only in his boxers. Jim removed them, revealing Toby's erection.

Oh, God, Toby thought, let this be okay. And then he felt it for the first time, an experience he would have hundreds, thousands more times: his penis in another guy's mouth.

He tried to relax and immediately came.

"Shit," Jim said, spitting onto Toby's navel. "You should have told me you were going to do that."

"I didn't know it was going to happen," Toby said. "I'm sorry . . . can I get you a towel or something?"

"Naw, it doesn't matter." Jim rolled over onto his back and Toby began to massage Jim's penis with his right hand. This was the time to conquer the inevitable, to do the thing that would make him truly gay. He went down on Jim.

His crotch smelled of sweat and laundry detergent. It wasn't bad, actually; Jim's penis had the texture of chewing gum. Like a big, fleshy piece of chewing gum.

Toby kept removing hairs from his mouth. That was the most surprising part, the taste of pubic hair on skin.

After Jim came, the two of them lay together for a few minutes. Toby ran his hands across Jim's chest. Here it was, a real live boy. His fingers went to Jim's right ear, its lobe pierced by a single stud.

"When did you get your ear pierced?" Toby asked.

"Two days before I left Wyoming," Jim said.

"Do you want to spend the night here?" Toby asked. He and Jim were going to be boyfriends, so their roommates would surely understand. My Wyoming boyfriend, he thought.

"No," Jim said. "I should take a shower."

"Do you want to take one together?" Toby asked. He wanted the evening to last longer than this.

"No," Jim said.

Toby woke up the next morning and opened one eye. Steve was getting ready for class.

"Hey," Toby muttered. He was hung over and wished he could continue sleeping.

Steve looked at Toby in disbelief, as if Toby had just told him he had murdered his baby sister.

Two can play that game, Toby thought, so he said nothing else.

The day went by quickly. Toby threw on sunglasses to ward off the sunlight on Beineke Plaza and fired up a cigarette before his 9 A.M. class. He was a little shaky as he got his breakfast at Commons, but happy. So this is what it feels like, he thought. I've gotten it out of the way. I'm now a member of that elite club of people who have had sex. It was a distinction that, at age eighteen, still carried some weight.

Unlike previous days, when the suite had been abuzz with activity, when Toby got back to the dorm that afternoon, he was met with silence. He holed up in his room and tried to work. At 9 P.M., Steve and Colin appeared at Toby's door. Steve was an Upper East Side brat who had gone to school in the city and seemed to know everyone. Colin, who in Toby's opinion was dumb as a brick, was at Yale on a baseball scholarship. What distinguished both of them was that they were big guys: each six-foot-three, with broad shoulders and thick, tanned necks. Compared to Toby and Jim, they seemed more like seniors than fellow freshmen.

"We need to talk to you about something," Steve said.

Toby cringed, sensing he wasn't going to like this conversation. It would be something like, *We're okay that you're gay and we just want you to know that,* or *We're okay that you're gay, but please don't use the common room in the future.*

"Sure," Toby said, wanting it to be over with as quickly as possible.

"About last night: We asked Jim what happened."

Toby looked up.

"Jim says you raped him."

Toby felt the floor drop out from under him. A few days earlier, the four of them had been to a sexual assault seminar (foreboding police officer, dated video presentation) that defined rape and urged people to speak out if they had been assaulted.

"I, I don't know what to say. I mean, that couldn't be further from the truth," Toby said. He wanted to run to the bathroom and throw up.

But what if he had taken advantage of Jim? What if he had, and didn't know it?

He wondered if anyone in the courtyard could hear the conversation through his open window.

"Well, that's what he's claiming. He's going to talk to the dean tomorrow. We just had a meeting with our freshman counselor." Their freshman counselor was an affable jock—only serving as a counselor in order to get free housing, Toby thought—who was sure to think the whole thing sordid and disgusting. And tomorrow Jim was going to talk to their college's dean, a stern French professor with painted-on eyebrows, a woman who was responsible for 500 students. The idea of involving such authority figures in his personal affairs was unbearable.

"Look, if you don't believe me, then I don't know what to tell you. The whole thing was completely consensual."

"It's not about who's right or wrong," Colin said. "We just don't want that kind of shit going on here."

Toby looked at Colin. What the hell did a baseball player from Tennessee know about things like this anyway? He was probably the type who had committed a dozen date rapes, who hit his girlfriend and then went to church with his family on Sunday.

"Of course you don't," Toby said. It was so much easier for them to turn it into a gay issue. No one would have been claiming rape if someone had hooked up with a girl in the common room.

"Where is Jim now?" Toby asked. "I'd like to talk to him about this."

"He's at the library. He's really angry at you," Steve said. "You two can talk it over with the dean tomorrow."

The dean would never understand. Now everyone would know: that he was gay, that he was foolish enough to sleep with his roommate, that he was a rapist. He would be forced to wear a big lavender R on his lapel.

Toby gathered a few of his books in a backpack and went outside to smoke a cigarette. There was no one he could talk to about this. His parents in San Francisco wouldn't understand. His classmates from boarding school who were at Yale wouldn't understand. He wanted to disappear, to find a way to escape.

He wanted to end his life.

It seemed like the only solution. Toby imagined that there was no way he could recover from this accusation. Once Jim went public with his claim, once it was out there, Toby would forever be labeled as a sexual predator—and a gay sexual predator, at that. It didn't matter that it wasn't true. No one would believe his story. He needed a way out.

Toby wanted to talk to someone, anyone, who would be on his side. He could talk to a counselor, perhaps even spend the night in the infirmary. He needed someone to defend him, so that he might be able to survive this ordeal.

He decided to go to University Health Services. It was 11 P.M., and Toby wasn't comfortable walking alone at night in New Haven, a city known for its homeless, its junkies, its crime. As he walked down Grove Street, he saw two campus policemen.

"Hey, can I get a ride to UHS?" he asked.

"Sorry," one of the cops said. "Can't do that."

Toby ran the rest of the way through a light drizzle up Hillhouse Avenue, where he explained to the night guard that he needed to speak to a counselor. After waiting for forty-five minutes, Dr. Yolanda Sanchez showed up. A short woman with dark brown hair pulled back into a ponytail, she looked annoyed that she had to come in to work at this hour. Her nametag read "Resident" below her name. Toby wondered if she was a real doctor.

"I've been thinking about suicide," Toby said, after explaining the situation. The words surprised him. Thinking about it was one thing; saying it aloud, in this setting, seemed so extreme, so final.

She made some notes in a file. "And how did you plan on doing that?"

"I don't know . . . I saw a movie where a guy hung himself with a belt," Toby said. "I guess I could do that." He smiled, just a little. While the idea seemed viable, saying it aloud sounded ridiculous.

Dr. Sanchez looked up briefly and then down again at her pad. She was nothing like the counselor he had sometimes spoken to in high school. Dr. Sanchez hadn't asked him a single question about what had happened, hadn't said anything to make him feel better about it, to get him thinking logically about the situation.

All she had said was, "Rape is a very serious accusation."

After finishing her notes, she asked Toby if he thought he could go back to the dorm.

He shook his head. "I'd rather not."

Toby waited another half an hour while the doctor made a few phone calls and prepared some paperwork. He could stay away from the dorm for the night, and talk to the dean in the morning. She would see how upset he was by Jim's claim. She would see he was not the kind of person who would do such a thing.

"You'll just need to sign these forms," Dr. Sanchez said.

Toby signed them all, skipping over the small print. He caught the phrase, "Patient is a danger to himself or others."

Dr. Sanchez called an ambulance to take Toby to the hospital. He said he would rather take a cab, but this was policy, she explained.

"Did you attempt anything?" the ambulance guy asked Toby as he helped him into the vehicle.

"Oh, God no," Toby said. In the three or four times he had thought about suicide in his life, he had never actually tried to do it.

"You're one of the lucky ones," the guy said.

The ambulance left the health services building. The sirens started flashing and shrieking.

"Do they have to do that?" Toby asked.

"We want to get you there quick, right?" the guy said. "So what happened to you?"

Toby stared out the back window. "I had a sexual experience with my roommate," he said.

"Did he force you to do something?" the guy said. "That is so sick. You hang in there, buddy."

"I'll try," Toby said.

At the emergency services wing, they took Toby up to the fifth floor psychiatric unit in a steel-walled elevator. It was now 2 A.M. After making Toby wait for an hour, two fat nurses performed a battery of tests on him, drawing blood, testing his reflexes, and asking him a series of questions, like what the capital of Connecticut was. Toby was so tired, he could barely remember.

They put Toby in a room with a boy, sixteen or seventeen years old. The boy was lying on his bed with his face to the wall. Maybe he has the same problem, Toby thought. Maybe he's gay, too, and someone accused him of rape. Maybe the two of us will become lovers here in this little room.

Toby closed his eyes for two hours of sleep.

At 6 A.M., a nurse woke them and announced that blood tests and meds would be administered in fifteen minutes.

Toby's new roommate stirred. His name was Billy, Toby could see from the tag on the end of his bed. As Toby looked at him, Billy turned around to reveal two enormous gashes across his chest. Toby stared at them in horror.

"What, you never seen a cutter before?" Billy asked, yawning. "Yeah, I got the deepest wounds they ever seen. I almost bled to death, you know."

"Wow," Toby said.

Toby's blood was taken for the second time in four hours. He was given a white pill that the nurse said would relax him. He slipped it under his tongue and then spat it out when no one was looking. Breakfast was juice, fruit, and a muffin, all served in wrapped containers with plastic utensils that couldn't cut a baby. Toby could barely hold down half a cup of orange juice.

Around him, teenagers swarmed.

"I've been here for six weeks," one girl said. "I'm going to get out soon. My parents are coming to pick me up." She wore sweatpants and an oversized T-shirt; her hair was greasy and unkempt.

"She says that every day," her friend said, turning to Toby. "I've been here all summer. Sheila says I'm the best on the floor."

"She says that 'cause she knows you're psycho," Billy said, blowing bubbles in his orange juice with a straw.

"Whatever, Gash Boy," said the girl.

Sheila, the head nurse on the floor, came out of the glass-enclosed nurses' station to talk to Toby. "Toby Griffin, right? We're moving you upstairs. Since you're eighteen, you really don't belong on this floor. It was the only available bed we had, and we had to put you somewhere last night."

"What are you here for?" the girl in sweatpants asked.

Toby looked at her. "Suicide," he said.

"What'd you try?"

"I didn't try anything," Toby said.

"Oh, that is so lame," Billy said.

* * *

Toby was moved to the sixth floor, the adult floor. Like the fifth floor, it had steel-bolted doors leading to the elevators, separated by glass three inches thick. The nurses' station was a glass-walled cubicle that looked out on the main common room.

Toby was asked to hand over his cigarettes, lighter, keys, and belt. They must have forgotten to do this last night, on account of it being so late, he thought. I could have burned the place down by now.

A nurse wrote Toby's name on his cigarette pack and threw it into a basket with fifteen other packs, all labeled with the names of their owners. She put the rest of his belongings in a plastic bag. Toby saw that his name had been written on a whiteboard, last in a list of thirty patients. Next to each name was a series of check boxes, outlining privileges and med schedules. I am becoming part of a system, Toby thought.

"Okay," the nurse said. "Make yourself at home. We don't have a bed for you yet, but we should by this evening."

"I don't think I'll be staying that long," Toby said. "I just need to talk to someone."

"The counselors don't come in until four," she said. "Until then, we have TV and a whole mess of magazines."

Toby looked over at the TV area, where a group of patients sat watching a sitcom. In front of them was a coffee table piled high with back issues of *National Geographic* and *People*. Like the magazines, the patients—they ranged in age from early twenties to late sixties—looked like they had been sitting there for years.

"Can I talk to the head nurse?" Toby said.

Gladys, the head nurse on the sixth floor, was an older woman who wore thick glasses and a patterned nurse's uniform that was supposed to cheer up the patients.

"I need to find out what's going on with my, er, case," Toby said. "I mean, I don't plan on spending the night here."

"I really can't comment on that," Gladys said. "You need to wait until the counselors come in at four."

"But I have classes today. I have a lecture at one."

"You're going to have to miss that," Gladys said. "You don't have pass privileges yet."

"How long does it take to get those?"

"Two weeks," Gladys said.

It was 9 A.M., still too early to call his parents in California. Toby knew there was no way he could miss two weeks of classes. How had it come to this? How had he managed to screw up so completely? It was homophobia. If Jim hadn't freaked out, if he hadn't wanted to be accepted by Steve and Colin, he would have taken responsibility for what happened. It sounded so dramatic. Homophobia: like a big black monster that threatened to destroy everything in its path.

But it was his own fault he was here. Why had he mentioned something as drastic as suicide?

The thought, the fantasy of killing himself, wasn't foreign to him—hell, he doubted any teenager who hadn't had a suicidal thought once or twice. In boarding school, when he was resolutely in the closet, the reality of being gay had seemed too horrible, and he had fantasized a few times about what it would be like to end his life. He wouldn't have to worry about coming out, about what his parents would say, about what other people would think. Whenever he had felt that way, he talked with the school counselor, and she would assuage his fears. Simply mentioning a suicidal fantasy hadn't meant that he would be sent to the hospital. That was all he wanted now: to be talked down from the proverbial ledge.

But this wasn't boarding school. This was Yale University, an organization that held not being sued as a primary concern alongside light and truth. Of course they were going to hospitalize him if he cried suicide. From now on, he would have to keep such thoughts to himself.

Toby rifled through the books in his bag. For his American Studies class, he was supposed to read *The Yellow Wallpaper*.

At 10 A.M., he saw the dean of his college, Dr. Nicole Sexton, enter the doors of the floor. She was ushered quickly into a glass-walled conference room where she met with several other doctors.

An Asian girl, probably a student, sat at the end of the table. Maybe the dean was used to deciding the fate of her charges.

Toby kept watch over the meeting. When it was over, he jumped up and bounded across the room.

"Dr. Sexton," he said, "I'm Toby Griffin." He was embarrassed to be seeing her under such circumstances, as if she were going to give him detention for being here when he should have been in class or studying in the library.

"Yes, of course," she said, even though they had met only once before, at the college's welcome dinner. They sat down together. "Jim came to speak with me this morning."

Toby explained what had happened, explained how he needed to get off the floor.

"Jim says you took advantage of him."

"Do I look like I could take advantage of him?"

Dr. Sexton looked him up and down, as if evaluating the question.

"No," she finally said. "I know this is about Jim, not you. But I can't promise that you can go back to the suite."

"I don't want to," Toby said. "I'm disgusted with all of them."

"Let's not speak too soon about that," she said, sighing. "Jim said how well things were going otherwise." She seemed sad that one of her artificially created living units had spontaneously combusted so early in the semester.

"That girl in the meeting, she's a student, right? Will she get to leave?"

"Some people need to stay in here longer than others. Some are not ready to be normal students again."

Toby desperately hoped he was not one of those people.

"Please," he said. "I can't stay here another night."

"I understand." She paused, considering her options. "You may have to stay the weekend." As she stood up, she said, "You realize this is coming right in the middle of registration. This is absolutely the worst time for this."

Yeah, right, Toby thought: he should have considered her schedule first before sleeping with Jim.

*   *   *

An hour later, Toby called his parents from a phone booth on the floor. After explaining what had happened with Jim, Toby told his mother he was bisexual. He knew he was probably gay, but he thought this would be an easier way to break the news to his parents. Toby didn't realize this made the issue all the more confusing for them.

"But you slept with a man," his mother said. "That sounds like gay to me."

Toby decided to focus on the more important issue.

"We'll come out immediately," his mother said. "Can we leave tomorrow?"

"Sooner," Toby said. "You've got to get me out of here."

His mother was a woman who believed in working quickly. Within an hour she had booked herself and Toby's father on a red-eye to New Haven. She then proceeded to get in touch with Dr. Sexton and the head nurse on the floor. But it was clear to Toby that it was up to him to get out of the lockup.

Two hours later, Gladys came over to talk to Toby. "I spoke with your mother," she said. "I told her you're doing fine."

"But I'm not doing fine," Toby said.

"Sometimes we need to keep people here under observation for a few weeks to see how they do."

"Everyone keeps talking about a few weeks, two weeks, the weekend," Toby said. "I can't stay one night here. The people here are crazy. Their wires are all crossed."

"The people here are not crazy," Gladys said. "They just need a little help getting readjusted to normal life."

Toby wondered if he had foolishly insulted the patients under her care. He was getting agitated, and he realized he needed to control himself.

"It could take two weeks, or it could take years," Gladys said. "It depends entirely on the person."

There is no fucking way, he thought to himself, that I'm going to let myself become *Boy, Interrupted*.

Toby remembered a toy he had as a child, a small colored woven tube, something called a Chinese finger trap. The idea was to stick an index finger in either end and then try to pull the fingers out. The more he pulled, the tighter the tube clamped onto each finger. The only solution to freeing himself was to relax and then wriggle out.

Daily group started at 3 P.M. The residents of the floor, the TV watchers, the previously bedridden, the patients who shuffled through the halls on an endless loop—everyone except for the student Toby had seen earlier in the meeting—gathered around the common room in a large circle. Toby imagined the missing girl had been sent off to solitary confinement or shock treatment.

The group was led by one of the nurses. Toby wondered why it wasn't led by a counselor.

"Today we're going to start by discussing a goal we have," the nurse said.

They went around the circle.

"I'm going to try to eat dinner tonight," said an anorexic girl.

"Good!" the nurse said.

"I promise not to wake everyone up when I go to the bathroom," said an old man with three days' growth of beard.

"I'm sure everyone will appreciate that," the nurse said.

"I'm taking all my meds," said a thirtysomething woman in a sweatsuit.

"Wonderful!" the nurse said.

Some of the residents didn't answer, because they didn't understand the question. Sometimes the nurse prodded them for an answer; other times she just let it go. An old black woman seemed comatose when it was her turn.

"That's a very nice sweater, Trudy," the nurse said, referring to the woman's red sweater decorated with a grinning Santa Claus. "Are you getting ready for Christmas?"

The woman had no response.

When it was Toby's turn, he said, "My goal is to leave. My parents are coming tomorrow to pick me up."

"Yeah!" shouted one of the patients.

"Now," the nurse said, "is that a very realistic goal?"

"I think it is," Toby said.

"But you just got here, didn't you?" the nurse said. "Maybe after group, some of you could speak to Toby and welcome him to the floor."

"I don't need welcoming," Toby said. "I'm about to leave."
But no one heard him.

"Has anyone here seen *One Flew Over the Cuckoo's Nest?*"
the nurse asked. "Well, we like to think being here is nothing like
that."

But it was exactly like that. Sure, it was co-ed, and there was
carpeting, and no one was getting the shit shocked out of them
or having their frontal lobes removed, but the inactivity, the rest-
lessness, the feeling of being trapped—it was all the same.

After group, a patient named Gloria sat down next to Toby.
She was a mousy woman with short hair. "You're a Yale student,
right? Do you want to talk about why you're here?"

"I'd rather not," Toby said. He was sick of talking about why
he was there to people who had no interest in helping him get
out.

"I think you'll find it's not so bad. I've been here six weeks
and I've found this environment very healing once I accepted it."

"Why are you here?" Toby asked.

"Now, you're not going to tell me, so why should I tell you?"
she said with a triumphant smirk. "But you hang in there. I
know you'll be fine." She gave Toby an awkward hug, and then
went to sit with someone else.

Toby sat reading for a few minutes, and then Gloria came
back. "You didn't mind that I gave you a hug, did you? Because
I'm just like that, you know, I like to show my feelings, and
sometimes other people don't like that, so I just wanted to make
sure it was okay with you."

"It's fine," Toby said. "Don't worry about it." Just go away,
he thought.

A girl with hollow eyes ringed with too much eyeliner sat
down next to him. She had a dancer's body, and was wearing a
skirt over a black leotard. "I heard you talking to Gloria," she
said. "I'm from Yale, too. The pharmacology school. I'm Cassandra."

Toby introduced himself. Cassandra had been there for six
weeks as well, and had been hospitalized for an attempted suicide. "I wanted to read the copy of the *PDR*—you know, the
Physicians' Desk Reference—that they have in the office, and

they wouldn't let me. I mean, I'm a graduate student; I need to have something interesting to read. They eventually let me go home and get my books."

"You went home?" Toby asked.

"I told them I had to go home to feed my cat. If I didn't, he would die."

"Why did you come back?" Toby asked.

"I didn't feel like I was ready to leave," she said.

At that moment, the residents on the floor with smoking privileges were being marshaled together for their hourly trip outside. "My whole life revolves around cigarettes," muttered a man waiting in line. Toby had been dying for a cigarette for the past eight hours, but he didn't have smoking privileges, so it was useless to think about it.

"Last week there was a jumper during the smoke break," Cassandra said. "Someone jumped over the fence into the parking lot and ran away."

"What happened to him?" Toby asked.

"Nothing," Cassandra said. "Everyone cheered."

The time went slowly, as if life were going by at twelve frames per second. Toby was hungry, but he refused to eat the food given to him at lunch and dinner. He had gone to the bathroom twice, but all that had come out were long streams of diarrhea, as if the stress in his body had stopped him from solidifying his bowel movements. He noticed the bathrooms didn't contain real hooks for towels and clothing, but safety hooks that could only support the weight of a towel or article of clothing before they gave way on their hinges. Toby thought about the ways he could kill himself in this environment. Surely the shower curtain could be twisted into a rope, and the doorknob could be used as a hook. He didn't want to commit suicide, but the place made him think about it.

Toby knew he could not give in to his natural reaction to scream and sob and break things. If he did that, he would be here for six months. The people running this place were sick, sick people, he decided, nearly as sick as their patients. It gave them power to tell normal people they belonged in the lockup.

Toby realized he would have to fake sanity if it killed him.

* * *

At 7 P.M., Toby met with Dr. Steinberg, the head of psychiatry, along with Dr. Sexton and a few other doctors. Dr. Steinberg was a little bald man with glasses, perhaps nearing fifty.

This was the most difficult thing Toby had ever done in his life. He had to convince these people, these people who had every reason not to believe him, that he was sane and did not belong here.

"I understand you don't want to be here, Toby, but you've entered into a system," Dr. Steinberg said. "Now, why don't you tell me your side of the story?" He had a nasal, slightly whiny tone.

Toby told his entire story. He was logical, penitent. This is the best acting job I've ever done, he thought. I want to scream and cry in rage at these people, but instead I'm coming off as clearheaded as the next undergraduate.

"Have you met your new roommate yet?" Dr. Steinberg asked.

"I don't need to meet my new roommate," Toby said. "Because I'm not staying here. I need to be let out, or at least be allowed to stay in the infirmary."

"That might be a possibility," Dr. Sexton said. Toby was surprised they hadn't thought of this before.

"I spoke with your mother," Dr. Steinberg said, changing tack. "I understand your parents are flying out tonight."

We're making progress, Toby thought. "Yes," he said, "they're picking me up. I'll go anywhere until then, back to the infirmary, wherever, but I can't spend the night here. I'm not crazy; I don't belong here."

"Of course, Toby, that's a natural reaction to this situation," Dr. Steinberg said, smiling.

Toby wanted to kill the man.

"Do you feel you can handle going to classes alongside Jim?" Dr. Steinberg asked.

"I have nothing against Jim," Toby said. "I mean, I'm upset about what he said, but I know he did what he did because he was embarrassed."

"Are *you* embarrassed, Toby? What are you embarrassed about?" The way he asked the question made it seem prurient.

"I know I shouldn't have slept with Jim, and we shouldn't have used the common room. I'm embarrassed that I had myself committed without knowing what it meant. And I'm embarrassed that I've taken up so much of your time and trouble." There, that should be enough, Toby thought. I have laid myself down at your feet.

Toby sat outside the meeting room and tried to look as stable as possible while they discussed his case. He fantasized about the enormous lawsuit he would like to file, but he knew he would have no case, that he had signed his life away the night before. It was such a simple thing to do, as easy as signing a credit card slip. Now he feared that if he stayed one more night, this could become permanent.

In the hallway off the common room, a woman was screaming, and two aides were throwing a blanket over her to keep her quiet. Toby averted his eyes.

Dr. Sexton sat down next to him.

Oh, God, please, Toby thought.

"Do you have all your things?" she asked.

Toby nodded and exhaled.

"I'm taking you to the infirmary. Your parents can pick you up tomorrow."

Toby's parents arrived at the infirmary at eleven the next morning, fresh from their red-eye. His mother and father embraced him.

"Let's just get out of here," Toby said.

By the time they had checked into the Holiday Inn, it was nearing lunchtime. Toby didn't want to be seen on campus, especially not with his parents. His father went out to get pizza for the three of them.

"I wish you could explain all this to me," Toby's mother said, as the two of them sat together in the hotel room. "What does this mean? Did you really rape this guy?"

"No!" Toby shouted. "Don't you understand anything about what happened?"

"Explain it to me, then."

Toby did his best. His mother started to cry.

"This is such a shock to us," she kept saying, as she blotted her face with tissues and then attempted to repair her makeup. "I mean, you can't just go around telling people you're going to commit suicide."

"I know that," Toby said. "I'll never do it again."

That evening, a Saturday, they had dinner at the best restaurant in town, a restaurant students rarely dined at without their parents. Toby was terrified he would see one of his classmates. His parents were under strict instructions to say they had been passing through the area and thought a visit would be nice. No one could ever know the truth.

Lubricated by the wine, Toby's father made a last-ditch attempt to explain the allure of the female anatomy.

"I just wish you knew," his father said in a low voice, "how good it feels to put your prick inside a woman's cunt."

"Oh, Simon!" his mother said. "Just leave him alone!"

"I'm trying to get him to understand this. Maybe he doesn't know about it."

Toby's mother turned to him.

"What I don't understand is the whole bisexual thing," she said. "Does this mean you might start dating a girl?"

"I don't know!" Toby said. "Do we have to talk about this now?"

"We're just trying to understand," Toby's father said. "Homosexuality is a very new thing to us."

"He's *bisexual!*" Toby's mother shouted across the table. "That means he likes men *and* women!"

"If you both don't shut up, I'm leaving and going back to the hotel," Toby said. He never spoke this way to his parents, but they were getting out of control.

It took years before they ever understood.

Surely this wasn't the best way to do this, Toby thought at the time.

But how else could he have done it?

On Monday, Toby met with the dean, the college's shrink, and his three roommates. He hated them, but all he wanted was his freedom. Everyone agreed that Toby would move into a new room. Steve and Colin helped him move his belongings up to what was generously called a "psycho single" on the fifth floor of the dorm. Psycho or not, Toby was thrilled. He didn't want roommates anyway, he decided, and he was happy to have a room of his own, though that didn't quell his shame and embarrassment over what had happened.

Over the next few months, Toby fell into a deep depression. Nothing in his freshman year had turned out the way he had hoped it would; he kept kicking himself for screwing up what was supposed to be the start of a new life: new friends, new experiences, a boyfriend. Toby's fear—irrational as it was—that everyone knew what had happened with Jim made it difficult for him to be social, and the resulting solitude drove him further into his despair. He felt like he was being forced right back into the closet.

He started seeing a shrink who put him on Paxil, one of the panoply of antidepressants currently medicating the student body. Buoyed by the medication, Toby slowly made new friends, whom he appeased by spinning a tale of his own voluntary selection of a single room; he was tired of roommates, he explained, after four years at boarding school. He didn't have a close-knit group that went on beer-drinking parties, but he found friends who occupied his free time with coffee at the Daily Caffé or drinks dates at the Anchor Bar. He adopted a cat at the pound that he kept illegally in his dorm room.

As the school year progressed, he thought about the lockup every day, though each time the memory faded more and more, like an outline of reality that is not the thing itself. Within a year, it was like something that had happened to another person.

In January of his freshman year, as Toby was traversing the icy flagstones in front of Branford College, he ran into Dr. Steinberg.

"How are you doing, Toby?" he asked in his nasal-tinged voice.

"Fine," Toby said. "I still think about it sometimes, but for the most part, things are okay."

"Just remember, Toby, you're a normal student at Yale University. Totally normal. A normal student." The doctor kept repeating it over and over like a mantra, even as he waved good-bye. Toby wished he would shut up.

As he walked back to his dorm room along the paths of Old Campus, Toby looked at his fellow students for hints, for clues. They were the best and the brightest, the smartest in the nation, right?

They know nothing, he thought. They know nothing at all.

4

That afternoon, when the mail arrived at the CityStyle offices, there was a large envelope with my name on it. I opened it and out slid a pair of cheap-looking magenta panties. I stared at them in horror.

"Fan mail?" Donovan laughed, as I blushed.

I held the sheer undergarment up to the light. Attached was a tag, inviting me to a "Naked Halloween Party" hosted by an important downtown designer, to be held at a club in the meatpacking district the following week.

"That party's going to be amazing!" Donovan said. "The entertainment is sponsored by a site for hustlers that just launched—the boys will be really hot."

Indeed, at the bottom of the invite was printed, "Entertainment provided by Rentaboy.com." I was both mortified and intrigued.

"Hustlers?" I asked. "Isn't that kind of dangerous?"

"You can look, just don't touch," Donovan said.

"Holy shit!" Sonia came running into the office with a copy of the *Daily News*. I saw Sunny, the office manager, behind her, glaring at Sonia's exuberance. "Our article is in here! I can't believe I didn't find out until now. One of our investors called to congratulate us."

She spread the article out on our work table. "Web Journos Dish Downtown Dives" read the headline. There was a large photo of us all, and quotes from every staff member.

"This is amazing," said Sonia. "You can't pay for publicity like this! Well, you can, but the point is, we didn't, and we got written up anyway!"

One of the guys from finance ran out to get a bottle of champagne, and we had a mid-afternoon toast.

"This should definitely help the funding situation," Donovan said.

"Let's hope so," Sonia sighed. She took a sip of her champagne and noticed the panties on my desk, draped across my keyboard like the remnants of an illicit fling. She flipped over the tag.

"You, my friend, will be covering this. I've been waiting for this invitation all week."

That evening, I met up with Jamie and Donovan at Flash, a new lounge Ariana was representing. True to its name, the interior was all mirrors and plush black velvet. Ariana had given us a bundle of drink tickets and put us on the guest list for the VIP area. When we got there, however, we were told we could sit in the VIP room only if we purchased a bottle of something from the drinks menu. Since the cheapest item was a bottle of Absolut for $250, we settled for hanging out at the bar. Soon after we arrived, the lounge started to fill up with a crowd that was distinctively Ariana: girls toting cell phones and Gucci handbags, guys in Dolce & Gabbana suits smoking cigars and waving around money clips.

"This place is awful," Donovan said. "I can't believe what I just heard in the restroom. Some guy was going on about 'faggot this' and 'faggot that' to the attendant. I mean, this place is supposed to be A-list, but it's breeder central already."

"You know how she packs these places," I said. "A sprinkling of celebs and society kids, and then it's B-list all the way."

As I looked toward the front, I saw the PR queen herself entering with Jordan Gardner and Cameron Cole. Trailing behind the three of them was a photographer Ariana had hired for the night. I waved to her, and she came over after arranging a photo op with Jordan and Cameron that would surely show up on the *Post*'s Page Six on Monday.

"What are you doing out here?" she asked, teetering on her heels. "*No one* parties out here." Apparently, the throngs crowding the bar added up to no one. "Come to the VIP room."

She waved for us to follow her and her party, and this time we were whisked past the velvet rope that separated the plebeians from the elite. Jamie glared at the bouncer we had argued with earlier.

Ariana had a banquette waiting for her, and the seven of us crowded into it. A waitress began to pour champagne as Cameron, Jordan, and Ariana immediately got up again. Ariana said she had to check on some guest list details; Cameron and Jordan were headed for the restroom.

"They're going to do lines," Donovan whispered to me. "I heard they were both cokeheads."

"Shut up," I hissed back. "He's a major producer."

"Oh, please," Jamie said. "He's not *major*. He wouldn't be anywhere if his mom hadn't given him his own company."

Jordan came back first from the ladies room, noticeably wired. Jamie, Donovan, and I smiled awkwardly at her as she sat down. We had seen her movie several weeks ago, and though the film had been entertaining, her performance consisted of little more than pouting in bed, slinking around in skin-tight dresses, and showing off her surgically enhanced breasts.

"Let me get a shot of all of you together," said the photographer, getting out of the booth and motioning to the four of us.

"Oh," I said, "we're not really—I mean—oh, what the hell!" Why not? The picture could be used when *Vanity Fair* did a story on my screenwriting career, demonstrating that I had been running with a fast crowd from the beginning. We all got closer together as his camera flashed at us several times. Other people in the VIP room gave us envious stares.

Ariana appeared behind the photographer and reprimanded him for wasting film. We were worth a few free drinks, but she drew the line at the use of her photographer.

Ariana and Cameron sat down again.

"Toby's mother is Isabella Griffin," Ariana said, in the general direction of Jordan.

Everyone nodded in appreciation. A lot of good it does me, I thought.

"I love her work," Jordan said, brushing aside a strand of

hair. "I wanted to wear something of hers to the Oscars last year, but my stylist said we couldn't get anything."

Though it hadn't been apparent in the film we had seen, Jordan had a slight Cockney lilt to her speech, the kind my mother often derided as vulgar.

"My mother doesn't believe in dressing celebrities," I said, realizing after the words came out of my mouth that I was in entirely the wrong company to be making such a statement. "I mean, she loves celebrities, but she just feels like her work is a little more understated, like it wouldn't look right on a celebrity."

"Well, your mother is wrong," Ariana said. "You should put her in touch with me. Her sales could go through the roof with the right endorsements. I know celebs who would kill to be associated with a brand like your mother's. These days, a brand can help a celebrity just as much as a celebrity can build a brand."

She made the proclamation as if she had come up with the philosophy on the spot. But the truth was that other publicists had been using these tactics for years. They had turned Manhattan into a giant celebrity-infested playground, where nothing held any meaning without a bold-faced name attached.

Ariana paused to take a drag on her cigarette. "Oh, my God!" she suddenly shrieked, jumping up to greet a slew of friends and nearly knocking over the ice bucket. Cameron and Jordan joined her, the photographer followed with his camera, and we were left sitting alone.

I realized that for Ariana, her entire career had been an extension of high school, an endless parade of parties and friends. The only difference was that instead of sneaking out of her parents' apartment and going dancing downtown, she was now running the show.

We decided to kill the second bottle of champagne. As the Publicist, the Movie Star, and the Producer—it was like a Manhattan version of *Gilligan's Island*—carried on with their Upper East Side prep school reunion, it became clear that Ariana didn't care about getting to know us, if I enjoyed myself at the club and wrote a good review, or even if my mother gave her clients free dresses. She was just paying attention to us until something better came along.

I had always hated half-assed attempts at VIP treatment. I would rather be left on the sidewalk than be treated well one moment and ignored the next. She had made us feel like what we were: interlopers, posers, no better than the people outside the velvet rope who were so desperate to get in.

"Let's go," Donovan said once we had drained our champagne flutes. "This place blows."

As we got ready to leave, Cameron pulled me aside. "You guys taking off so soon? Look, give me a call sometime. Here's my card."

"What do you think he wants?" I asked Jamie and Donovan once we were safely in a cab. "It was so ambiguous: 'Give me a call sometime.' Sex? Friendship? A business meeting?"

Donovan piped up. "Toby, he doesn't know you write screenplays, and the guy's got enough friends. He has one thing on his mind."

"He wants you for sex," Jamie said grimly. "But I don't think you should call him."

Cameron's proposition—I wasn't sure what else to call it—thrilled me, mainly because it was unclear. Even if he just wanted to sleep with me, getting to know Cameron would undoubtedly be a boon to my career. The exchange made me wonder if I had been overly judgmental of Ariana. Maybe we should have stayed behind and hung out with her friends. There was nothing worse, though, than trying to have a good time at a party when you clearly didn't belong.

The next day, a brilliant Saturday, I received a copy of my high school's alumni magazine in the mail. I flipped to the class notes. An item caught my eye among the usual slew of grad school acceptances and job offer announcements: "Frederick Brandt, who graduated last spring from USC's Film School, reports that he just sold his feature screenplay *My So-Called Sex Life* to Paramount for an undisclosed sum." Freddy and I had been friends when he was the treasurer and I was the president of our film society in high school; we had stopped talking after I dis-

covered he was using the society's funds to finance his video collection. Now Freddy had sold a screenplay about his sex life?

I hated him for it, but I knew it was a sign. I had to write the
piece about Real World Guy, because people were looking for
that kind of candor. I would write the definitive article on the
Naked Halloween Party, even if it meant sleeping with every
hustler in the joint. And I would get back to *Breeders*, pitching it
to Cameron Cole when I was done.

I gave Sonia a call at home to find out what she was looking
for in the piece about Real World Guy. The angle she wanted
was that I was a brazen starfucker, a ruthless slut just out to cut
another notch on my bedpost. "The whole relationship thing,"
she said, "no one will believe that anyway. This is about fame
and celebrity and the lengths to which people will go to have a
taste of it."

Though I wasn't sure I agreed with her angle, I knew I could
manipulate the facts in order to suit it. I started making notes on
my experience, and by the end of the afternoon, I had a pretty
decent first draft.

What I hadn't mentioned in the piece was that while I would
have enjoyed a relationship with Real World Guy, I had gone on
the date to make Donovan jealous, or at least to attract his attention. On the second count, I had succeeded; I just wasn't sure
it was the kind of attention I wanted. Now that he regarded me
as a player, I was privy to his every sexual exploit, the details of
which often made my stomach turn.

"Did you know the Cock's back room is open again?" he
asked me, referring to a divey gay bar in the East Village that fa-
mously advertised itself with a red neon rooster.

It was Monday, and the two of us were at lunch.

"I went there last night, just for kicks. The whole room is
dark, just lines of guys standing up. This guy asks me if I want a
blow job, so I'm like, 'Sure, why not?' "

"Please," I said, "I'm eating."

"Come on, you like giving head."

"Very funny," I said, annoyed. "It's just so public and exposed. And you don't know what kind of trash is floating
around there—I mean, anyone who hangs out in a back room is

bound to be doing it on a regular basis. You're just increasing the odds, don't you think?"

"I guess so. But don't you think that kind of public sex is really hot?"

"No," I said defiantly, and we finished our meal in silence. As much as I was attracted to him, this side of Donovan's personality made me sick.

When we got back to the office, I keyed in my review of Flash: "The latest entry to Manhattan's lounge scene is Flash, a young Hollywood hangout on the edge of Soho that epitomizes style over substance with its slick decor. In two months, when it becomes strictly B-list, the door policy may not be so forbidding; for now, wear your best Prada and claim nascent celebrity if you want to be let in."

I made a few clicks, and the review went up on the site.

By mid-afternoon, Cameron Cole's card was burning a hole in my wallet, so I decided to give him a call. I knew the Monday after a Friday seemed soon, but I didn't want him to forget who I was.

I left a message with his assistant, a fey-sounding boy who asked me to spell "Griffin."

As I hung up the phone, Ariana stormed into our office, holding a printout from the site. "Toby, what the fuck is this? I give you VIP treatment and you write this shit? I can't show my client a clip that says they're going to be B-list in two months! That's why they fucking hired me—so that doesn't happen!"

Sonia appeared in the doorway. "Ariana, I'm sure we can do something about this," she said coolly. "I'll talk to Toby and we'll come up with an equitable solution."

What the hell was Sonia talking about, "an equitable solution?" To what? To a club that sucked to begin with? I couldn't believe Ariana was asking us to be part of her spin machine, and Sonia was agreeing with her.

"This is ridiculous," I said. "I'm going to go have a cigarette."

Ariana's outburst reminded me of the time in high school

when our newspaper's advisor had told us we couldn't print a cartoon that was critical of the school's administration. I argued our case, but it had no effect. Ultimately, we triumphed by photo-copying the cartoon and surreptitiously inserting it in 550 copies of the paper.

After I had calmed down, I went back into Sonia's office. "This is bullshit," I said. "I can't change a review that I've al-ready put up on the site."

"Toby, the review has been up for all of thirty minutes," Sonia said. "No one will notice. Just tweak it a little bit to make her happy."

"But that's not journalism," I said. "We might as well be writ-ing her press releases for her."

"Toby, the reality of running something like this is that we're dependent on people like Ariana to give us access to venues. And she's our landlord."

"We pay our rent. That doesn't mean we have to write nice things about her clients."

Sonia took a deep breath. "Actually, we're several months be-hind in our rent. And Ariana has offered to help us look for ad-ditional investors. You might say we have a mutually parasitic relationship."

"Well, that's fucked," I said.

Sonia raised her perfectly tweezed eyebrows at me.

"I'm sorry," I said. "I know you're doing your best to keep this thing going. It's just that—I mean, everything I've ever been taught—"

"Toby, I know. Just change the review, okay?"

I went back to my desk.

Donovan was watching me with an amused look on his face.

"I don't know what she was so upset about," I said. "I thought she would love the 'style over substance' comment!"

"I know," Donovan said. "Some people work their entire lives to achieve that kind of notoriety."

While I was composing the article about Real World Guy, all I could think about was what my parents would say. I prayed they wouldn't scrutinize the site too closely that week; I could only imagine how my mother would feel about my writing for a column called "StarFucker."

After the article went up, though, the only person I was worried would see it was Real World Guy himself. I was terrified he would contact me or, even worse, I would run into him somewhere and have a confrontation. I felt like a sell-out, exploiting a date as fodder for an article. I thought about using a pseudonym on my byline, but that wouldn't change what I had done. I had disguised him so he wouldn't be recognizable, moving him from Queens to Brooklyn, changing his hair color, stuff like that. But he would know I was writing about him. I had committed a cardinal offense: I had kissed and told.

That evening, a Thursday, I met up with Donovan and Jamie and we went to the Naked Halloween Party in the meatpacking district. David and Alejandro were supposed to join us, but they were, in Jamie's words, "too busy fucking."

We should all be so lucky, I thought.

Donovan wore a denim vest with nothing under it as his nod to the "naked" part of the invitation; I wasn't about to go naked in any form, but I did wear a tight leopard print T-shirt by the designer who was hosting the party, while Jamie wore his usual gay-preppy-by-way-of-Diesel garb. When we got to the door, I pulled the panties out of my bag, held them up like court evidence, and we were whisked into the VIP area, no questions asked.

Once inside, the three of us commandeered a plush settee. The club's dance floor and lounge were decorated like nineteenth century drawing rooms, with Oriental rugs, lush curtain swags, enormous gilt mirrors, and bad copies of paintings chronicling the lovemaking of nubile water nymphs. Though there wasn't much actual nudity among the attendees—we figured that would come later—both rooms were filled with club kids, drag queens, leather daddies, fashion fags, and an assortment of personalities who didn't fit into any category at all. It was a Halloween party, but that was a moot point for most in attendance; it was a crowd that dressed in costume every night of the year. Gorgeous college kids who belonged in Bruce Weber photographs danced with Lola (who was, indeed, the only one completely naked, save for a pair of Lucite stilettos) and her transsexual posse, all of them wed together in a society of mutual admiration.

Amidst the crowd on the dance floor, I spotted the boy I had seen a week earlier on the train. As Subway Boy danced with his friends, he tossed around his long hair like a runway model. I couldn't tell if he was gay or not; he seemed masculine, though I was sure he could go either way.

I pointed him out to Jamie.

"Brett may know him," he said. "But I don't think he's that good-looking."

I would have to remember to ask Brett about Subway Boy.

While Jamie went to the restroom, I told Donovan my worries about the column.

"Don't stress about it," he said. "The piece was fabulous. Besides, he sounded like a jerk."

"I don't want to get a reputation for selling my dates down the river."

"It was one piece, and it had to do with who he was, not the date itself. There's a price to pay for fame; he should know that as well as anyone."

"What do you think?" I asked Jamie when he returned.

"I didn't read it," he said.

"Bullshit. Of course you read it," said Donovan.

"I skimmed it; I really can't make a judgment." He went to find a cocktail waitress.

"*Jamie* can't make a judgment? He's the most judgmental person in Manhattan. What the fuck is that about?" I said, though I knew exactly what the fuck it was about. "I'm not married to him! We've never even dated."

"That," Donovan said, "is exactly the problem."

Jamie returned. "God, the guys here are so fucking hot!"

"They're probably all messes," Donovan said. "You know, alcoholic, drug-addicted, growth-hormone-popping, dysfunctional faggots."

"Don't be bitter or anything," I said.

Donovan continued. "Or they have 'the voice.' You know, you see a guy who's cute and you go talk to him, only to discover he has a voice about three octaves higher than the average guy."

Jamie agreed. "See Tarzan, hear Jane."

Donovan tugged at Jamie and me, asking us to dance. The three of us went out to the dance floor and formed a circle. As I danced with Donovan and Jamie, I kept looking for signals—the way Donovan moved his eyes, the swiveling of his hips. I had to do something, anything, to get his attention.

I wanted to save him from his profligate lifestyle, from back rooms and online hookups and dates with waiters and busboys and guys he met at the gym. I imagined that we would live together in our large rent-controlled one-bedroom in the West Village, eating out on the dime of the publications we were writing for. Donovan would publish his first cookbook and negotiate a development deal for his own food show. Under his nurturing, I would finish my screenplay, and it would be produced by Cameron Cole and become the first gay blockbuster in history. We would be interviewed by the E! channel. "I'd like to thank my partner Donovan," I would say. "I kept him from turning into a complete sleazeball, and he kicked my ass into finally finishing something." I would accept the Oscar that year for best screenplay and would dedicate the award to him. . . .

Donovan was poking me. "What's up with you? You've been staring into space for the last five minutes. Do you want another drink? I'll buy."

I was on my third cocktail of the evening, so I was feeling pretty loose. As Donovan went to get more drinks, I wondered if I should make a move.

By now, the parade of rentboys had started. They were perched on go-go boxes around the dance floor and lounge, tight, muscular boys wearing little more than g-strings or Calvin Klein briefs. I pulled out my notebook and started taking notes.

I was nervous about interviewing the guys; I didn't think I had ever even seen a hustler before, let alone spoken to one. I thought about getting another drink first, but I remembered Donovan was already at the bar.

Jamie rolled his eyes at me as I scribbled in my notebook.

"I have to go talk to some rentboys," I told him.

"Are you crazy? Those guys'll tear you to shreds!"

"Good," I said, grinning with false bravado. "I can't wait."

I approached one of the go-go boxes and waited until there was a break in the music. The boy on the box had dark floppy hair and was wearing a pair of white boxer briefs. Even though he was dancing in a smoky nightclub, he still looked sweet and clean-cut, like a buff version of Elijah Wood.

He sat down on his box and sized me up.

"I hate this trance shit, you know?" he told me. "You can't dance to it." He slipped on a pair of sneakers as he took a break from the evening's work.

I asked him if I could get a few quotes from him for my article.

"You gonna pay me for it?" he asked, his beady eyes examining me with suspicion.

"Well, I—" I stammered. Why was I nervous about this? He was just a stupid hustler. He was probably younger than I was.

"Don't worry, I'm just fucking with you."

We sat down together on a nearby couch, and I gave him a cigarette, his fee for our twenty minutes together. From close up, I could see his body was completely shaved; his stomach, so smooth from a distance, was covered with a slight layer of stubble. I imagined the razor burn I would get during sex.

"Do you shave your whole body?" I blurted out.

"Yeah," he said. "Even my pubes. You wanna see?" Before I could protest, he pulled down his briefs to show me his entire pubic area, right up to the shaft of his cock, completely shaved, bare like a little child's.

My curiosity more than satisfied, I lobbed a number of questions at him, and, like a media pro, he answered them with aplomb. He told me about the new Rentaboy Web site and how it would change his business, bringing him a more upscale clientele. He said he was originally from Rye, New York, and was now a student at Fordham; he was hoping to break into the music management business. His name was Tyler, though in his ads he went by the name of Stephano.

"People like that, you know. It sounds European. I'm half Italian, so I figure it's okay," said Tyler-Stephano.

"So, what do you do with these guys when you're, like, with them?"

"Me? Oh, I do everything," he said.

"You mean, everything everything?"

"What are you talking about? You mean, like *fucking?*" he said, as if it were a concept foreign to him. "Yeah, I do that, sometimes."

"Have you ever had any really scary, um, clients?"

"Scary tricks? No. I've never slept with anyone I wouldn't have for fun. I'm a big slut anyway." Though I didn't doubt his last statement, I had trouble believing he had never encountered any difficult clients. "So," he continued, "what are you doing after this? You got plans?"

"No," I said, "I'm not doing anything."

"Maybe we could hang out. You're cute."

I laughed. "Are you going to charge me for it?"

"No, not for you," he said.

"I thought it was bad business for hustlers to give it away."

"Oh, I make plenty the rest of the week," he said. "What other business do you only have to work an hour a night to make this kind of money?" He was surely pulling in more each month than I was, but I didn't want to think about that.

"I have to get back to my friends," I said.

"What, you don't want to hang out?" He seemed incredulous at being turned down.

"Not tonight," I said. "Sorry."

"Well, you know where to find me." He got back up on the go-go box and started working it again.

I put my notebook back in my bag and stood up. When I turned around to look at him, he gave me a half-wave and a grin.

I was shaking; I wasn't used to being propositioned by hustlers. Should I have been flattered? Embarrassed? Scared?

I made my way back to where Jamie and Donovan were sitting. As I passed the dance floor, I looked around for Subway Boy, but he had disappeared.

"I need that drink," I said.

Donovan pointed to it.

"Fuck," I said to Donovan. "I just turned down a hustler. He was hot, too! Dumb and tacky, but hot."

"Where is he?" Donovan asked. "I might be interested."

"That's a mess I'm not letting you get into," I said. I'm not letting you, I thought, because I want you for myself.

"You're right," he said. "I should be getting home; it's almost one."

We all exchanged goodbye kisses and Donovan took off. I had blown another chance to make a move on him. It wasn't the same when we were in the office together; things felt more intimate under the cover of night.

Jamie lit a cigarette.

"I want to hook up," I said to him, realizing after I said it that he was going to misinterpret the statement.

"Me, too," he said.

"I mean, with someone else."

"Why do you torture me like this?" He cupped his hands to his face in mock despair.

"Look, Jamie, if we're going to be friends, we have to be able to talk about stuff like this. I really like you, but I don't want to ruin our friendship by sleeping together."

"But you sleep with people all the time! Why not me?"

"I do not sleep with people all the time!" I said. The article was causing my reputation to balloon exponentially. "I haven't slept with any of our friends." I cocked my head toward him. "But give me time, I'll get to some of them."

"You're a slut," he said.

"So? What's your point?"

"I'm leaving," Jamie said. "I hope you find what you're looking for."

After Jamie left, I got up to use the restroom. On my way past the bar, I saw Donovan talking to a guy I didn't recognize.

"I thought you were leaving," I said.

"I was. I just ran into an old friend." Donovan had a fresh drink in his hand.

Someone else was worth another drink and I wasn't? I shrugged and tried not to look annoyed. I didn't want to act the way Jamie had been acting toward me.

There was a line for the restroom. I waited behind a late-career drag queen who had once dubbed herself "the toast of New York" in *Time Out*. She was wearing a tight black dress and fishnet stockings. Her makeup was caked on hard in an attempt to cover her wrinkles and 2 A.M. shadow.

"Hey, baby," she said, her voice husky.

"Hey," I said.

"You want a blow job?" she asked, grabbing my crotch. My dick was about as hard as a piece of warm brie.

"No, thanks," I said, grimacing.

"Your loss," she said.

When I left the restroom, I saw a guy I knew from going out, a hunky NYU student I wouldn't have minded getting with.

"It's been a really weird week," he said to me. "I lost my ferret."

"What do you mean, you 'lost your ferret'?"

"My ferret. He died."

"I'm sorry to hear that."

"Hey, do you want some coke?"

It was turning into that kind of night. I decided to push everything else out of my mind and focus on what mattered at the moment: partying and the pursuit of sex.

"That guy over there, the bleached blond, he'll give you some. Just tell him you're a friend of mine."

I found the guy by the bar. He was in his thirties, muscular and beefy, and had spent too much time in the sun. His face was pockmarked, though I guessed he had once been handsome.

I told him my name was Tyler and I was a student at Fordham.

He was an interior decorator, originally from Atlanta. We discussed a past boyfriend of mine who had wanted to be a decorator. After about five minutes, I decided I needed the drugs, since I couldn't bear the conversation any longer.

"Do you have any coke?" I asked. "I, uh, had some earlier, but I ran out."

"Sure," Decorator Guy said, smiling. "All you had to do was ask."

I followed him into a private handicapped restroom, and he handed me an amber vial. I scooped out two bumps with my old post office box key from Yale Station and snorted them into each nostril, licking the key afterwards and rubbing the coke dust into my gums. As usual, it tasted bitter, like uncoated aspirin dripping at the back of my throat.

Infused with a burst of energy, I suddenly didn't care about anything else that had transpired. There was a party to be had and I was going to enjoy it. Even though the night had been disappointing, it was only 2 A.M., and there was still plenty of time to salvage it.

The crowd was starting to strip off its clothes, turning the dance floor into a meat parade, a mass of writhing bodies, flopping breasts and penises. Tyler the Rentboy, I noticed, had started flashing anyone interested in a peek.

I had a few more drinks with Decorator Guy, which he paid for, since I had depleted my cash reserves by this point. Compared to what I could have scored that night, he was a shitty catch, but I felt like I owed him my company—in exchange for the drugs, the drinks, the companionship he had given me after my friends had left.

We stumbled back to the restroom several more times, the second and third time to do full lines off the top of the toilet tank. I had done coke in college, but this was nothing like the New Haven crap I had tried before. I had never bought it; if it was available, though, I was the first in line.

Decorator Guy told me that he used to be married to a woman and that I reminded him of her, in a good way. I told him I had just come out and hadn't been with too many guys.

I put my arms around him and we started sucking face. His body was thick and built, the product of many hours at the gym. If he hadn't been there to hold me, I might have fallen over right there at the bar, a drunken, quivering mess.

"Let's go to your place," I slurred into his ear.

When we got to his apartment, we were greeted by his large

Doberman, Willie. The first-floor apartment consisted of a long hallway with a bedroom, bathroom, and a galley kitchen that reeked of air freshener. The walls were stained and the carpets frayed. "You're a decorator and your apartment looks like this?" I asked.

"You little brat," he said, slapping me on the ass.

"Sorry," I said.

He took me to his bedroom, where the bed was a double-size futon. I was exhausted, so I flopped down on it. Willie promptly joined me at the foot of the futon and stared at me expectantly, as if I was supposed to perform tricks for him.

"Shit," Decorator Guy said. "I think Willie pissed in the bathroom. Let me go clean it up."

I closed my eyes and tried to pass out. My head was throbbing from the booze and the coke and I couldn't shut my eyes without seeing the spinning lights of the club.

When I woke from my catnap, Decorator Guy was on top of me and kissing me. He took my clothes off, which was a relief, since I didn't feel like doing it myself. He pulled my boxers off and started sucking on me vigorously.

"Your dick," he panted, after coming up for air. "It's the perfect size for blow jobs."

I tried not to laugh. "Thanks," I said.

I felt I should reciprocate, so I let him straddle my face while I gave him the most dispassionate blow job of my life. His crotch smelled musky and I wanted to get it over with. I stopped just shy of the obligatory sixty seconds. I didn't want to be rude.

Like Tyler, Decorator Guy was also a shaver, and his crotch was rough and stubbly, so I got the razor burn I had been wondering about. Guys with shaved pubic hair were bad news.

Across the room, Willie was curled up in a corner, licking his balls. I wondered if the two of them slept together in the bed.

Decorator Guy decided to do some licking of his own: he flipped me over and tongued my ass. I tried to pretend I was on the brink of passing out again, that I didn't have control over what I was doing. But it felt good.

"I want to fuck you," he whispered.

He put on a condom and pulled some lubricant out from

under his futon. I straddled him and positioned myself. It had been a while, but I was too tired to say no.

As I held onto his dick and tried to slide it in, my ass tensed up. Even though his cock was small, my body wasn't having it.

"Just relax," he said, as if it were a simple bodily function to control, like making a fist when you give blood.

After a few deep breaths, his cock was inside me; small as it was, it was in me, part of me. Was this worth it? The condom breaking, slipping off when he pulled out, exposing me to the blood and semen of this man who sticks his dick God knows where and keeps condoms and lube right next to his bed? I wondered what Tyler the Rentboy was doing right now, and wished I were with him.

I rocked up and down a few times, but I was getting no pleasure from it. "I don't think this is a good idea," I said, getting off him. I pulled the condom off his dick and threw it on the floor.

"Don't put it there," he said. "The dog will eat it."

I slept for a fitful two hours. As it was getting light outside, I slipped my clothes back on and let myself out. I had spent all my money on drinks, and I was too tired to find an ATM, so I decided to walk home. Rain had started falling in giant drops. By the time I reached Washington Square Park, I was soaked.

5

After showering and changing at home, I dragged myself into the office, arriving at quarter after ten.

"You look like you've been partying all night," Sonia said. "Did Lola take you to an after-hours?"

"Bad night," I said, shaking out my umbrella.

"I hope you took a lot of notes for your story."

"Oh, yeah," I said. "I got notes."

I hadn't realized Sonia wanted the article up by that afternoon, so I was forced to relive the evening, moment by moment. I kept thinking about Tyler the Rentboy, and about Decorator Guy and how disgusting he was. What was the difference between sleeping with a hustler and sleeping with someone like him? After spending the night at Decorator Guy's apartment, I felt cheap and sleazy, whereas I imagined myself feeling sexy and fabulous after a free night with a rentboy. But Tyler probably had to sleep with people like that all the time. Who knew what diseases either of them was carrying? I resolved never to let anyone fuck me on the first date. Oral, yes. Anal, no. Maybe I could keep that in my wallet as a mantra.

After I wrote the article and put it up on the site, complete with some images Sonia had purchased (including a tasteful photo of Tyler the Rentboy thrusting his crotch toward the camera), I felt strangely cleansed. I had shed the skin that had been bothering me last night. Sure, I hadn't written about my activities after the party, but that was no one's business. I was free to start afresh. Afresh with a wretched hangover, but afresh nonetheless.

Sonia wasn't crazy about the piece, but she said it would do. "I think you could have done more with this," she told me.

I realized I had to stop fucking around. If I was going to do proper nightlife reportage, I couldn't scrawl drunken notes and hope it would all come together in the morning. And if I was going to be a screenwriter, I had to use my time outside of the office more effectively.

I decided to continue working on my screenplay as soon as I got home that night.

I left the office at six and walked home. I would take a short nap and then resume work on *Breeders*. The short nap turned into a long one, and I woke up at ten to the sound of the phone ringing. It was Donovan.

"Do you want to go out to Mirror tonight? I heard Ariana saying she and Cameron might stop by."

"I need to get some work done," I said. "I'm really behind on my—"

"All work and no play makes Toby a dull boy," he said.

"Yeah, and all play and no work puts Toby's career in the toilet," I said.

"Whatever," he said, hanging up.

After I went to the bathroom, the phone rang again. It was my friend Elizabeth, who was working in film development in Los Angeles. We had been best friends in college; she had graduated the year before me.

"You're home," she said. "I thought you'd be out carousing."

I told her about the screenplay I was trying to finish.

"It sounds fabulous," she said. "I should set up some meetings for you. I mean, it's very, you know, alternative, so it's probably not right for us, but I can think of a few people who might be interested. New Line, maybe."

"Really? Do you think you could send it around?"

"I'd have to look at it, but yeah, totally, we could do something. Just finish it first."

Elizabeth was a rich girl from Connecticut I had met during my sophomore year in college. She became the friend I always called after a drunken hookup, the confessor who absolved me of my guilt. Elizabeth was the closest thing I had to a fag hag, though there was nothing haggy about her. She was pretty, with almond-shaped eyes and a button nose. She had no problem getting men into bed; she just had trouble keeping them there.

Elizabeth was, in her own words, a "Westport JAP," a high maintenance strain of the species that required frequent trips to Barneys, Tiffany, and, now that she was in Los Angeles, Fred Segal. As a development executive who had been at her studio for over a year, she was my in to the film industry. But I didn't like to think of her that way. She was my friend, and I felt terrible that we hadn't spoken since my graduation.

After I hung up the phone, I reread the opening scene of *Breeders:*

FADE IN:

EXT. GOTHAM STREET—NIGHT

A MAN and a WOMAN, both breeders, exit a basement level nightclub and walk down the street together.

                    MAN
I didn't know you were such a good dancer.

He affectionately puts his arm around her. She wriggles out of his grasp.

                   WOMAN
Not here. You know we can't—

                    MAN
Oh, come on!

                   WOMAN
Just wait, wait until we get home.

                    MAN
Fuck that! I'm not going to be afraid anymore!

He embraces her and gives her a kiss. Two POLICE OFFI-
CERS pull up in a black squad car. They are dressed in
military-style uniforms and speak through a megaphone.

POLICE OFFICER
You! Breeders, stop!

The police officers jump out of the car and pin the two
against a wall.

OPENING CREDITS ROLL as the two are beaten sense-
less.

I had made it to page sixty, and I resolved to finish by the end of
the weekend. I worked all day Saturday, stopping only to run to
the Korean deli for Tab and cigarette refueling. By that evening,
I had a workable first draft. I spent all Sunday editing, and by
Monday morning, I had a finished screenplay to send to Elizabeth.
The process was exhilarating and exhausting. It was the first weekend I could remember during which I hadn't gone drinking. The
phone had rung half a dozen times, and I had let every call go to
voice mail. Messages from Jamie, Donovan, David, my parents.
Plus two from Decorator Guy.

"When do I get to fuck you again?" said the first message.
Gross. Delete.

"What do I have to do to get you to call me back?" said the
second one. I didn't have an answer, so I deleted that one, too.

I decided I wouldn't give my number to anyone sketchy from
now on. I would just get theirs. The ball would be in my court.

But I had more important things to consider than my career in
bed. I thought about sending the screenplay over to Cameron's
office, but I was annoyed he had never called me back. He could
bid for my work if he wanted it. Anyway, it was just a first draft,
and probably had massive problems that Elizabeth, a comp lit
major who was brilliant at dissecting screenplays, would illumi-
nate.

I arrived at work on Monday morning after dropping the

screenplay off at Fed Ex. Donovan, as usual, was sitting at his terminal. "Where were you all weekend?" he asked.

"I told you: I had to work. I finished it, though. It's done and off to California."

Before Donovan could answer, Sonia came into our office. The dark rings under her eyes were only made worse by her eyeliner habit.

"I need to speak with you two," she said. "We've been asked to cut back our editorial budget."

"What does that mean exactly?" Donovan asked, turning around.

"A few things. I can only let you expense two restaurant reviews per week, instead of the usual five. You'll still be able to do five; some of them will just have to be comps."

"Comps?" Donovan said. "You know I can't do real restaurant reviews with comps. It totally ruins the integrity of the piece if the restaurant is giving you a free meal. Can't you cut in other areas?"

"Actually, we are. We won't be having Friday staff lunches anymore. We're going to do our freelance payroll on a net thirty days basis to conserve cash. And we're not buying photographs anymore; we're going to get images from the venues, or you guys can shoot them with the digital."

"I'm sure we can handle this for now," I said. "But what does this mean long term?"

"This is just a temporary solution to conserve our resources," Sonia said. "I'm meeting with investors almost every day, and they want to see that we can keep our burn rate low. Once we get additional financing, things will go back to normal."

I wasn't sure I believed her, but I wanted to.

Elizabeth called me at the office on Wednesday. "Toby, I just finished reading it. I really like it. I have some notes for you, and there are some parts that need work, but I think you should plan to come out here and meet some people."

I took a deep breath. I had finally finished something, and it was getting a positive response. Why had I been so afraid of this in the past?

I asked Sonia if I could have a few days off before Thanksgiving, which she said would be fine, as long as I filed my reviews ahead of time.

I spent the next two weeks preparing for my trip to Los Angeles. I continued to revise my screenplay, showing drafts to several friends, and I went shopping for a few LA-friendly items for my wardrobe. I arranged for Gus to be boarded. I read up on meeting etiquette, stuff like "Always go to the restroom before your meeting begins" and "Don't sit in the most comfortable chair." I rented every movie I could find on Hollywood culture, even the ones I had already seen: *The Player, Swimming with Sharks, Sunset Blvd*. I just hoped I wouldn't meet my end floating face down in a swimming pool.

I stopped by Sonia's office the day before I left for LA.

"Look, Toby," she said, "I think it's really great that you're doing this, and I'm sure your work is fabulous, but don't get your hopes up. It takes a long time to sell a screenplay. Even if they take an option on something, it can be years before it ever sees the light of day. I don't mean to be discouraging, but believe me, I've been there. A few years ago, I sold options on two pieces I wrote, and nothing ever happened with them. It made me some quick cash, but it's not the same as getting your work produced."

"I know," I said. "I don't have any illusions about it. I just want to get out there and see what the business is all about."

Of course, I wanted much more than that: recognition, fame, to tell a story.

I got up to leave.

"Oh, I almost forgot," she said. "Are you stopping off in San Francisco?"

"I'll be there for Thanksgiving," I said.

Sonia closed the door to her office. "There's something I've been meaning to ask you about. Do you think your parents would be interested in investing in the site?"

"I don't know," I said. "What kind of money are you talking about?"

"Right now, we're offering $200,000 minimum investments. Let me give you the PPM and you can show it to them. Seriously, even two hundred grand would allow the expansion we're look-ing for. You know, a few other cities, beefing up this operation, a bigger editorial budget, the whole bit."

She handed me a spiral-bound book of a hundred pages or so, CityStyle's private placement memorandum. I wasn't sure what to think. I knew $200,000 was a lot of money, but I had no idea how that would figure in my parents' world. Perhaps foolishly, they believed it wasn't a good idea for me to be privy to their fi-nancial matters. While it meant that—unlike many of my peers in grade school—I never went around the schoolyard telling peo-ple how much money my parents had, I was also woefully unin-formed when it came to matters of finance.

After thinking about it, I figured it couldn't hurt to ask my parents about CityStyle, though I did feel a bit put upon by Sonia's asking me to solicit an investment. Mostly, though, I couldn't believe she and the company were so desperate for cash.

When I arrived in Los Angeles on Saturday afternoon, Elizabeth met me at the airport in her Range Rover. As soon she stepped out of her car to help me with my bags, I tried to figure out what had happened to her. In the past year, she must have gained about fifteen pounds. While previously she had been stick-thin, she had now reached a more normal weight.

She started in on the topic after pulling away from LAX and lighting a cigarette.

"You noticed," she said. "I gained weight. I got sick of being thin but not enjoying myself."

"You look great," I said. "But how did you do it?"

"Started eating more regularly. Stopped going to the gym like a maniac. Now it's just yoga twice a week. I know that com-pared to some of these girls, I look like a heifer, but I don't care. I'm at my ideal body weight now."

We came to a stoplight. She looked at me.

"You're looking a little skinny yourself, you know."

"If I get fat, I'll never find a boyfriend."

"Yeah," she sighed. "I guess it doesn't matter for me, since I have Chad."

Elizabeth had told me briefly about her new boyfriend, a twenty-five-year-old personal trainer with model-actor ambitions whose claim to fame was appearing in *Playgirl* several months earlier. I was surprised that Elizabeth, who had been Phi Beta Kappa at Yale, was dating someone like Chad, but I tried not to judge. Maybe this was what people did in Los Angeles, more so than in New York: dating as arm candy. Maybe people picked out boyfriends like they would a new handbag. A girl wouldn't judge her accessories for their intelligence, would she?

Elizabeth had made a dinner reservation that night at the Avalon, a mid-century-styled hotel with a restaurant and cabanas surrounding its figure-eight-shaped swimming pool. Chad was at the white vinyl bar finishing a call on his cell phone. We were introduced and the three of us sat down.

"How are you all doing?" asked the waitress, a strawberry blonde in her early thirties.

"Great. How are you?" Elizabeth said.

"Oh, whatever," the waitress said, sighing and waving the question away.

"Welcome to LA," Elizabeth said to me with a smile.

When the waitress had left, Chad asked me about my screenplay.

"That is so cool," he said after I finished telling him about it. "Maybe there will be a role in it for me once you sell it."

"Of course there will be!" Elizabeth said. "I've introduced Chad to a friend who does casting for the soaps and he just loves his work."

I asked Elizabeth and Chad how they met.

"At the gym," Chad said. He worked at the Crunch on Sunset.

"Were you Elizabeth's trainer?" I asked.

"I haven't actually gotten my training certification yet. I've been working at the shake bar. I was talking about my modeling portfolio with one of the trainers, and, uh, uh . . ."

"Elizabeth?" I said helpfully.

"Yeah, Elizabeth—she said she knew a casting director."

"Chad is studying to be a Level I trainer."

From my gym in New York, I knew that was the entry level. "That's fantastic," I said, feeling obligated to praise the most meager of accomplishments.

"I spend so much time at the gym anyway, that I figured, why not be a trainer?" He shrugged and grinned.

"What were you doing before?" I asked.

"Test screenings for films, you know, where you invite people to watch and then they fill out surveys."

"Really?" I asked. "What kind of films?"

"Oh, the big ones, mostly. Biggest flick I did was *Titanic*. Man, that was so good. I saw the four-hour rough cut and I cried and cried."

Elizabeth patted him on the shoulder affectionately. What was she doing with this meathead?

When it came time for the check, I put down my debit card.

"Toby, you don't have to do that," Elizabeth said.

"No, really," I said. "It's my treat." I felt it was the least I could do for her.

"That's so sweet of you, man," Chad said.

Five minutes later, the waitress came back, saying my card had been declined. I was sure I had enough money in my account; my latest check from CityStyle should have been automatically deposited two days ago. I fumbled with my wallet and gave her a credit card, the one I had sworn I would stop using.

"What do you think of him?" Elizabeth asked me as soon as the two of us were safely ensconced in her Range Rover. Chad was following us home in his own car.

"He's adorable," I said. What was I supposed to say? That he wasn't the brightest bulb on Hollywood Boulevard, but he had the body of a god?

"It's like, all those years I dated guys who were such smarties, they were into playing so many head games, and then this guy comes along, and he's just simple, you know? He says what he's thinking, he just wants a good solid relationship. I know he's not exactly a rocket scientist, but who needs that anyway?"

Maybe Elizabeth was right. Perhaps I had been setting the bar too high. If I could just find someone who was simple, honest— did it really matter what school someone went to?

"What do you guys talk about when you're alone?"

"Mostly movies," she said. "I've been trying to get him to read more, but he's not a big reader."

On second thought, I didn't know if I could bear it, no matter how beautiful the moron was.

"And he wants to have children! You know how much I want to have kids. I mean, I'm twenty-four years old, and I'm not getting any younger."

"How long have you been together?" I asked.

"Almost two months," she said.

"Does it bother you that he posed naked?" I asked, though the idea secretly turned me on.

"Wouldn't you if you looked like that?" she said.

Once we were back at her bungalow in the Hollywood Hills, Elizabeth set me up on the pull-out couch in her living room. During the day, she had a view of the Hollywood sign; at night, the most prominent feature of the landscape was an enormous lighted cross perched high in the hills.

As I drifted off, I started to understand her relationship with Chad. From the direction of her bedroom, I heard the distinct sounds of sex. Either Elizabeth and Chad wanted me to hear every machination, or they had no idea how thin the bedroom door was. There were loud, heartfelt groans, bedsprings squeaking, the moving around and repositioning of sheets and pillows. Just when I thought I could no longer contain my combination of laughter and embarrassment, I heard her scream it: "Oh, shit!"

It wasn't a bad "Oh, shit!" either. It wasn't an it-slipped-out or the-condom-broke sort of "Oh, shit!" It was an ecstatic you-surprised-me-and-I'm-on-the-brink-of-orgasm "Oh, shit!" What new surprise would warrant that exclamation with someone Elizabeth had already had sex with dozens of times? What new technique could Chad have employed that she hadn't already experienced in his tongue's endless exploration of her body?

Whatever it was, it was something good, something my sex life was sorely missing.

On Monday morning, I called my bank. My CityStyle check had never been deposited. I had taken out a cash advance on my credit card to last me through the weekend, and Elizabeth had lent me some money. I left a voice mail for CityStyle's financial guy so he could correct the problem.

Elizabeth was able to take a few hours off from work each day in order to accompany me to my various meetings.

"I wasn't able to get meetings with everyone I sent it to, but we have plenty to start with," she told me. "I'm being very careful about sending it out. People like to think they're reading something no one else has seen."

Unfortunately, the meetings were disappointing. A large studio told us the story was too gay; a small indie producer said audiences would think the message of *Breeders* was homophobic. A gay producer said the screenplay was not gay enough, while an agent said it was too cerebral. At a smaller company, a producer only a few years older than we were said they could consider it with some capital investment on our part. Elizabeth rolled her eyes and quickly brought that meeting to a close. At another large studio, when a smug producer sat behind his desk and said, "It's very well written, but I really don't think anyone would want to see this movie," I had the urge to jump across his desk and throttle him.

On Monday, I got a call on my cell phone as we were leaving a studio lot. It was Jamie.

"I've got business in San Francisco tomorrow," he said. "I can be routed back through LA and we can hang out. I probably should just head back to New York—I've been working twenty-hour days on this deal—but it would be really fun to see you in a different city."

I asked Elizabeth where he should stay, and she said he should get a room at the Standard, a hip hotel in West Hollywood.

"I can't wait to see you!" Jamie said, though I had just seen him four days ago. His phone clicked. "I gotta jump."

"You'll get to meet the famous Jamie. Maybe he can expense dinner for us," I joked to Elizabeth. I hadn't heard back from CityStyle about my check, and I had made another cash withdrawal from my credit card. I was starting to get worried.

"Don't worry about it; I can cover it," Elizabeth said. "Hell, I do it for Chad all the time. We have a deal: he pays for the little stuff—parking, movies, whatever—and I pay for the big stuff, like dinner."

"Do you ever give him money?"

"I've lent him a few hundred dollars. I know he'll pay it back, though."

I didn't want to say anything, for fear that she might not lend me any more money.

Our last meeting, on Tuesday, was with a short film Web site whose producers said they might be interested in serializing *Breeders*. The idea of my work appearing on a three-by-four-inch box on someone's computer screen—on a site that would most likely be out of business before the end of the year—was not appealing. At the end of the meeting, we were given yo-yos advertising the site, probably as a consolation prize for being so desperate. We gave them to the parking attendant along with a tip. He looked like he had seen them before.

That night, Elizabeth and I met Jamie at the poolside bar at the Standard after he checked in. I immediately noticed there was something different about him. His usually animated face seemed placid and calm.

When Elizabeth was in the restroom, I asked him about it.

"You seem so mellow," I said. "Are you on something?"

He shook his head.

"What, then?"

"You can't tell anyone, okay? I got Botox injections in my forehead," Jamie said. "My dad gave them to me over the weekend."

"Why?"

"Wrinkles. Partly preventative, but I *am* aging at a faster than normal rate. My dad confirmed it."

"Jamie, that's absurd. You're twenty-two!"

"I knew you wouldn't understand," he said. "You have it easy."

"You looked fine before. You could end up hurting yourself with this stuff. No one knows the long-term effects, do they?"

We noticed Elizabeth heading across the lobby and back toward the bar.

"I'd rather not talk about it, okay? I can't help it if I want to look good."

After having drinks, we drove to Matsuhisa for sushi. I was already loaded on vodka cranberries by the time our food came.

Elizabeth and Jamie started gobbling up the thin pieces of sashimi from the platter on our table, but I wasn't hungry.

"Toby, don't get discouraged," Elizabeth said. "It takes a lot of time to make a sale."

"They weren't meeting with us because they liked the script; they were meeting with us because you had sent it to them. I mean, it's fabulous that you have all these contacts, but I want people to like my work for what it is." I didn't want to seem ungrateful for what she had done for me, but I couldn't deny that the trip hadn't turned out how I had imagined it.

"Look, there are a few other places that still have the script, and I'm sure I'll be hearing from them after the holidays," Elizabeth said.

Right. It was about as likely she would field any more calls about *Breeders* as it was that Cameron Cole would call me back. He still hadn't, nearly a month after I had left him the message. I hadn't wanted to call again; that would seem pathetic. What was I calling Cameron for anyway? A date, a pitch meeting, a future? I was desperate for all these things.

Maybe tonight I would finally hook up with Jamie. After four cocktails and more on the way, my faculties for reasoning weren't as strong as they should have been. And Jamie—wrinkle-free forehead and all—was on his best behavior in the presence of a member of the opposite sex. I also felt more relaxed with Chad not around; he had told Elizabeth he had to work late. It would have been far too embarrassing to have him there, and would have completely ruined Elizabeth's credibility. Of course, Jamie would have enjoyed the eye candy.

The check came, and I put down my credit card, partly to show my appreciation to Elizabeth and partly to show that I may have been down, but I certainly wasn't out.

Again, my card came back declined. "I'm sure it's a mistake," Elizabeth said. "Sometimes they cut you off if you spend too much in another city, just to make sure the card isn't stolen."

I knew that wasn't the case. I was dangerously close to my credit limit on both of my cards. Apparently, I had just reached it on one.

Jamie magnanimously put down his card and offered to pay for everyone. Elizabeth seemed pleased. It was probably the first time in two months that a guy had done that for her.

Even though it was late, I was determined to make the most of my trip, so Elizabeth dropped Jamie and me off at a strip of bars on Santa Monica Boulevard. Jamie got money from a cash machine and lent me two hundred dollars. Considering that I might sleep with him tonight, it made me feel like a prostitute.

We stepped inside a huge, whirling disco emporium that could have been the set for a music video.

I fetched drinks for both of us, since I felt like I owed Jamie something for his generosity. Standing at the bar was a guy who couldn't have been more than twenty. He wasn't my usual type; bone thin, he fashioned himself as a goth-punk with dyed red spiky hair, a leather jacket, and an ear pierced in five places. He was adorable, like a little baby punk who had recently come into punkhood.

"Hey," I said, because I was sloshed, and it just came out.

"Hey," he said, offering a pale hand.

Goth Boy was an art student who was, not surprisingly, into the goth music scene. He had come to the bar tonight with several friends, but they were nowhere to be found.

When I brought Goth Boy over, Jamie gave me a sideways glance that said, *You've gone crazy, picking up trash like this*. But Goth Boy wasn't trash. He may have been pierced a few too many times, but he was a sweet kid.

As we talked, I realized what would make me feel better. I pulled Goth Boy aside and asked him if he knew where to get some coke. My buzz had started to wear off and my mood was heading downhill.

"I know someone here who can get it," Goth Boy said. "How much do you want?"

"Just forty dollars' worth," I said. "I hardly ever do it." I handed him the money and he went off to find his friend.

Jamie glared at me. "I just want you to know, for the record, that I don't approve of this," he said.

"Okay," I said. "Your disapproval has been noted."

Fifteen minutes later, Goth Boy came back with a tiny plastic envelope. "Your C," he said. "I never do it either, but I might partake tonight." With his emaciated frame, he looked like he did it all the time.

We stumbled towards the restroom, where we shoveled out the coke with my key. Goth Boy was about to unlock the door when I tugged at his sleeve. I pulled him towards me, kissing him, trading our bitter saliva. I felt the fluorescent lights of the restroom bear down on us in the stall.

Through his black jeans, his erection pressed against my leg.

"How old are you anyway?" I asked.

"Nineteen," he said.

"What's a nice boy like you doing in a place like this?" I teased.

"Where else am I supposed to hang out?" he asked.

I realized we shouldn't ignore Jamie, so we hurried back to where he was standing near the bar.

"I'm getting tired," he said. "I think I'd better be getting back to the hotel."

"Come on," I said. "We just got here."

"It's almost closing time," said Goth Boy. "But I know a cool after-hours on Sunset."

The three of us hitched a ride with a friend of Goth Boy's. He knocked on the door of the club and a guy in leather pants unlocked it for us. The black-walled dive, complete with a pool table and jukebox, stank of beer and sweat. Even though the place was illegally serving drinks, everyone still obeyed California's smoking laws, crowding onto a small porch in the back.

As I watched Jamie, I realized he was hanging around entirely for my benefit. He was exhausted from work, he had a plane to catch in five hours, and this was probably the last place in LA where he wanted to be spending his time.

"Why don't we go back to the hotel room?" Jamie asked. It was almost 3 A.M. and he had to leave for the airport at six.

We piled into a cab and cruised up Sunset to the Standard. Jamie showed his key card to the doorman and we headed upstairs.

Jamie's room was decorated like a fantasy 1960s motel room, with an orange Formica bathroom, Warhol cow-print curtains, and a bed with a blue vinyl headboard. Goth Boy and I collapsed on the silver beanbag in the corner.

Jamie flopped down on the bed and half-heartedly told us we could help ourselves to the mini-bar.

I felt awful that Jamie seemed so defeated, but the situation had already gone too far. I had brought my date back to his hotel room, the hotel room he had reserved specifically to see me, so we could hang out in LA together, away from the madness in New York. And instead I had brought all the madness with me.

"You guys can stay here if you want," he said. "I just need a few hours of sleep." Jamie dimmed the lights and passed out on the bed, fully dressed, his good ear to the pillow.

Goth Boy and I started making out on the beanbag, which wasn't the most comfortable arrangement, since one of us fell off onto the deep shag carpet every thirty seconds. After this had happened several times, I crawled up onto the bed. Jamie was barely occupying half of it. Goth Boy clambered on top of me and we started kissing again, the kind of wet, messy kisses that only happen when people are drunk and hungry for contact. His mouth tasted like sour milk.

As we kissed, I looked over at Jamie, who was lying less than two feet away from us. He had his eyes half closed, but I could tell he was watching.

As soon as Jamie stepped into the shower, we took our clothes off and crawled under the covers. I felt awful about it, teasing him like this. But we had to be out of the room by eleven, and there wasn't a moment to waste.

Jamie emerged from the bathroom fully dressed. He packed up quickly and waved goodbye to us from the foot of the bed. It was as if he had barged in on us, not the other way around.

After Jamie left, we both stripped out of our underwear. Goth Boy's uncircumcised dick was skinny, not very long, and had red veins running down its side. I wasn't looking forward to putting my mouth on it.

"You're like the sweetest guy I've met in, God, since I don't know when," Goth Boy said.

"Thanks," I said. I wasn't sure what I had done to deserve the compliment.

"No, really," he said. "I hope I can see you again."

"I may be out here more if this screenplay thing works out." I knew there was no guarantee of the elusive "screenplay thing" working out, and if it did, I certainly wouldn't be spending my time with the likes of Goth Boy. I hoped he realized that, but I had the feeling he didn't.

I went down on him for thirty seconds, segueing into jerking him off, kissing his chest and rubbing his pierced nipples. After two minutes, he came onto his stomach in short spurts. Part of his semen formed an X, like the frosting on a hot cross bun.

Of course he would come like that, I thought. I wiped his stomach down with the sheet, erasing his handiwork.

"Do you want me to . . ." he asked. He started trying to jerk my dick to attention.

"Don't worry about it," I said. "It's been a long night."

"But I want to," he said.

"Really, it's fine," I said, even though it wasn't. "Let's just order breakfast."

I called room service, since Pelham Robertson was paying for it, and ordered as much as two people could possibly eat. It was punishment for all the late nights Pelham had been making Jamie and David work over the past several months.

As Goth Boy and I wolfed down our breakfasts, I noticed he still had a raging erection.

"Must be since I'm diabetic and I have poor circulation," he said. "Once the blood gets to my dick, it just wants to stay there for a while."

After showering and getting dressed, I surveyed the room. The bed was stained with Goth Boy's red hair dye on the pillows, his semen on the sheets, and the room service orange juice I had spilled on the duvet. In an effort to create some ambiance, Jamie had turned one of the wall lamps so it faced the headboard, and there was now an enormous welt where the blue plastic had melted.

We had pulled a Johnny Depp on the room, or as close to a Johnny Depp as ordinary civilians could come.

I left five dollars for housekeeping and we headed downstairs.

Goth Boy and I sat on the steps outside the Standard, feeling more like two vagabonds who had spent a night on the street than two people who had just bunked at a chic hotel. We exchanged numbers.

Elizabeth pulled up in her Range Rover and Goth Boy sauntered forward and put his hand on the rear door.

Thinking he was some kind of drifter, Elizabeth instinctively power-locked the doors as a horrified look crossed her face.

After she realized Goth Boy was the person I had just spent the night with, she unlocked the doors again and we got in.

Goth Boy, who had suddenly become shy, grunted a greeting. He told her he lived in an apartment building near Mann's Chinese. Elizabeth drove him home.

"I'll give you a call," he said after getting out, seeming genuinely sad that the night was over.

"Cool," I said, though I was sure I would never see him again.

As we pulled away, he stood on the street waving to me.

"My God, Toby, he was so young," Elizabeth said. "Did he have braces? I saw something that looked like braces!"

"It was probably just his tongue piercing," I said.

"Kiddo," Elizabeth said, "you are out of control."

Right after Elizabeth dropped me off at the airport, my cell phone rang. Sometimes, I thought as I pressed SEND, you know you shouldn't answer.

"Toby?"

"I'm about to check in," I said. "This isn't really a good time."

"I was just thinking about when I would get to see you again."

I asked Goth Boy if I could call him back later.

With the same naïveté I had exhibited at his age, he was now sure we would be long-distance boyfriends. I had known, though, from the moment I had met him, that this would be a one-night-and-one-night-only deal.

Still, his needy phone call spurred my conscience. Did I owe him something? What was it?

I feel like this every time, I reminded myself.

Every time I slept with someone, part of me felt guilty.

6

When my plane landed in San Francisco, I experienced a familiar sinking feeling as I anticipated seeing my parents. It was the feeling that there was a continental divide between us that had to be crossed, a gap of understanding to be bridged.

I thought of them as sophisticated people, though San Francisco is a city that tends more toward the provincial than the cosmopolitan. To a longtime San Franciscan, New York carried with it a whiff of sin, of ill intent. My mother had always lived in large cities; she grew up in Rome, the product of an Italian mother and a German father. She attended the American University of Rome, making that choice, she said, because she wanted to marry an American. After completing a major in dance, she moved to New York with her boyfriend, a young man with a trust fund, and they lived at the Plaza Hotel for three months. She failed to find work as a dancer, instead becoming fascinated by the machinations of Seventh Avenue. After the romance faded, she enrolled at F.I.T. and found herself an apartment in the Village with three other Italian girls. In the spring of her senior year, she was rushing several bolts of fabric down to her studio on Twentieth Street on a Friday afternoon when she ran into my father, who was visiting from California. A native of Palo Alto, he had just completed his M.B.A. at Stanford. She showed him the town that weekend, and six months later, they were married. Glad to be freed of New York's sticky summers and biting winters, she set up her household in San Francisco in 1975.

Thus it was with a mix of fear and regret that my parents

viewed my current situation. My mother, after all, could have stayed in Manhattan. She could have married a New York banker and ended up on Park Avenue. She could have started her own boutique in the Village and continued to live as a quasi-Bohemian. My father could have chosen to move out to New York himself. But none of those things had happened. They were now Californians, and I was on my way to becoming a New Yorker, which meant I was a different breed entirely, one not to be trusted, regardless of the fact that I was their only son.

My father greeted me at the gate at SFO with an obligatory grin. He looked the same as always: a little paunchy, soft around the edges, though still handsome.

"How's New York been treating you?" he asked, the question he always asked.

"Great," I said, since the truth was too hard to explain.

"Your mom wanted to pick you up, but she's been busy with her Thanksgiving preparations. You know how she always tries to do a little too much each day."

He asked about the Web site, and so I told him about the funding crisis, leaving out the part about the possibility of his investing. Explaining it all, combined with the previous evening's debauchery, was making my stomach turn.

"I don't know, Toby, it doesn't sound very stable. How about something more traditional, like marketing or PR? You're good at that sort of thing."

"I want to be able to write," I explained, though he already knew this.

"That's fine," he said. "But we don't always get to do the things we want to do. Sometimes you have to pay your dues."

When I arrived at my parents' house on the edge of Pacific Heights, it was filled with the aroma of multiple meals being prepared: a cioppino for tonight, cornbread and pumpkin pie for tomorrow. Mercedes, my parents' housekeeper, was busily stuffing the turkey, her small hands stuck up its ass. My mother, who still enjoyed cooking, was preparing a salad. She was dressed in

a slim pantsuit under an apron; her figure was the result of diet-
ing, yoga, and a complicated liposuction procedure done several
years ago that had put her in a girdle for ten days. Her shoulder-
length hair, which she still had highlighted every two weeks, was
a rich honey blond whose variations she had asked her colorist
to copy directly from a real leopard coat of hers.

"My darling," she said, hugging me. "You look good. Have
you lost weight?" My mother's Italian accent, as much as I was
used to it, never failed to surprise me when I hadn't seen her in a
while.

She opened a bottle of champagne. "Our hero has returned
from New York!" she exclaimed, toasting me. My stomach was
feeling a little better—perhaps simply due to making it home—
so I took a sip. I wasn't looking forward to explaining about
CityStyle, about my check not coming through, about borrow-
ing some money to tide me over.

Instead of worrying, I did what I always did when I returned
home: I ate.

Despite my mother's propensity for thinness, she was a master
when it came to orchestrating meals. We all dug into the rich red
cioppino, spooning out mussels, clams, and prawns into large
bowls.

"This Web page," my mother said after we had been eating
for a few minutes. "I don't really understand it. Every time I pull
it up, I find it hard to read. The color combinations, the type: I
suppose it is not for people my age."

"They do try to push the envelope a bit on the design," I said.

"Readability should be key," my father said.

"Is it my imagination, or does it have a column called
'StarFucker'?" my mother asked.

"I don't write for that," I said, hoping they hadn't seen my
piece about Real World Guy.

"This woman who says she slept with Mick Jagger? What's
the big deal? Everyone slept with Mick Jagger at some point or
another!"

My father laughed. "You never did."

"I just think there are more important things to write about."

"I don't see how the site makes any money," my father said.

"Actually," I said, "they're looking for additional investors. I wanted to ask you two if you were interested."

"Ha!" He laughed as if I had suggested he jump off the Golden Gate Bridge. "You think we would invest in an Internet venture!"

"Toby, we really don't have the money right now to do such a thing," my mother said.

"Isabella, don't say—"

"I think it's important Toby understands what our situation is."

They explained to me that revenue at my father's company was down 40 percent, and my mother's company was nearing bankruptcy.

"How can that be?" I asked. "I thought the label was doing well."

"Everyone thinks that," she said. "We're a private company, so no one ever sees the figures. But people aren't buying couture anymore. It's a dying breed of fashion."

"Why don't you do what everyone else is doing?" I asked.

"And what would that be?" She looked at me sternly, as if I had no business making such suggestions to her.

"Branch out. Do a bridge line. Do fragrances, accessories."

"Toby, that takes a tremendous amount of money. And you know I've never taken on investors. Besides, all those bridge lines are just shit, pardon me." She started waving her hands around for emphasis, something she did whenever she was excited. "They are just watered down versions of the original vision! If I'm going to do that kind of thing, I might as well not do it at all!"

"You can't close down the company," I said. It was impossible to imagine my mother not running her studio.

"There are a number of people interested in buying. I just had a meeting last week with LVMH, though I'm not sure I can meet their terms."

"You're going to sell to LVMH?" I couldn't imagine my mother's label becoming part of a bigger operation. However, owned by a company like LVMH, it would be visible alongside the Guccis of the world.

"Let's not presume anything," she said.

"The important thing," my father said, "is we would prefer you come home. Your rent every month isn't cheap, and I want to see you creating a solid future in something. All this Web site stuff can be fun, but how different is it from working on the college paper? It just seems frivolous."

"It's not frivolous," I said. "It's serious journalism. I know it's not politics or business reporting, but people use the site as a resource. They rely on us."

"Just think about it," my father said. "Six months from now, what do you want to be able to say you've done with your time in New York? I was talking with the father of one of your classmates—what's her name, the Carr girl?—and he said she's been working as an analyst at Goldman Sachs."

"What an experience!" my mother said. A classmate of mine could be digging ditches and my parents would think it was fabulous.

"A lot of my friends do that sort of thing, and they hate it," I said. "They would kill to be doing what I'm doing." I looked at my mother. "You should understand. I'm not the type who can just do what everyone else is doing."

"He has a point, Simon. It wouldn't be fair to tell my own child he has to be like everyone else."

"I'm afraid you're living in a fantasy world. You have no idea of the things that comprise daily life."

There was no arguing with them. And I certainly couldn't ask them for money. CityStyle not making payroll would just be one more nail in the dot-com coffin.

"Let's talk about something more pleasant," my mother said, and I knew exactly what we wouldn't be talking about.

The thing about coming out to my parents—after all the explanations, the fighting, the tears—was that it was still impossible to discuss relationships or dating. The phrase "I'm seeing someone" brought up a multitude of disastrous images: the AIDS-ridden guys my mother pictured me falling into bed with, the sodomy my father imagined me committing. They hated thinking about the lack of societal acceptance, the inability to have children. To a liberal mind, these were all barriers that could be overcome, but to my parents, two people whose primary contact with homosexuals prior to my coming out was with the florist, the tailor, and the hairdresser, these were not lifestyle choices to be taken lightly. True, my mother had employed a handful of gay guys at her studio over the years, but she regarded them similarly, as members of a service industry whose practices in the bedroom were not for her to comprehend.

It took my mother longer than my father to accept that I was gay. While my father saw it purely as biology, of winning the gay gene in the genetic lottery, my mother always thought it was her fault, that she had made me gay. She even once told me I was gay because I hated her and therefore hated all women, both of which I assured her were not true.

All this, along with the introduction of a variety of boyfriends of dubious quality through the years, had made it all the more difficult for us to relate to each other.

There was a simple way around it: They didn't ask, and I didn't tell.

There were insinuations over the years, like the time my mother returned from Costco during a vacation with a jumbo box of condoms "for your promiscuity," she said, an assumption she made based on my proclivity for coming home at five in the morning. Or the times my father would ask me in the middle of the evening news "what the gays think about this," as if I could be responsible for the opinions of the entire world's homosexual population.

It wasn't that my parents were squeamish about sex, either. Unlike many parents, mine actually introduced me to the idea of sexuality, explaining the mechanics at an early age. For them, sexuality—as long as it was heterosexuality—was a comfortable issue, not a source of embarrassment but a fact of life, as it should be.

Still, even after I had come out, my father continued to harass me for several years, hoping I would come around to the right side of the fence. When I told my parents about my plans to adopt Gus during my freshman year of college, my father said, "Why don't you worry less about getting a cat and more about getting some pussy?"

I knew it wasn't worth it to make them understand.

7

Because it was a celebration she had never experienced as a child, planning a Thanksgiving feast that would make her husband and son proud was high on my mother's list of priorities. When planning for any holiday, my mother embraced multiculturalism—and shopping—with a vengeance. She and my father always returned home from trips loaded down with twice as much as they had brought.

The two had traveled through most of Europe together in the seventies and eighties, and had since moved on to farther flung destinations like Africa, India, China, Japan, Russia, and South America. This year, it had been Mexico, which, though they had visited before, my mother felt they had never "done properly," and so our table was decorated with little dolls made of corn husks and brightly colored wooden animals, including a grotesque army of little turkeys whose heads bobbed up and down obscenely when tapped.

Since a photographer from *Elle Décor* had stopped by earlier to record this spectacular display of colonial fetishism, the table had been set for twelve, even though it would just be the three of us. My mother's parents lived in Italy and did not celebrate Thanksgiving, and both of my father's parents were dead. Some years, we would do Thanksgiving with my godmother and her children, but this time they had decided to take a trip to Hawaii. So it was just the three of us sitting at an enormous table decorated with sweatshop-produced Mexican handicrafts.

We always started eating around four and were ready to pass out by eight from all the booze and food. Just as my father had finished carving the turkey Mercedes had prepared, the phone rang.

I answered it.

"Is Toby there?"

For some reason, the fact that Goth Boy was calling didn't surprise me. I clutched my glass of champagne.

"I think you turned off your cell phone, so I called directory. Thank God you're listed. So what's going on?" He asked me the question as if there was sure to be something unusual and spectacular happening on Thanksgiving.

"Well," I said, I hoped not too condescendingly, "we're just about to sit down to dinner. Aren't you going to do the same?"

"I'm not having Thanksgiving dinner," he said. "I was going to go to my sister's, but she had to leave town." I had forgotten; he had mentioned something about his parents living in Illinois.

"Don't you have any friends you can hang out with?"

"Not really," he said. "Thanksgiving is not a very goth holiday."

"No," I said, "I suppose it isn't."

There was a long pause. I heard a video game being played in the background.

"Anyway," I said, "I've got to get going. We're sitting down to eat."

"Call me," he said.

"Sure," I said, and hung up.

"Who was that?" my mother asked. "Imagine, calling on Thanksgiving! How strange!"

"Just someone I met in LA."

"Really?" my mother said, and I knew what she was thinking. "Does that Elizabeth hang out with strange people?"

"No," I said. " 'That' Elizabeth has very nice friends, actually. She's currently dating a model."

"What a mistake," my mother said, as she poured the gravy into a tureen. "I always tell my girls at the studio, 'Never date anyone who is better looking than you are.' "

I wondered what my mother would think if I ever dated Donovan.

* * *

Since my mother insisted every vacation at home be stretched to its greatest possible length, I didn't arrive back in New York until the following Sunday evening. Though the LA meetings hadn't gone well, and I would have to tell Sonia my parents weren't interested in investing, I had never felt so glad to be back in Manhattan.

On Monday morning, though, something had changed. Sonia looked beaten down, not rested, by the few days' vacation we had all been granted. She told us we would be having our weekly staff meeting a day early.

"What's going on?" I asked Donovan as we both scrambled to gather our notes so we could report on the coming week's reviews.

"Beats me," he shrugged.

The eight of us squeezed into Sonia's office and waited for her to begin.

"I think many of you have sensed this day was coming," she said, and with those words, we all knew.

"The site, I'm sorry to say, will be shutting down, effective immediately. I had a number of meetings with investors during the first half of last week, and continued to have follow-up discussions over the weekend." She let out a sigh. "We simply don't have the funding to keep going, and the venture capital situation is not getting any better."

I looked at the faces around me. The staff, even Donovan, was stoic. Had they expected this? Why weren't they angry? Perhaps there was nothing to be angry about.

"As you've probably realized, our last payroll didn't go through. I want to make sure you are all compensated as soon as possible for that pay period. We can't offer any severance, but at least we can give you that."

Great. We were being offered our back wages as if they were some sort of grand consolation prize.

"More importantly," she continued, pepping up a bit, "I want you all to be able to get good jobs in the field. The job market is not easy these days, especially in editorial, but I'm going to do everything I can to make sure you can find something. Ariana has graciously allowed us to use these offices through the end of the year. You are free to take advantage of the office for resume submission and to field calls until December fifteenth."

She leaned up against her desk and folded her arms, but it was a gesture of resignation, not defiance. I felt sorry for her.

"Guys, I'm really sorry about this. I know we all thought we could create something really great here, and I think we did the best we could, but the reality of it is that the money just isn't there." She looked like she was about to cry. "I'll be available all day to field questions."

"Let's grab a cigarette," Donovan said to me.

As we walked out of the office, Sunny gave us a patronizing smile. She was probably glad to be rid of us as tenants.

"This fucking sucks," Donovan said once we were out on the sidewalk. "I'm going to have to dig into my savings to make rent for this month."

"So what next?" I asked.

"I don't know," he said. "Start making offerings at the great shrine of Condé Nast?"

After stopping at the coffee place down the street, Donovan and I went back upstairs. Like obedient drones, the rest of the staff had started doing job searches on the Internet or packing up the contents of their desks. The two of us joined Sonia in her office. She looked like she had been through a war.

We put an iced coffee on her desk.

"Thanks," she said, taking it gratefully.

"So what are you going to do?" I asked.

"Go home and sleep," she said.

"Seriously," Donovan said.

"Ariana needs someone full time to write press releases, create media kits, stuff like that. It'll tide me over while I look for something else."

"And what should we do?" I asked.

She pointed to Donovan. "For you, I have a contact at *Gourmet*. I think you're ready to move on to a place like that. You know, serious food writing. Not all this scenester crap."

"And where does that leave me?" I asked.

"Definitely not doing nightlife reporting. You're too smart for that. I mean, there's only so many times you can review clubs before it gets old. I've got a few leads for you, people you should call. Nothing full-time, but some people who can give you freelance work."

We paused, in the silence that occurs after a disaster, as we reflected on CityStyle's final burnout. I thought about how much this would please my parents, how much it would confirm their world view. But I didn't care. I would be destitute and living on the streets before I would take the kind of job they wanted me to have.

"I think we were trying to do too much," Sonia finally said. "I mean, sometimes you guys were working twelve-hour days! Other magazines, even other Web sites, have huge staffs to take care of everything: fact checking, research, listings. How did we ever think we could compete?"

"We had something good going for a while," Donovan said. "Our editorial was awesome when we had enough money to pay people."

"I know . . . it's just that no one gives a shit about editorial. How was I supposed to explain to some venture capitalist that our site was better because it gave people the real deal on downtown? They don't care what you're serving up, as long as there's a revenue stream. And who am *I* to be talking about revenue stream and profit margins and return on investment? I don't know the first thing about that sort of stuff! I was an English major at Vassar, for Christ's sake!"

Jamie knew what we should do to help ease the blow of our recent unemployment. "Donovan's birthday is coming up. We'll throw him a party, and you can host it. You're the only one with tolerant neighbors."

"I can host it? I'm completely broke," I said, which was true.

"Exactly," he said. "That will be your contribution. The rest of us will pay for liquor, food, entertainment."

"Entertainment?" I asked.

"You'll see," Jamie said.

Within a day, Jamie and the boys had composed an email invitation and divided up the responsibilities. David and Jamie would handle the liquor, Donovan would deal with music and entertainment, Alejandro would do the decorations, and Brett would create the guest list.

With Jamie's help, I described Subway Boy to Brett to see if he could invite him. Having gone to NYU, Brett knew every boy in the city.

"I think I know someone who knows him," Brett said. "I'll try to get his email address." Brett reviewed the list, his version of Mrs. Astor's Metropolitan 400. "Between the five of us, we have almost three hundred people on our email list. I've narrowed it down to two hundred. If half show up, then we'll have a good turnout."

"You realize," I said, "that my apartment can only hold about thirty people, tops."

"That's good," Brett said. "People like intimacy."

The next morning, email invitations were sent out from the five of us, inviting people to "A Dot-Com Crash Party, In Celebration of Donovan's Birthday, Hosted at the Swank East Village Digs of Mr. Toby Griffin."

Since Alejandro spent more time at his sewing machine than he did at his laptop, he had not entirely understood the dot-com theme. The theme he did understand, however, was camp, and so he decorated my apartment with a combination of Mylar sheets, votive candles, and 99-cent Ken dolls spray-painted silver. By the time he was finished, my apartment looked like the second coming of Andy Warhol's Factory. I hoped my sublettor, who had the habit of showing up at all hours, wouldn't see what had become of her East Village love pad. David and Jamie had six cases of assorted premium liquor delivered that afternoon, which made an impressive display laid out on my kitchen counter. At 7 P.M., I realized we had forgotten something.

"What about food?" I asked.

"Food?" David looked at me quizzically.

"You know, like munchies?"

"Do people really eat at these parties?" Jamie asked as he fixed himself a drink.

"Sure they do!" I said. "We at least should have a cake."

"He does have a point," David said. "Donovan will be really insulted if we don't get him a cake."

"I thought he might be insulted if we *did* get him a cake," Jamie said. "You know, like implying he was fat or something."

"Oh, this is ridiculous!" I said. "I'll go buy him a stupid cake!"

Jamie handed me two twenties, which meant I wouldn't have to take another advance off my credit card. I went to a Ukrainian bakery down the street and picked up a sheet cake and candles.

Brett arrived armed with a clipboard of confirmed guests ("in case things get out of hand," he explained), and Alejandro showed up with an "emergency decoration repair kit" of tools, tacks, tape, and, alarmingly, a glue gun.

Donovan arrived last, with two binders of CDs. In honor of Alejandro's décor, he put on The Velvet Underground & Nico:

> I'll be your mirror,
> Reflect what you are,
> In case you don't know.
> I'll be the wind, the rain, and the sunset,
> The light on your door to show that you're home.
>
> When you think the night has seen your mind,
> That inside you're twisted and unkind,
> Let me stand to show that you are blind.
> Please put down your hands,
> 'Cause I see you.

"What is this?" Brett yelled from the kitchen. "It's too mellow!"

"Just something to get everyone in the mood," Donovan said with an impish grin. He shook his head. "I can't believe he doesn't know what this is."

"I know what it is," I said.

Donovan raised his hands in the air. "Thank you—finally someone who listens to stuff outside of the gay canon!"

"Still never heard of it," Brett said, as he came into the living room.

"Just relax," Donovan said. "We've got all night to get to

Whitney, Deborah, and Britney. I'm not going to deprive you of your pop divas."

As the party got under way, my two-room apartment started to fill up with nearly a hundred Diesel-clad, heavily primped boys. I could count the number of females on one hand, not including Lola, who was a gay man at heart anyway.

"Hi, Toby," Lola purred, sidling up to me after having a cocktail brought to her by one of her admirers. "Gorgeous party."

She was wearing a hot pink satin kimono-style robe, cut just above her thighs. She looked like a female wrestler about to disrobe and take on an opponent.

"You look amazing," I said, giving her a peck on her waxy cheek. Flattery will get you everywhere, she'd once told me.

I asked her if she was going to take her CityStyle column elsewhere.

"I won't have time, actually," she said. "I've been talking with several producers about optioning my life story."

"Really?" I said. "Which ones?" I was sure they would be small indie companies, not even at the level of those Elizabeth and I had recently met with.

"Some people at Miramax," she said. "But I don't know if I want to go with them. New Line is also interested."

I could feel my eyes widening.

"Do you have an agent?" I asked.

"Yes," she said. "I just signed with CAA."

I took a large gulp of my cocktail. I couldn't believe that Lola, who was far more adept with a g-string than she was with a keyboard, was repped by CAA. I hated her for it.

"I've been meaning to talk to you," she continued, delicately sipping her drink. "They feel my writing isn't . . . well, it isn't quite strong enough to be produced. But they really like the story. I was wondering if you would take a look at what I've written so far, and maybe help me out a bit."

"Are you looking for a co-writer?" I asked. I hated to be blunt, but I was drunk and unemployed, a lethal combination.

"They did mention something about bringing in a co-writer, actually." She perked up considerably, as if she had come up with the idea herself. "You could be my co-writer!"

She had been carrying a cassette tape, and now she handed it to me. "This is for my show," she said.

"Your show?"

"Donovan said I should do a show. You know, for his birthday."

My living room was packed with boys: boys with drinks, boys with cigarettes, boys with other boys. I had no idea where Lola was planning to perform her show. Then again, until a few months ago, I hadn't known anyone with a vagina constructed from a penis, either.

After Donovan blew out the birthday candles on his cake, bump and grind burlesque music cascaded out from my speakers. Lola cleared a space in the center of my living room with the help of an assistant who had just arrived, a three-and-a-half-foot-tall midget named Trixie.

"She's a porno actress," someone told me.

"A midget porno actress?" I asked.

"That kind of thing is huge in straight porn."

Trixie handed Lola the equipment for each of her illusions in succession. They were garden-variety, dime-store tricks: coins produced out of the air, scarves that appeared out of Lucite tubes, needles stabbed through balloons that didn't break. Lola's exercise in irony was putting me to sleep; I'd seen better magic at children's birthday parties. Nonetheless, there was something charming about it, as if Lola was trying to prove she could entertain in a traditional manner.

For her last trick, Lola slipped off her robe to reveal a slinky bikini set. She started pulling a multicolored paper chain out of her mouth, handing it to Trixie, who pulled it across the room. After the chain had been thrown to the delighted audience, Lola slid down her bikini bottoms so they were dangling at her ankles and sat on a chair as if she were getting ready to pee. She spread her legs, proudly displaying her surgically engineered orifice, and began pulling dollar bills from it.

The audience went wild, grabbing at the money as Trixie tossed it to them.

"Fuck the dot-com economy!" Lola cried, and the crowd cheered.

When the money had reached its end, as a final "That's all folks!" Lola stood up, removed her bikini top and, now fully nude, shimmied her sizeable breasts to the beat of the music. The crowd of guys hollered and shrieked. They had never seen such a sight, transsexual or otherwise.

Donovan's cake sat on my kitchen table, uneaten.

Half the people at the party were friends-of-friends-of-friends, which was fine, since a secondary—if not primary—goal for the party was to get us all laid. Rico was a twenty-four-year-old guy who someone said was a hustler with an ad in one of the bar rags. He was supposedly a friend of a friend of Donovan's, though the exact connection wasn't clear. Whatever it was, he had decided that night he wanted Jamie, who, I noticed, was completely blitzed. At 1 A.M., Rico pulled me aside and asked if he and Jamie could use my bedroom. I refused him, partly on principle and partly because the living room crowd had spilled into the bedroom and would be impossible to clear without making a scene.

"It'll only take us ten minutes," he said. His hair was slicked down with gel, he reeked of cologne, and he had a faint mustache that he clearly thought was suave. His face was fixed in a permanent snarl.

"Forget it," I told him. "It's not that kind of party." Of course, it was exactly that kind of party, but letting Rico and Jamie use my bedroom would have made me feel like I was running a brothel. If I wasn't having sex, then no one else would be, either.

It surprised me that Jamie would be interested in someone who wore a gold chain around his neck. In that way, though, that Upper East Side trust fund fags will fantasize about screwing gas station attendants or deliverymen, Jamie saw something in him, because an hour later he rushed into the bedroom with tears streaming down his cheeks. I had procured a few bumps of coke from someone and was in line for the bathroom when I saw him.

I asked him what was wrong.

"Nothing," he said, wiping his face. "I need to use the bathroom."

The door opened, and I slid in with Jamie.

"What the hell is going on?" I asked. "You're a mess!" His hair was disheveled, his belt was undone, and his face was flushed.

"I let him—Toby, you can't tell anyone, okay?"

"Fine," I said.

"I let him fuck me."

"Where?"

"In my ass, you idiot, where do you think?"

"No, I mean, where in the apartment?"

"In your coat closet. Oh, God, Toby, I'm so embarrassed." He reached out to hug me as he continued to sob.

"Clean yourself up first," I said, gently pushing him away. "And tell me you used a condom. Please tell me you used a condom."

"I don't know what he used," he said. "I was so drunk . . . I am so drunk." He looked like he was about to fall over.

"Dammit, Jamie, why the hell did you do that?"

"I had never before . . . I had never let anyone fuck me before. I wanted to try it."

"But with that guy? He was so nasty! Come on, you must have had other opportunities!"

"Look, I don't get all the chances you do," he said. "It was nice for someone to, you know, want me . . ." He doubled over in pain. "It just hurts so much!"

I felt like this was my fault, for rejecting Jamie for all these months. All he wanted was one night of passion, something he probably hadn't had since his fling with his boyfriend in college.

"Jamie, I want you . . ." I said, as I tried to steady myself. "I mean, maybe not always in that way, but I care about you. Look, you wash up, and I'm just going to—"

I turned toward the wall and started doing the bumps of coke.

Jamie dropped his pants and started wiping his ass. He groaned in pain.

It was too late and we were too far gone to worry about propriety.

"Are you doing what I think you're doing?" he asked.

"Yes," I said. "Because I can't deal anymore."

We heard pounding on the bathroom door. "Open the fucking door!" someone yelled from the bedroom.

"It's him," Jamie said.

We both finished up and I opened the door. The rush hit me, and I felt like things were going to be okay.

"Damn," Rico said. "I got shit on my dick, and you guys are in there having a lovefest! Let me use the bathroom."

"I don't think so," I said. "You're leaving—right now."

"Dude, I did him a favor. He was practically begging for it. 'Fuck me, fuck me.' " He imitated Jamie in a shrill voice.

I could feel the blood rushing to my face. "Get out," I said. "Go clean up somewhere else."

"Nice way to treat your guests," he said.

"Tough shit, asshole," Brett said, standing behind Rico and looking every bit the bouncer. Donovan and David were with him. "You want us to carry you out?"

The three of them escorted Rico to the door, him whining all the way.

I took Jamie over to the couch in the living room and got him a glass of water. "Everyone knows," he whispered. "Everyone knows what happened."

"No one knows," I said. "Everything will be fine."

By the end of the party, though, everyone did know. As the last remaining party guests straggled out, Jamie curled up on my couch in a fetal position. David, Alejandro, Brett, Donovan, Lola, and a few others were going to split cabs home. No doubt some of them would end up in bed together.

At the beginning of the night, I had thought I wanted a hookup myself. I had thought Subway Boy might show up, though I wasn't sure if he had ever gotten an invitation.

Now I didn't want anyone touching me. I wanted the loneliness.

I started cleaning up in the kitchen.

"Toby," Jamie croaked from his spot on the couch. "Can I sleep here tonight?"

"Sure," I said. "But wouldn't you rather be at home, in a clean apartment?"

"I'd feel better not being alone," he said.

I got him a blanket and turned off the light in the living room. He took off his shoes and Gus started licking his toes. I sat down next to him as he sprawled out on the couch, his skinny frame barely occupying its surface.

"You're going to be fine," I said. "Just fine." I stroked his hair and gave him a kiss on the cheek.

The worst part about it was that after denying him the use of my bedroom, Rico had asked me for a condom.

I had refused him on both counts.

8

Though I had only done a few bumps of coke, I fidgeted for hours before finally falling asleep at 6 A.M. At ten, I woke up in a panic, unable to rest a moment longer. Jamie was still out on the couch. He was lying on his right side, so I knew whatever noise I made wouldn't wake him up.

I started cleaning the apartment, but was disgusted by the mess. I hoped I would be able to call the boys and get them to help me later.

I went downstairs to sit on my stoop and smoke a cigarette. Up the street, a small church was letting out services. Every time I had passed it since moving in, I had thought about going in, taking a moment to be still, to think about what was going on in my life. But there was always something pulling me along, something that prevented me from being absolved of my sins.

After the CityStyle crash, I wasn't sure if writing articles was what I wanted to be doing. Reviewing nightclubs had been a boon to my social life, but I didn't see it as a long-term vocation. I had gone out nearly every night for the past two months, and all the drinking wasn't helping my health or sanity. If I was going to write, I couldn't wake up every morning with a brain pickled in vodka.

I got up early on Monday and went to the CityStyle office. I sent out a few pitches to Sonia's contacts and a few of my own from my days as a freelancer. At one, I checked my voice mail. Along with a message from my parents, there was one from Sherry Merrill, the owner of a boutique literary agency in Beverly

Hills. She had read *Breeders* over the weekend and wanted to discuss the possibility of representing it.

I called Elizabeth immediately.

"Sherry Merrill called you? That's fabulous!" she said. She gave me the rundown on who else she represented. They were respectable clients, writers with solid credits to their names.

"What should I tell her if she asks if anyone's seen it?"

"Don't tell her about all the meetings we had. Just say I've shown it around to a few people, just informally, no decision-makers involved. We want her to think she's the first to see it. I'm so excited! This will be big, Toby, this will be big!"

Buoyed by Elizabeth's enthusiasm, I called Sherry Merrill back. Her assistant put me through.

"Toby?" She was on speaker phone. "I loved your story. Very original. *Quirky.*" She said the word as if it were a delicacy. "And funny. I think we can find a home for it somewhere."

"Really?" I said, trying not to sound too skeptical.

"Yes! The scene at the end when your hero leads the breeder liberation march? Fabulous."

"Thanks," I said. "That means a lot to me."

"You managed to show metaphorically how ridiculous homophobia is by turning it on its head. I think it's an important piece that should be seen, something that has the potential to touch people." She paused. "Now, has anyone else seen it?"

"Not really," I said. I gave her the line Elizabeth had instructed me to.

"You just never know where this stuff is going to come from. I mean, I deal with Elizabeth's office all the time, but you get something over the transom, and you just never know. Everyone always has a friend who's a screenwriter."

"I'm sure," I said.

"I'm going to send you some notes, just a few suggestions for ways we can tweak this, and then we can start sending it out. Is this Seventh Street address correct?"

I told her it was.

"You're in the Village! I grew up on Long Island, and I used to love coming into the city. Then I left for California thirty years ago and never looked back."

I smiled to myself. I liked her; she was down to earth. We went over a few more details before saying goodbye.

After I hung up, Sonia popped her head in the doorway.

"Was that Sherry Merrill? A friend of mine used to be repped by her."

"Really? How is she?"

"She's a doll, really. Not exactly at the top of her game, but she has some strong clients. And she'll take care of you. I think you'd be smart to work with her."

I didn't need any convincing.

Lola and I met the next day at her apartment. She lived above a store on Eighth Street that specialized in large-size high heels for transvestites. Her entire apartment was painted Barbie pink, except for the kitchenette, which was baby blue.

"I never go in there anyway," she explained.

On a coffee table in her living room she had organized a series of file boxes containing stacks of press clippings and other notes. She had several scrapbooks of photos from her many years on the scene. I was surprised to learn she had been profiled by many major magazines, had written a column for the old *Details,* and had appeared in the *New York Times* party pages, an honor usually reserved for uptown socialites, not downtown transsexuals. She even had a copy of an NYU master's thesis that spent twenty pages analyzing the mother-womb relationship in her work. Her notes and files, while not organized, were certainly extensive.

The two of us sat down on her fluffy sheepskin rug and sorted through everything. She had put together a box of essential materials to start me off on the process, including a rough draft of the first half of her screenplay.

"What do you think this story is about?" I asked her.

"It's about freedom," she said. "It's about discovering one's true identity."

I suggested we meet with her agents to discuss my working as a co-writer on the project. I also told her I now had an agent I would have to cut in on the deal.

"Let's talk about that after you finish a draft," she said.

The project had fabulous possibilities, and I had already been provided with amazing source material. I was hesitant to mention it to Sherry, as I didn't want to bombard her with too much information while we were still establishing our relationship. I would wait until I had finished a draft, and then surprise her with what a strong client I was.

Later that afternoon, I stopped by the CityStyle offices. Sonia's desk was now out in the open with Ariana's other employees. Her old office was only halfway dismantled.

"So you have two offices now?" I joked.

"Yeah," she said, "I wish." Though she looked worn out, she also seemed hopeful. If everything went well, she thought she could find something in editorial soon. She knew she wasn't meant to be working in PR.

"You got some mail." She handed me a stack.

On top was a crudely lettered envelope addressed to me. I opened it and out slid a handwritten letter on binder paper. It looked like it had been written by a twelve-year-old. It could only be from one person.

Goth Boy had written me a long, rambling letter, all about what he was doing for his semester projects in art school, how much he missed me, and how he couldn't wait to see me again.

"Jesus Christ," I said aloud.

Sonia started reading over my shoulder. We went back into my old office and I told her about Goth Boy.

"Reminds me of what a friend of mine once said," she mused. " 'Sometimes it's not about finding someone who loves you as much as it is about finding someone you can love back.' "

"Should I call him?" I asked. "Or at least send him an email?"

"If you want to be nice, you'll write him back. Would I write him back? No. He could be a psycho. But what do I know?"

Why couldn't I be getting letters like this—well, not exactly like this—from someone like Donovan? Or from Subway Boy, whom I hadn't seen in more than a month?

I decided not to write Goth Boy back. I didn't want to encourage him.

"Hey, you know," Sonia said, "Ariana's looking for junior

publicists. It would be fun to have you working here. And I know she likes you."

"She likes me? She barely even knows me."

"To her you're cool by association. You know, the whole thing with your mom."

"Right," I said. "As much as I'd love to work with you . . ."

"That's okay," she said. "I know the rest."

I found a temporary job editing the nightlife listings at another Web site. Unlike CityStyle, where I wrote full reviews, these listings were simply a matter of which party was being promoted on which night, which DJ was spinning, and what the cover charge was. It was somewhat akin to editing the phone book. I had to branch out.

Most of the editors I sent pitches to never returned my calls. One editor called me back and, after learning that I had a connection to Ariana, wanted me to do a short profile of her client Jordan Gardner. The interview consisted of my meeting Jordan at the Four Seasons and chatting with her for fifteen minutes, followed by a forty-five-minute briefing from one of Ariana's account execs on what I could and couldn't say about Jordan's career.

Sonia never would have made me do a puff piece on Jordan Gardner. Unfortunately, I didn't have the luxury of being choosy.

I kept searching the job listings for permanent openings in editorial. Since it was two weeks before Christmas, the pickings were slim.

I spent the rest of the time working on Lola's story. The draft she had written was a disaster, and I realized I would have to start over. I made copies of the materials she had lent me and marked them up extensively. By the end of the week, I had an outline that incorporated the key events in her life and fictionalized most of the major players. I felt I had a handle on the tone: I didn't want to alienate mainstream audiences, but I also didn't want the whole thing to come off like a made-for-TV movie on transsexualism.

I asked Lola when she wanted to get a first draft to her agents.

"Not before the holidays," she said. "Let's wait until after."

I decided to put off finishing Lola's life story until Christmas break.

I got my own early Christmas present in Chad's issue of *Playgirl* that I had bought from a seller on eBay, a Florida dealer who specialized in soft-core male porn. I turned eagerly to the pictures of Chad. Maybe they would hold the answer to Elizabeth's attraction to him.

The explanation was simple: he was hung, if not like a horse, at least like a donkey.

Chad's cock, fully erect, was at least ten inches long, and as thick as a can of Red Bull. It curved a little to the right, and looked less like a penis and more like a monster from one of the *Alien* films. The copy accompanying the photo of "Buck" confirmed his size: " 'Yeah,' Buck says with a shy smile, 'I've been told it's pretty big.' Our roving reporter pulls out her measuring tape: ten inches! 'I guess that's about right,' Buck says modestly."

The copy may have been cheesy, but I let the fantasy fly. I unzipped my jeans and got to work.

Later that day, I called Elizabeth.

"Chad and I broke up," she said coldly. "He had another meeting with that casting director, and it didn't go well. I should have known he was just using me for that contact. I suspected it all along, but I wanted to pretend it wasn't true. The bastard." I heard her exhale a stream of smoke. "Oh, God, the sex was so good. That's what I'm going to miss most of all."

"Yeah," I said, as if I would miss it too. I remembered something I wanted to ask her. "Listen, I know you may not be in the mood, but my friend Donovan is going to be in LA on vacation and I thought you two might want to meet up for a drink."

"Sure," Elizabeth said. "Since we all know I'm the queen of the fag hags."

"That's not true," I said. "I just thought you would enjoy meeting each other. He said he'd like to take you out for a drink." It sounded stupid, as if the promise of a free drink held any allure for Elizabeth.

"Give him my number," she said. "I'm available."

* * *

Ten days before Christmas, I had dinner with the boys. Despite my abundance of free time, I hadn't seen them since the crash party two weeks earlier. We ate at a slick new gay restaurant in Chelsea. All around us there were old queens tossing around bon mots. Someday, I feared, that would be us.

By the time I arrived, Jamie was already on his second gin martini. Brett and Donovan nursed vodka cranberries while Alejandro and David sipped Diet Cokes. I wondered if being in a relationship made people drink less.

Everyone ordered food except for Brett.

"Are you not eating?" I asked.

"Already had a protein shake at home," he said.

"You shouldn't be replacing meals. You have like two percent body fat as it is, right?"

"My abs need more definition. The supplements in the shakes will help me do that."

"The vodka you're drinking sure won't," Donovan said.

"You can't expect me to make too many sacrifices at once," Brett said.

"The important thing to decide tonight," Donovan said, changing the subject, "is what we're doing for New Year's. I've done some research on the matter." He handed us a few Web printouts with a number of options, from prix fixe dinners to mega-dance clubs to private parties.

"We'll be in Argentina," David said.

Alejandro's parents were millionaires in Argentinean beef, and they owned an enormous compound outside of Buenos Aires.

"Do they know you guys are together?" I asked.

"Oh, sure," Alejandro said. "They're fine with it."

"I'm just glad I don't have to deal with the cows this year," David said, and everyone laughed. "I was replaced by an emergency generator."

We all knew the story. David's parents owned a cattle ranch in Minnesota; by contrast to Alejandro's, it was so small they knew each cow by name. In the region where David grew up, blackouts were endemic during the holiday season, and David's father worried about their electric fencing system going down. The previous year, David had to eschew the New Year's revelry with his college friends in favor of spending the evening in subzero temperatures with a flashlight and a cattle prod.

Like David, I wasn't planning on sticking around at home for New Year's Eve. I would be heading back to New York a few days after Christmas, so making plans was in order. We decided on a prix fixe dinner at Marion's on the Bowery, followed by several private parties in the East Village.

"So that's settled," I said. "But what are we doing tonight?"

"This'll be an early night for me," Donovan said. "I've got an interview tomorrow at *Gourmet* and then I leave for LA in the afternoon."

"You should just do what I do," Jamie said. "I go into all my interviews hung over. That way, I'm not as nervous. It worked for me at Pelham."

"I don't know," I said. "I think it's better not to go in looking like a fuck-up."

Our entrees arrived and we ordered several more bottles of wine. Jamie poured himself a glass, even though he was now working on his third martini.

"Jamie," Donovan said, "shouldn't you be watching yourself a bit? You're such a mess." He turned to me and muttered, "He's drinking so much these days."

"What did you say?" Jamie said. "Don't think I didn't hear that!"

"Nothing," we said.

"No, you said something. You said something about the party. Well, fuck you. If you're going to say something, say it to my face."

Everyone looked at Donovan and Jamie uncomfortably.

"I have no idea what this is about," Brett said.

"What this is about is that I can be whispered about right in front of my face," Jamie said.

"Jamie, relax. I really—what I said, it was nothing." Donovan tried to wave away Jamie's concerns.

"Oh, yeah? At least I'm not sleeping with transsexuals."

Jamie looked smug, as if he had just delivered the *touché* of the evening.

I put down my fork and looked at Donovan. "What was that?"

"Nothing. He's drunk. He doesn't know what he's talking about."

"Have you become a trannie chaser?" Brett said. "I knew this guy at school who was into that."

"What's a trannie chaser?" Alejandro asked.

"I have not become . . . one of those," Donovan said.

It hit me. "You slept with Lola! That night, the night of the party, you slept with Lola!"

"Look, it was late, I was drunk, I didn't know what I was doing, she asked if I wanted to see her place, and one thing led to another." I didn't know which was more upsetting: that he had done it, or that he had done it without telling me.

I was annoyed at Lola as well. I had been working on this woman's—this *person's*—life story and she had slept with one of my best friends, the friend I would never get to bed.

"Did you use protection?" Please, I thought, please.

"Yes, we did. Jesus, it's not like she's going to get pregnant or something."

"That's not the point." It surprised me how my friends could be so stupid about safe sex.

"And then," Jamie said, triumphant now that he had the upper hand, "he did it again!"

Everyone looked at Donovan in horror as he turned the color of Lola's lips.

"There was a second time," Donovan said. "It wasn't a big deal."

"You're a regular trannie chaser," Brett said, partly joking and partly in twisted admiration for Donovan's adoption of this new sexual fetish.

"I am not," Donovan said. "I just wanted to see what it felt like."

"Sleeping with a transsexual?" I asked.

"No," he said. "Sleeping with a woman."

* * *

Donovan went home after dinner to prepare for his interview and pack for his trip. On our way out of the restaurant, I picked up a free copy of one of the local bar rags. I flipped through it, looking for something interesting to do that night.

On the back page, there were pictures from parties and club nights around town. I recognized one of the faces: Subway Boy, in a picture from B Bar. I checked the captions, but no name was listed. Did the photo mean he was a regular partier? Or even worse, a circuit queen?

No, I decided, he wasn't either of those things. I was sure he went out less than I did. He led a healthy, active lifestyle. He was an intellectual. He didn't go to sleazy bars or engage in risky sex. Or maybe he already had a boyfriend and was permanently un-available. He had found someone who was perfect, someone wholesome and pure.

I had to stop obsessing and projecting my fantasies onto him. He was probably none of these things.

I tore out the back page of the bar rag and stuffed it in my pocket.

Like the night I first met Jamie, we ended up at G. Amidst the weeknight crowds at the circular bar, I started talking to a guy who claimed he had recently left the U.S. Army, where he had been stationed in Virginia.

"I thought the army would make a man out of me," Army Guy said. "Instead, it made me into a faggot." He smiled goofily, revealing huge teeth that were like tombstones.

He was now working at the Abercrombie & Fitch store at South Street Seaport.

Jamie swooned over him, but I told him to back off. He had a way of scaring people away.

Around 2 A.M., Army Guy came home with me. We had de-cided on my place, since he lived with two roommates in the fi-nancial district. When we arrived at my apartment, Gus sidled up to him, purring. Even my cat was impressed.

"Here, puss puss," Army Guy said.

We fell into bed together, tearing each other's clothes off.

Though we were the same height, his build was so much bigger that I felt dominated by him. I liked it.

He had big hands, strong hands I was sure could snap my neck at any moment. He kept rubbing his cock against my ass, tickling it, lifting me up as he flexed his enormous biceps. He was like a wild beast recently escaped to civilization.

It was a score, to be sure, and renewed my faith that I hadn't lost my touch, that I wasn't destined forever to pick up over-the-hill decorators and nineteen-year-old goths.

Even if he was lying about the army (or about working at A&F, which I had soon conflated into his being an A&F *model*), I bought into the fantasy. I had an army brat in my bed—well, an army-brat-turned-retail-queen. He was my own Chad. If I could just set this up to be a regular thing, if he could come by weekly to service me . . .

"I want to fuck you," he whispered in my ear.

I wanted him—a hundred times more than I had ever wanted Decorator Guy—but I knew the aftermath might not be pretty.

I also didn't know if it would fit.

I decided he could come back for seconds tomorrow. I wasn't going to give it all up in one night.

As a consolation prize, I let Army Guy push my head down to his crotch. It was a meal that might have to be taken home in a doggie bag.

When he came, he did it loudly, as if he hadn't in a week. He smelled like ammonia.

After he cleaned himself up, he said, "You can jerk off if you want. I'll just watch."

Like Real World Guy, he was another one who didn't blow. Lying there naked on my bed, though, he was like my own private centerfold. Unlike some of the other guys I'd been with, he had no qualms about hanging out in the nude with a complete stranger. It was live eye candy.

Unfortunately, I was too drunk to do anything. I had jerked off earlier in the day, rendering my dick about as useful as a wet towel.

"I can't," I said. "I think I had a bit too much to drink." I knew it had more to do with the Paxil, but I didn't want to complicate things. He probably wouldn't have understood anyway.

"No big deal," he said. "So what time do you want to get up?"

After setting the alarm, I wrapped myself around his naked body and covered us both with my down comforter. Lying with him, I thought, *This is how it's supposed to be.*

I woke up before he did, so I used the time to take in every inch of his body. I had a hangover, but having him in my bed seemed worth it. I grazed my fingers over his pubic hair, stroked his morning erection. He stirred and smiled.

"Hey," he said. "What time is it?"

It was eight.

"I should get going," he said.

I could have gone for round two, but I didn't want to keep the guy from his job.

He got up and threw on his clothes. I wrote down my number for him and he did the same for me. Before he left, he gave me a full kiss on the mouth.

I could get used to this. True, working at the A&F store wasn't exactly the height of ambition, but when you were that gorgeous and built, it didn't really matter, did it? Army Guy was a booster shot to my self-esteem.

I slept for a few more hours and then got ready for my day. I decided I wanted Army Guy to stay over again, and I would have sex with him, real sex. Maybe he wasn't boyfriend material, but I still wanted more of him than I had already had.

I went to the drugstore and bought a box of extra-large Trojans.

I left him a message that evening, around seven, when I knew he would be getting home.

By 10 P.M., I hadn't received a call back.

I called him again.

He answered.

"Hey, it's Toby. I was just wondering how you're doing." If he was home, why hadn't he called me back?

"I'm just chillin' tonight," he said. "It was a long day at work."

"Did you get my message earlier?" I asked.

"Yeah, I got it. I've just been busy."

"Maybe we can hang out sometime," I said. I sounded pathetic.

"Sure, maybe," he said. "I'll give you a call."

I knew he wouldn't.

I hung up the phone and suddenly felt sleazy. I had been used as a sex object, just as I had used him. But I wanted something more meaningful than that. I wanted more than a box of condoms, sweaty sheets, a crumpled up phone number. I wanted to be remembered.

Though Army Guy might have been annoyed, I was still glad I hadn't let him screw me. It wasn't worth feeling like a tramp and then not getting called back. At least this way I hadn't given everything up.

Maybe he had been disappointed by my sexual inadequacy. I knew I was always upset when a partner didn't have an orgasm, so it made sense that Army Guy would be, too.

I finally decided to call my shrink and deal with the problem.

Dr. Laemmle's office was in an older building on Fifth Avenue in the lower twenties. He always seemed slightly embarrassed by his profession, as if it was unseemly that he had to ask his patients such personal questions. I also had no idea what his own sexuality was. There were no pictures of a wife, no pictures of kids, no pictures of a partner of any sort, so in the two times I had seen him since I moved to New York, I had avoided comments of a sexual nature. He knew I was gay, which seemed to make him uncomfortable. I just wasn't sure from which side of the fence his angst came.

"So," Dr. Laemmle said, peering over his glasses at me, "you're experiencing sexual side effects from the Paxil?" He shifted in his chair and continued. "Though it's not uncommon, you've never mentioned this before. I don't believe it's anywhere in your files." He flipped through a folder filled with papers, the entire emotional history of my last four years reduced to chicken scratch and faxed from New Haven.

"Actually, it's been going on the whole time," I said. "I was just embarrassed to mention it before."

I stared anxiously at the beige carpet.

"So the entire time you've been on medication, you haven't had an orgasm with someone else?" he asked.

"No, I have, a few times," I said. "It's just, if I've had any alcohol, even one or two drinks, it's nearly impossible. And most of the situations I'm in . . ." What was I supposed to say? I'm a big lush, and I can't separate sex from drinking? I don't have the balls to hook up with someone unless lubricated by alcohol?

I didn't need to say anything, as he seemed to understand.

He prescribed me a new antidepressant, Wellbutrin. It sounded so touchy-feely.

"I think you'll find that as far as the depression goes, the transition will be pretty effortless. It may take several weeks, however, for the sexual problems to be resolved, so I'm going to give you something else in the meantime. You can take it if you need to, usually half an hour before any sexual activity. It should be good for at least four hours."

"It's Viagra, right?" I asked. I felt stupid being prescribed it.

"Now, don't get scared by this," he said. "You're not impotent. You're just having problems brought on by your medication. It's not you, just remember that."

As if it mattered, I thought. It was all the same thing in the bedroom.

A few days later, Donovan called me from his cell phone. "LA is fabulous," he said. "The boys are incredibly hot. I think we should all move out here when we get sick of New York."

"I'll never get sick of New York," I said.

"There's something I need to tell you. Your friend Elizabeth?"

"Yeah?"

"Well, we had a few drinks, and we were having a really good time and one thing led to another . . ."

I couldn't believe this. "What is it with you?" I said. "One thing always just leads to another, doesn't it? You're fucking transsexuals, you're fucking women. Next you're going to be into bestiality?" I was disgusted and furious, but also strangely attracted. Donovan was like a sexual adventurer, exploring new lands.

"She was really upset about her boyfriend dumping her, and she kept going on about how all her male friends are gay and beautiful and they won't sleep with her, and I figured, since I'm sort of exploring this new side of myself . . ."

"What new side is that? The 'I'm a bisexual slut' side?"

"Toby, that's not fair. It's just, you know, I had sex with Lola, and that was fine, but then I was thinking, Lola's not a real woman, and I wondered what a real woman would feel like."

"So you're using my friend as a test subject for your personal Kinsey Report?"

"No, I think we really had something together."

"Oh, whatever, you really 'had something together.' I really have something with my cat, but I don't fuck him! You can't play with people like this, Donovan. Elizabeth is very fragile right now; she doesn't need added complications in her life."

There was silence on the line. "Are you done ripping me a new asshole?" he finally said.

I had never spoken to him like this before. "Girls take this kind of thing seriously, at least the girls I know. They don't just sleep with guys and not expect to be called again."

"There's something else you should know. I'm telling you this because I don't want you to hear it from her."

"Yes?"

"She asked me not to use a condom."

"Jesus Christ. Did you come inside her?"

There was a pause. I could hear the traffic in the background.

"No, I pulled out," he said after a moment.

"Oh, that's really safe," I said sarcastically.

"The whole thing was really weird, because afterwards she kept talking about how much she wanted children. But she said she was on the pill."

"That doesn't stop you from spreading diseases."

"Excuse me, 'spreading diseases.' What the fuck is that supposed to mean?"

"I meant catching diseases. I'm sorry, that came out the wrong way."

"Damn straight it did."

"Well, have you had an HIV test?" This increasingly seemed like a strange conversation to be having on a cell phone.

"I haven't been tested recently," he said. "But I'm going to get one soon. And don't worry, I'm not going to stop sleeping with guys."

"Oh, I feel much better now," I said. "But for God's sake, please be more careful."

Elizabeth was a complete idiot. What kind of woman would have unprotected sex with a bisexual man from New York City? Was Donovan even bisexual? I felt like he had deserted us, had gone to play for the other team, or at least had started switch-hitting. I felt like my chances for being with him were now cut in half.

While Donovan was busy sticking his dick in new territories, I was having a sexual crisis of my own. In the several days before I left for my Christmas break, I had noticed a burning sensation in the tip of my penis. Whenever I went to the bathroom, it felt like I was pissing glass shards. I was terrified there would be blood, but there wasn't. I tried to limit the amount of water I drank so I wouldn't feel the pain as often.

I've got AIDS, I thought. All this fucking around and I've finally got it.

Or maybe it was a less serious STD, like gonorrhea. That was treatable, right?

After the pain continued on my second day back home, I told my mother I needed to see the doctor. I said I had an earache.

Dr. Angelika, our family doctor, had an office in our local medical center, the same facility where I was born. In his waiting room was a Zen-inspired rock fountain that dribbled water at a somnolent rate. It was supposed to be soothing, but it only made my pain worse, like listening to running water with a full bladder.

The doctor himself was a jovial balding guy who had once told me that if I only slept with Ivy League girls, chances were pretty good that I wouldn't have a run-in with an STD. I had not yet told him about being gay.

"So you're having a problem with the plumbing," he said. "Are you sexually active?"

I told him I was.

"And you're gay, straight, undecided?"

How did he know?

"I'm gay," I said.

"How many partners have you had in the last six months?"

"Um, let's see . . ." I counted mentally. "Six?"

"And you're using protection?"

"Yes. Only one was, um, penetration."

"When was your last HIV test?"

"Last year."

"And?"

"Oh, it was negative," I said, as if this were obvious.

He asked me to drop my pants. He took a sample from my urethra, which meant he had to stick a thin swab into the slit in my penis. After he did it, I was almost in tears. It was the most painful thing I had ever experienced. It felt like a razor blade slicing off the tip of my dick.

"We'll send this out for testing," he said. "In the meantime, I'm going to give you some antibiotics. They will hopefully clear up whatever the infection is."

"But could it be something worse?"

"Could be gonorrhea, could be chlamydia, could be a number of things. I'm also going to send you downstairs for blood work. I'd like you to have an HIV test."

"Do you think it could be HIV?" I asked. "Is this a symptom?"

"No, it's not a symptom, but you're in a high-risk group."

I know that, I thought to myself. Doctors always talked about the "high-risk" factor as if you had the option of putting yourself in a lower-risk group.

We went through the rest of the standard HIV pre-test counseling. He said he would ask the lab to rush the tests. I took the elevator down to the lab on the first floor, where a swishy black male nurse drew several units of blood. I must have looked shaken.

"Honey, just relax," he said to me. "You ain't dyin' yet."

I tried to work on Lola's screenplay but found it impossible. I had no interest in sex, not even in masturbation. I wanted to purify myself, to cleanse myself of everything. I even decided to quit smoking.

Two days later, I went back to Dr. Angelika's office. As I sat in the waiting room, I was sure my test would be positive. I wondered if it might be better not to know.

After an interminable wait, he admitted me to his office.

"Let me see what we've got here," he said. I hated how doctors always did this, as if they hadn't looked at the results themselves until then. He flipped through several pages.

"You tested negative for HIV and nothing showed up on your sample. It could have just been a minor infection. Has the burning gone away?"

"It's getting better," I told him, breathing a sigh of relief.

He gave me a few dusty pamphlets and dismissed me. I had already made my decision, though. I had been playing fast and loose with my health for too long, and it scared me. From now on, I would be like a monk: no sex, no drugs. No more one-night stands. Just the thought of having that swab stuck into my dick again was enough to have me strapping on a chastity belt.

Besides, I needed a boyfriend, not just a bed partner. I would hold out for as long as I could without having sex. Anyway, a relationship would be safer: I would only be exposing myself to one person instead of many.

When I got home, my mother was putting the final touches on our Christmas tree. She usually hired a florist, but this year she was doing it herself to save money. I also noticed something odd about the decorations: they weren't new. The tree was a mishmash of ornaments from years past: silver balls from Germany, silk elephants from India, tribal figurines from Africa.

"Haven't we used some of these before?" I asked her.

"I thought it would be fun to recycle them this year," she said.

"And I didn't want to do Mexico for both Thanksgiving and Christmas."

This was unlike her. She usually bought enough new decorations each year to garnish several small villages.

On Christmas Day, after we opened our presents, I found out what was going on. Between the three of us, we were already working on our third bottle of wine, so my parents' tongues were loose.

"Your mother's company is going to be sold," my father explained to me as we were eating Christmas dinner.

"That's great!" I said. "How much are you getting?"

"Twenty-five million dollars," my mother said. "It's low, because they have to buy all our debt."

"Still, that's amazing," I said.

"In stock," my mother said. "We can't sell it for five years. With the way the economy's going, we don't know what it'll be worth then."

"No cash?"

"I'll get a salary, but no cash for the sale," my mother said, resigned.

We continued eating. I was desperate for a cigarette and couldn't stop fidgeting under the table.

"So what are your New Year's resolutions going to be?" my mother asked me.

I had told my parents several weeks ago about losing my job, and they had been surprisingly understanding. I had a feeling they wanted my resolution to be about finding permanent employment.

"I don't know," I said. "To sell my screenplay. And to continue working on another one."

"That's not a resolution," my father said. "That's a goal."

"A resolution is like quitting smoking," my mother said. "How about that? I wish you would do that."

"I'm trying," I said.

"I don't know, Toby. This whole writing thing, I worry about it," my father said.

"What do you mean?" I asked.

"You're always jumping from one job to another. There's no

security. Your mother and I want you to get a stable job. Not this freelance stuff."

"But I want to write screenplays," I said.

"Toby, lots of people want to be artists, but few succeed," my father said.

"You both got your chance to do what you wanted. Why shouldn't I get mine?"

"You're forgetting that we both went to graduate school first," my mother said.

"How about that?" my father said. "Business school could be the perfect thing for you."

"Come on," I said, "you know I could never go to business school."

"What's going on with that agent?" my mother asked. I was grateful she was changing the subject.

"She's pitching *Breeders.* You remember that story, right?"

"I thought that idea was fabulous," my mother said, suddenly the expert on contemporary film.

"You know," my father said, "you don't always have to write about gay topics."

I couldn't take it anymore. I went outside to the deck and had a cigarette. Maybe now was not the right time to quit.

I worried about what my father was saying. After my tests had come back negative, I had been able to work on Lola's screenplay more steadily. But I didn't want to get pigeonholed as a gay writer. I wanted to write other films, silly romantic comedies and action adventure films. Sure, my life was a low-budget indie feature at the moment, but why couldn't I write popcorn movies?

I got back to New York the day before New Year's Eve. For the first time in two weeks, I felt like jerking off. Out of curiosity, I popped a Viagra and waited for it to take effect. Within twenty minutes, I started to feel warm and flushed. I thought about having sex with Donovan and Subway Boy at the same time. After I came, I fell into blissful sleep.

On New Year's Eve, there were four of us at dinner—Jamie, Donovan, Brett, and me—and it felt intimate, like family. The kitschy restaurant was extravagantly decorated in a 1960s Hollywood glamour theme. I was wearing a new pair of sparkly pants I had bought on sale at Patricia Field's store, though I wasn't feeling particularly sparkly myself.

As we drank champagne, the four of us went over our resolutions. Mine was to sell a screenplay, which I decided was a resolution, regardless of what my father thought; Jamie's was to be more responsible at work; Donovan's was to work for a major food magazine (though his *Gourmet* interview had gone well, they told him they couldn't make a decision until after the holidays); Brett's was to go to the gym more often. To each of these, we added, in earnest, "and find a boyfriend." It was a simple resolution, but it would change everything.

I thought about the coming year. I was almost finished with a draft of Lola's story, and Sherry was pitching *Breeders*. I had Jamie, my own personal cheering section, and I resolved to be nicer and more attentive to him from now on. I was still annoyed at Donovan, but I decided the things he had done weren't enough to break up a friendship.

At midnight, Brett celebrated by whipping off his shirt and dancing on a chair to the disco music, to the delight of most of the patrons and to the horror of one couple who had brought their children along. Donovan and Jamie each gave me a kiss and a hug. I wondered, though, if I would be getting a real New Year's kiss.

Around 1 A.M., after party favors had been handed out and the check had been paid, we headed into the freezing night. I wrapped my coat around me and put the flaps down on my red plaid hat. The four of us traversed the ice and snow as if going in slow motion.

On our way to the next party, I saw Real World Guy. I didn't realize it was him until we were close, in spitting distance, and it was only for an instant. He glared at me.

I told Donovan.

"What did you expect, Toby? You were going to see him eventually," he said.

After I had written the piece, he had become a mythical entity, the creation of a night fueled by red wine and marijuana. Now that I had seen him in the flesh again, I realized he was a real person. Somewhere, in the back of my own champagne-addled mind, another resolution was forming. Something to do with integrity. I couldn't figure out exactly what it was.

We arrived at the apartment building on Avenue C, a slick condo complex that had the neighborhood up in arms when it was built. There was a twenty-dollar cover to pay for the booze and the heated tent on the apartment's balcony.

The party was packed with boys. We made our way to the bar, and Jamie ordered me the first vodka cran of the new year.

"Toby," Brett said, "I think that guy is here, the one you liked? The guy you wanted me to invite to the party?"

"Subway Boy?" I asked.

"Yeah, yeah, Subway Boy."

"Shit," I said, even though this was a good thing. I looked over to the other side of the loftlike living room. He was talking with a group of friends. He looked thoughtful, composed.

"I'm going to go talk to him," Brett said.

"No! You can't do that. Don't talk to him," I said. I didn't want him to see me while I was drunk, tired, slightly depressed.

"Why not?"

"I don't know . . . it's just . . . it's not supposed to happen this way. I want to meet him when I'm at my best."

"I'm just going to say hello. I'll find out if he's single or not."

Brett made his way across the room, not an easy feat at a party this crowded. He seemed to have gotten stuck, though, because he was soon talking with another group of people. I saw Subway Boy go to the bedroom, retrieve his coat, and move toward the entrance with his friends. Was he with any of them? Was one of them his boyfriend?

I knew I shouldn't speculate, that I shouldn't impose a personality on a guy I didn't even know.

Subway Boy left and my eyes darted over to Brett. He shrugged to me, mouthing the word "Sorry."

I didn't feel like going to any of the other parties on the evening's roster, so I decided to make my way home. Once I was safely in my apartment, I stripped off my clothes and rolled into bed.

I caught a few hours of sleep and then woke up as the sun was rising. I dressed quickly in a pair of jeans and a sweater and went downstairs to sit on my stoop and watch the sun come up as the early morning stragglers trudged through the snow. I was alone and it was okay. I embraced the feeling, though it cut me like ice.

9

A few days later, Lola called me. I had finished a draft of her screenplay, and was about to send it to her.

"Toby?" she asked in her signature breathy voice, as if someone else might have answered my phone. "I need to talk to you."

"What's up?"

"I spoke to my agents about your working on the project. They want to package someone with the project, a screenwriter. I forget his name, Something Something. He wrote that movie that came out last summer about the Hamptons?"

"What does this mean for me?"

"They said there's only room for one screenwriter to do the adaptation. I'm sorry, Toby."

"I spent all this time working on your material and now you're kicking me off the project?"

"Toby, you know I don't have any control over this. It's the agents. I know it's unfair."

"Alright," I said, wondering if I had any recourse. "You can come pick up your stuff whenever you want." I hung up on her.

I was furious at myself for taking on the project without getting something in writing. I took Lola's files and threw them back in their box, taking the copies I had made and stuffing them in a drawer. I had just wasted several weeks writing 110 pages about a transsexual from Miami. I could mention it to Sherry Merrill, but I felt stupid for getting into a situation like this without a contract. I finally decided to keep the whole thing to myself.

* * *

A week later, I got a call from Sherry.

"Toby, let me start by saying I think your work is very strong. I've been getting lots of interest, lots of very respectable passes. The coverage you're getting is positive, but everyone I've spoken to feels it just isn't right for them."

"Do you still have other leads out that haven't responded yet?" I asked.

"Absolutely. I'm going to keep pushing this, because I believe in it. I think it's a great film that needs to be made."

It was hard for me to hear her words.

I called Elizabeth at her office. She seemed distracted.

I explained what Sherry had told me.

"Hmm," she said, "that's very odd."

"Do you think there's anyone else we can send it to?"

I heard her take a deep breath. "You know, Toby, I can't just keep mining my Rolodex for you."

"Elizabeth, I'm not expecting you to do that. I thought you were interested in the project."

I was shaking. What was this about?

"I got you an agent. Isn't that enough?"

"I'm very grateful to you for that," I said.

I didn't know whether to be angry or penitent at her sudden change of attitude. I felt a little of both.

"Toby, every time you call me, you want something. To show around your screenplay. Drinks with your friend. Job advice. I'm tapped out. This isn't a friendship anymore; this is like career counseling."

I didn't know what to say. "Elizabeth, that's ridiculous," I stammered. "Of course this is still a friendship. I can't believe you think of me that way. Does this have anything to do with Chad?"

"You, Chad, everybody—everyone wants a piece of what I have." Now she was being arrogant.

I knew what this was about.

"This is about Donovan."

"That's none of your business," she snapped.

"I don't understand. What prompted this?"

"I've decided to clear out my life of everyone who's using me. I need to start living my life just for me."

"Did your therapist tell you to do this?"

"I took a seminar over the weekend. It really opened my eyes to all the toxic relationships I've been maintaining."

"You're mad at me because of a seminar?"

"I don't think we can be friends anymore. I need some space."

"You have plenty of space," I said. "You're on another coast."

"I think you would really benefit from a seminar like this. They offer them in New York, too."

I laughed. "I'm going to take a seminar that's going to tell me to dump my friends?"

"You're exhibiting classic resistance," she said.

"If you were mad at me, you should have warned me while it was happening. You wanted to read my screenplay, remember?"

"I can't talk to you now," she said. "I'm very busy at work."

I didn't know what to say.

"Oh, and another thing," she said, before hanging up. "I don't think there's much of a market for serious gay science fiction."

I was stunned. Had a two-day self-help seminar caused her to go crazy? Was this my fault? Had I been using her, or had I simply become the scapegoat for her seminar-induced delusions? And was my screenplay really no good, or was Elizabeth just jealous that I had finished something?

I couldn't believe that after everything I had done for Elizabeth in the past, this was how she repaid me. After all the lunches, the dinners, the movies, the boyfriend counseling, she was ready to throw out our friendship like a dirty paper plate. We had trusted each other, helped each other, supported each other through everything. Had I asked too much of her as a friend? She had always been the one to offer first. I hated it when people did that, offering something and then slapping my hand for taking it.

Maybe Elizabeth and I had shared the kind of friendship that only thrived in college, the kind that couldn't survive in the real world.

I asked Donovan if he had any explanation, but he said he didn't understand it.

I left several messages for Elizabeth at her home over the next few days, but none were returned. I finally wrote her a long email explaining my position, saying I always valued her as a friend above anything else, and I had never intended to use her.

I couldn't help thinking, though, as I considered the loss of our friendship, about what a bitch she had become. All I really would miss were her film industry connections.

I took the calls from Lola, Sherry, and Elizabeth as a sign. If I wanted to be in the film business, I needed to get on the inside. I needed to work for someone who was doing things in the industry, doing the kind of projects I would want to be part of.

I needed to work for Cameron Cole.

Cameron had never returned my original call. While I was annoyed, I knew I couldn't afford to hold it against the guy. I composed myself and called Ariana.

Calling ARPR involved a complicated voice mail system that belied its company owner's own casual nature. I finally got through to her personal assistant, who remembered me. To my surprise, she put me right through.

"Yeah?" Ariana, like Sherry, had the habit of taking her calls on speaker phone.

I explained what I wanted.

"Cam did tell me he's looking for a personal assistant. The guy he had before decided to join the circus or something."

I couldn't tell if she was joking or not. "Do you think you could ask him?" I said.

"Sure, I'd be happy to," she said. "Hey, did I read that your mother's company was sold? Who can I talk to about getting some dresses for my clients?"

"I can have someone call you," I said.

I called my mother and she agreed to look into it, though she seemed resigned about it, as if she had no choice in the matter. I felt sorry for her. She had always wanted to maintain control over her product, over who wore her dresses, how her image was presented. Now she was at the mercy of publicists who were half her age.

Though Cameron's company was called Eastside Pictures, his office was in a brick factory building in Tribeca, which was most definitely on the West Side. I was ushered in by Margaret, his director of development. A serious woman with black-framed cat's eye glasses and bright red lips, she was surely a lesbian, and I felt more solidarity with her than with Cameron. She scrutinized the resume I had faxed over the previous week. Cameron barely looked at it.

I was wearing a threadbare Dolce suit I had bought at Century 21 several years ago. To my embarrassment, Cameron was in jeans and a tight designer T-shirt.

Cameron was one of those good-looking guys I would never talk to in a bar; handsome, but older than his twenty-six years, he gave off the sense that he had been around the block one too many times. He had the close-cropped haircut of the moment, and he clearly went to the gym every day. His office, which had a gorgeous view of the Hudson River, was a complete mess: framed movie posters that needed hanging, papers and files in stacks on the floor, an overflowing ashtray on his desk.

Directly across from his desk, there was a large mirror on the wall. I noticed him checking himself out several times during the interview.

I had prepared myself for the meeting, refreshing my memory on the film classes I had taken in college, coming up with informed opinions about recent movies, and doing research on all the films Cameron and his mother had produced. I was terrified that Cameron was going to ask me if I had any real experience working in the industry; the truth was that I had none. Still, I had prepared a few answers to show how well-versed I was in office protocol from my various internships.

Though I was armed with all this information, it was useless; instead of interviewing me, Cameron lectured for half an hour.

He moved around his spacious office with a manic energy that was infectious.

"When I started in this business, I was still in college," he said, waving around a burning cigarette with a perilously long ash. "I had no idea what I was doing. I was a business major, but I liked movies, and I knew the gay market could be exploited. My goal is to broaden the spectrum of gay imagery on film. What about an action hero? What about a light romantic comedy?

There have been a few, but there's so much more that can be done."

I could buy into this. It wasn't exactly high art, but it would sell.

"The important thing," he said, "is that you understand this company's mission. I ask everyone who works for me to come up with a definition that works for them."

I nodded in understanding, even though it sounded like a load of shit.

"Did you have any questions?"

The ash on his cigarette broke off and dropped on the floor.

"Why do so many of your films feature straight actors playing gay roles? Aren't there enough gay actors out there?"

"Oh, sure, there are plenty," he said. "But we have to do what's popular. Mainstream audiences can relate better to the main character if they know he's not really a faggot."

I was too stunned by his last statement to say anything.

"Anyway," Cameron continued, "when can you start?"

I had never had an interview during which so little interest had been taken in me.

"Today, if you want," I said. I realized I was coming off as a bit too eager.

"Well, that's settled," Margaret said, standing up abruptly, as if we were keeping her from her lunch hour.

Cameron introduced me to the other people in the office. There was Keith, the division's president, Stephanie, a creative executive who would soon be going on maternity leave, and Eric, Margaret's aloof assistant. Since there were only six of us in the office, we relied heavily on Katherine's larger staff and management, but in ethos and purpose, we were a unit unto ourselves.

What surprised me most was that of the six of us, Cameron and I were the only employees who were gay men.

Cameron, I soon realized, had always known success. He had been catapulted directly from summer intern to running his own division, where he was being groomed to take over his mother's job when she retired. His dad was an agent who represented writers and directors and funneled the appropriate talent Cameron's way. Cameron and his mother took a car to the office every day, he had a personal trainer, and his mother's maid cleaned his apartment three times a week. He had grown up among the Manhattan prep school set, with people like Ariana who had always known privilege.

I hated Cameron, because I wanted to be him.

I didn't want to be exactly like him. I wanted to be a smarter version of him. He never read books, and would often ask me to read bestsellers for him and then give him a synopsis. He didn't even read the newspaper, instead relying on me to tell him what was important. The only thing he read religiously were marketing reports and the trades; every morning he had his mother's Beverly Hills office fax him reams of daily movie grosses and tracking statistics.

Cameron was also completely disorganized. In my first two weeks, I helped streamline his operation. I cleaned up his office, hung the framed posters on the wall (*Jules et Jim* and *The 400 Blows,* both films he admitted to having never seen), arranged his phone list in a database, and set up a filing system. My cubicle was directly across from his office, and I controlled who got to see him and who didn't. I was supposed to listen in on phone calls and take notes on any action that needed to happen. Sometimes he would ask me not to monitor a call, but for the most part, he made very little distinction between his public and private life. He would ask me to fetch his dry cleaning, go to his apartment to meet the cable repairman, and pick up his car from the shop after he got into a fender bender. I had to make regular trips to replace his cell phone, which he had a habit of throwing against the wall when a call didn't agree with him. I arranged dates for him with a rotating roster of gay and mainstream celebrities, though I never got to meet any of them. He also asked me to make a few romantic dates for him, since he found chatting with potential boyfriends during the workday too time-consuming. I was even in charge of picking the restaurant.

Cameron's dietary needs were my responsibility as well; I would bring him breakfast, lunch, and sometimes dinner. Aside from his Marlboro Lights and the occasional line of coke he did at parties, he was a health junkie. In an effort to cancel out the tar in his lungs by eating only organic food, he was a strict vegetarian who subsisted on a diet of salads, bottled water, and the protein shakes I made for him in the office kitchen. At night, he might switch from water to vodka, but he would be back on the health kick by eight the next morning.

The only person Cameron was afraid of was his mother. A bottle blonde who, thanks to the wonders of plastic surgery, existed in that nebulous chasm between forty and sixty, Katherine ruled the company like a South American dictator. While she was always pleasant to me, I got the sense that she regarded me as an annoying, albeit necessary, appendage to her son's life.

I soon felt like as much of an insider as Elizabeth or any of my other friends who had gone into the film business. During the day, I handled administrative tasks and the minutiae of Cameron's life. I spoke to fifty people a day on the phone, though I had no idea what they looked like; often, my goal was to leave word for people without actually speaking with them, insuring that Cameron would stay on their call list without actually having to make any decisions.

While the job had solved my financial woes, I wasn't writing or doing anything remotely creative. When I read scripts, I gave thoughtful and informed coverage, but then decisions were mysteriously made from above. Scripts I loved lingered on the shelves for months; projects I thought were doomed to fail were swiftly greenlighted and moved into production. When I got home at night, I found myself too tired to think, let alone write. If I skipped dinner with the boys, I would tinker with a few pages at home, only to succumb to the more appealing prospect of an early bedtime or a DVD. I had turned into an avid film buff, even more so than I was in college, taking home stacks of titles from the office and watching five or six each week. In the first month, Cameron told me over lunch that he "would love" to see my writing, so I brought him a fresh copy of *Breeders* the next day. Weeks passed, however, and as his reading load got heavier and heavier, he never got to it, despite my several friendly reminders. Eventually, I just stopped asking him.

* * *

One day late in January, Donovan asked me if he could stay over at my place. His landlord was having the floors refinished in his apartment that week, and the dust was irritating his sinuses. He had been staying with a different friend each evening, and tonight was my turn.

The last few weeks had been busy for him; he had gotten the job at *Gourmet* as an editorial assistant, and was working long hours. The two of us met at my place at nine. He had a bag of groceries with him.

"I thought I would cook dinner for us," he explained. "I figured your kitchen should get some use."

He had bought a small chicken to roast. I found him a pan and he expertly seasoned the bird with olive oil, oregano, basil, and paprika.

"Just a simple recipe my mom taught me," he said, putting it into the oven.

I was impressed. The idea of cooking a whole chicken terrified me.

After preparing our salads, he joined me in the living room, where I was reading a screenplay I had brought from the office. He handed me a glass of red wine.

"It should take about forty-five minutes to cook," he said, looking at his watch.

Donovan had brought along a copy of *La Dolce Vita,* even though we had both already seen it. In the first several minutes, when the helicopter is flying the statue of Christ over Rome, he paused the DVD.

"I've been meaning to ask you something."

I turned towards him.

"Are you talking with Elizabeth?" he asked.

"No. Are you?"

"We speak occasionally."

"She got brainwashed by that stupid seminar," I said.

"She wanted me to take it, too," he said. "I told her to forget about it."

"I don't understand how a seminar can make you dump a friend."

"She's just crazy, Toby. You can't let her get to you."

As we watched the movie, we lost track of time and the smell of chicken roasting quickly turned into the smell of chicken burning.

"Do you smell that?" I asked.

"Smell what?"

"The chicken is burning."

He rushed to the kitchen and pulled the pan out of the oven. The chicken was charred on the bottom. He returned to the living room, embarrassed.

"I'm glad you caught that," he said.

"Couldn't you smell it?"

He blushed. "Oh. I guess you don't know. I figured Jamie would have told you by now."

"Told me what?"

"I can't smell."

"Why not?"

"I had my nose fixed when I was seventeen, and they fucked up my olfactory sensors."

"You had a nose job?" It must have been a good one, because I had never noticed.

"I had a deviated septum, and I was having trouble breathing. But honestly, I think I would have had it fixed anyway. I had a swell the size of a ski jump."

I started laughing. "You're a food writer, and you can't smell?"

His voice grew quiet. "Please don't tell anyone, okay? I could be fired if anyone found out."

"It makes no difference to me," I said. "I'll just have to warn you before you step in shit."

Both of us had long days to look forward to, so after finishing dinner and the movie, we got ready for bed. I took a set of sheets out of the closet so Donovan could sleep on the couch.

"Don't worry about that," he said. "I can just sleep next to you."

"Oh," I said, surprised. "Sure."

"I mean, you have a queen, right?"

I nodded, and tried to control my hard-on as I considered the possibilities. Maybe this would be the night we hooked up.

Donovan changed in the bathroom and came out wearing boxers and a T-shirt. He slid into bed next to me.

As we drifted asleep, I was careful not to let my body touch his, though I desperately wanted to.

When I woke up, my arm was wrapped around Donovan. I withdrew it in horror before he could notice. He stirred slightly.

After waking up, Donovan took a shower first. I kept one eye open as he came out of the bathroom in a towel and proceeded to get dressed. He put on a fresh pair of pink boxers by sliding them under his towel.

"Hey, do you have a sweater I can borrow?" he asked. "It's supposed to get really cold today."

"In the drawer."

He picked one out that I thought looked terrible on me. He put it on and looked great.

As soon as he left, I rolled over to his side of the bed and breathed in his scent. It was a combination of his hair, whatever he styled with, soap, deodorant, facial products, and sweat. It was sweet, like tanning oil.

I thought about him, being as close as I was, to the indentation he had left on the pillow, to his odor left on the sheets.

This, I thought, is all I will ever get of him.

While my relationship with Cameron started off curiously buddy-buddy, it soon became clear I was little more than a hired gun. One minute I would be his confidant, and the next minute he would have me picking up steamed vegetables for his lunch. I never got to accompany him to other companies' premieres, though I was permitted to sit in on the occasional meeting. I learned from Margaret that his previous assistant, the one who had reportedly joined the circus, actually *had* joined the circus. He and Cameron had been having an affair, and he was terminated once Cameron decided the relationship was over. He was given a confidential—though obviously not so confidential that the entire office didn't know about it—severance package of

$25,000, and decided to use it to fulfill his lifelong dream of attending Clown College. Perhaps because of this, Cameron went back and forth between treating me like a friend and treating me like the janitor. He wasn't above asking me to dump out his ashtray when it got too full.

One day in February, he asked me to stop by his apartment and pick up a screenplay he needed that afternoon. I was sure I had a copy of it on file, but he insisted he needed "that exact copy of that exact version," so I hopped on the subway and rode up to Chelsea, where Cameron lived in a co-op with units that went for seven figures. By now, I was on a first-name basis with his doormen, so I was let up without a fuss.

The other times I had seen Cameron's apartment had been right after his maid had given everything a thorough scrubbing. This time, however, the place was filthy. There were dirty dishes in the kitchen, a coffee pot left dangerously on, magazines and screenplays strewn all over the living room. I peeked into his bedroom and saw his bedsheets in a tangle. Had he had a tryst last night? Was my boss getting more play than I was? There were two condom wrappers on the floor and a bottle of lube nearby. I wondered if Cameron was a top or a bottom.

After I found the screenplay, I had to use the toilet. Cameron's bathroom was enormous compared to my East Village water closet, with mirrors on every wall. I lifted the lid to discover a mess of tissue and a used condom. At least Cameron had the good taste to throw away his condoms before he left for work in the morning.

I flushed, and the toilet let out an enormous gurgle. The tissue went down, and then came back up again. I flushed again. Water started rushing in as the bowl refilled at a rate that seemed faster than usual. Shit, shit, shit, I thought to myself. Soon water was spilling onto the floor and the tissue and condom were floating near the rim of the toilet like a little barge.

Even worse, I still had to pee.

Okay, Cameron, I thought, this is your fault for being such a slob. I relieved myself in his sink and then quickly rinsed it out with water. I looked for a plunger, but couldn't find one. I ran downstairs and had the doorman call maintenance. As I stood in

Cameron's bathroom while the maintenance guy shoved an industrial-sized plunger into the toilet, spilling tissue and the guilty condom everywhere, my cell phone rang.

"Toby, where are you? I need that script, dude." Cameron thought calling me "dude" made him more affable. I found it annoying; "dude" was an affectation I had left behind after eighth grade in California.

"I had to use the bathroom and the toilet got clogged. I mean, I didn't clog it up. I just had to pee, but there was something in there and—" I couldn't believe I was having this conversation with my boss.

"Why were you using my bathroom?"

"Look, I'm sorry. I'll be right back down as soon as possible. I've got the maintenance guy here."

"You called maintenance? Make sure you give them a tip or something."

The maintenance guy finished his work and proclaimed the toilet "good as new." I knew, however, that I couldn't leave the bathroom looking like this. Using wads of clean tissue as a buffer, I picked up the wet tissue and the condom and threw them in the trash. My stomach churned, and I nearly retched. Dealing with other people's bodily functions was not my forte, especially when it was my boss's shit I was cleaning up.

As I took the elevator down, I thought, it can't get much worse than this.

If I could just stick it out, though, I had the feeling success would be waiting for me.

That next meeting, that next phone call, that next drink.

It would be there, and then it would be gone.

On a Tuesday around the end of February, I called Jamie at his office. His secretary, who had strict instructions to give his friends his actual whereabouts and not the "he isn't available" line, told me she hadn't heard from him today. I tried his cell and home numbers, leaving messages in both places. It was unlike Jamie not to return a phone call, especially from me. I kept calling every few hours, but got no answer. At 6 P.M., I called Donovan at his office.

"What do you think is wrong with him?" I asked. "I mean, he could be dead for all we know, kidnapped or drowned in his bathtub!" I was overtaken with the melodramatic reaction Jamie would have toward his own disappearance. Underneath it all, though, I was really worried.

"I'm sure it's not that bad," Donovan said. "Maybe we should call his parents. I have their number if you want it."

"Let me go over to his building first," I offered. Jamie was still not out to his parents, and they had a notoriously difficult relationship.

I left the office just after six, earlier than usual, and caught a cab uptown.

Jamie's building was in the east seventies, a mid-century apartment building that had seen better days but still carried a hint of New York glamour. His parents had bought him the apartment as an investment when he moved to New York.

I spoke with Miguel, Jamie's Puerto Rican doorman. Jamie called Miguel "the hot one."

"He was out in the morning, but he's been home since then," Miguel said.

I had him ring Jamie's buzzer. There was no answer.

"Maybe he's sleeping," Miguel said. On his good ear, I thought.

I called him on my cell phone and started to speak into his answering machine. "Jamie, pick up the phone, we're all worried about why you haven't—"

He picked up.

There was no sound on the other end of the line. I went out onto the street for some privacy.

"Are you there?" I asked.

"Yes," he said. He sounded choked up, as if he had been crying.

"What's going on? Your secretary said you didn't even call in this morning."

"I had a doctor's appointment and I—"

"Look, can I come up? I feel so stupid standing here in the street."

"I don't want you to see me like this."

"Jamie, I've seen you much worse. Just buzz me up."

I went back into the lobby and Miguel let me up.

In the elevator, I wondered what it could be. Had someone done something to him?

I wanted to protect him, to wrap my arms around him and hold him. I wanted to be there for him where I hadn't been before. Jamie was the closest friend I had made since moving to New York, and I couldn't stand the thought of him in trouble again.

When he opened the door, Jamie was wearing sweats and an old Princeton T-shirt. He was unshaven and his face was streaked with tears. I sat down on his sofa while he stood.

"I went to the doctor this morning, and oh, God, this is embarrassing—"

"Come on, out with it. We've all done embarrassing things."

"I had this pain in my nuts, and it wouldn't go away, so I was worried, and I saw a doctor last week about it, and I didn't want to see my normal family doctor, so I picked this doctor from the company's insurance plan and—"

"And what happened?" I was getting impatient.

"He did some tests, and he tested also for, you know—"

"HIV?"

"It was just precautionary; he didn't think I had it or anything—"

"And?"

"And the test came back and it was positive." He said it all in one quick breath and then broke into tears as he collapsed onto the couch.

"Jamie, I don't know if—" What was I talking about? What could I tell him? What did I know about any of this?

"Don't you think it's too early for it to show up in a test?" I finally said. I had thought it took six months for HIV antibodies to be detected in a person's blood.

"It's borderline. It's been almost three months since that, that awful night, and sometimes these things show up early—"

"Have you been with anyone else in the past six months?" Please don't let it be from that night, I thought.

He looked up at me and started to cry again. "No," he finally said.

He had gotten it that night. It was my fault he had gotten it. I could have prevented this.

"Oh, my God," I said. "I'm sorry, I mean, that wasn't about your not, you know, sleeping with anyone, but just the whole thing—" I was becoming incoherent.

"Toby, you can't tell anyone. No one can know about this. Not Donovan, not Brett, not any of the others. This has to stay between the two of us."

I nodded. Of course, it wasn't between us. It was between him and himself. It was his body that had this disease, and his body that would have to fight it off. It was his body that would be vulnerable to everything from now on: every cough, every cold, every sniffle would be a sign of what was to come.

I had to get things under control. I grabbed a tissue and blew my nose. Every part of me wanted to cry, but I didn't. It would only have made Jamie feel worse.

I tried to pull myself together. This was like any other hurdle in life: diagnose the problem, find a solution. Of course, I knew this wasn't like anything Jamie or I had experienced.

"I just want to kill myself," Jamie said.

I looked at him closely. "Don't say that," I said. "You don't know what that means."

"You have no idea how it feels, Toby."

I took a deep breath. "We need to be pro-active about this. First of all, did you feel comfortable with this doctor?"

"No," he said. "His office was like a hundred years old and I don't think he knew anything about . . . you know. I don't think he'd ever even had a 429 patient before." I knew Jamie had a deep mistrust of doctors that stemmed from having two for parents.

"Look, you need to find a new doctor, someone you trust, someone who knows what he's doing with this sort of thing. And you don't know what's going on. Sometimes these tests are false. And there are medications you can take . . ." It was too awful to think about Jamie having to take those drug cocktails advertised with smiling gay couples who went rock climbing and celebrated their anniversaries as they popped pills every hour. No matter how fashionable the ads made it look, it didn't get around the fact that you had it. You were dirty, like an infected needle thrown in the trash. No one would want to be your partner. No matter how much the media played it all down, it was no different than it was fifteen years ago. Now there were just more ways to cover it up, to make people feel better about it. But it still wasn't okay.

I knew I was prejudiced about the disease, but I couldn't help it. I had always thought people like Jamie didn't get it.

After I left his apartment, I felt a surge of anger. How could he have been so stupid? It was basic knowledge that you didn't do it without a condom, ever. I knew there were uninfected guys out there who had unprotected sex with multiple partners, chasing the disease until it closed in on them. I knew there were guys who ended up in bed too high on crystal or coke to have any idea what they were being penetrated with. But I didn't include those people among my friends, and I didn't think my friends would ever be like those people.

I thought about Jamie, and Rico, and how it had all happened in my apartment, and how it was my fault there was no condom, and I felt sick to my stomach. I walked shakily through the lobby past Miguel and into the icy street. Holding myself up against someone's Lexus, I vomited into the gutter, first a stream of liquid, then a series of dry heaves that left my throat scratchy and hoarse. The entire time, Miguel stood there watching me.

10

In college, the guy I had drinks with on Friday night would usually be the person I was still with on Saturday morning, before sliding on stiff jeans and dirty socks and making the walk across campus, the infamous Walk of Shame, viewed only by early risers and the inevitable tour group. Traveling alone in those days, as I often did, I was braver about approaching guys. Advancing meant the possibility of sex, while doing nothing meant standing alone. Without a group backing me up, it was easier to make contact. Now that I was almost always accompanied by my clique, my Heathers, my junior-high-styled infantry of bitchboys, it was more difficult to advance. Why risk rejection when I could dish everyone in the joint to my friends? Sometimes the only remedy was to go out alone, usually in a state of intoxication, to have a few more for the road at some dark dive after I had bid farewell to my friends for the evening. There, at two or three in the morning, everyone was out for the same reason.

It was this impulse that landed me one Saturday night at Rocket, a hole-in-the-wall bar in the East Village no bigger than my bedroom. It only served the cheapest wine and beer, and featured nearly naked eighteen-year-old go-go boys who would pause in the middle of a song to do double duty as busboys. There were always a few lurkers, leering old men hoping for a piece of boy meat, but for the most part, the crowd was young and virile, freshly supplied by an underground pipeline leading directly from the dorms at NYU, Cooper Union, and FIT.

I always held out hope that someone like Subway Boy would

walk in the door on a night like this, we would hit it off brilliantly, and become boyfriends on the spot.

Instead, I met Xander.

"Like Alexander?" I asked after he had introduced himself.

"Nope," he said. "Just Xander." He had a slight Southern drawl.

"Did your parents name you that?" I had phrased the question rudely, I realized as I said it.

"Yeah," he said. "They were hippies." He was from South Carolina and, I was surprised to learn, was an architect who had gone to Harvard. He worked at a well-known firm with offices in Union Square.

The bar was closing, so I had to make my move quickly. "Do you want to, uh . . ." I faltered.

"Go somewhere? Sure."

He had boyfriend potential, so I decided to suspend my moratorium on sex.

I followed him out of the bar. His hair was cut military-style, the kind of haircut boys at boarding school would get to show solidarity with each other before an important game. But this wasn't any simple clipper job. He had been styled.

We went for burgers and milkshakes at Stingy Lulu's, a nearby diner that catered to the late-night club crowd. As Xander dug into his onion rings, I realized how much I liked that he ate. He was a real boy, not a waif who would order a green salad with dressing on the side as a main course. And he was good-looking and slim. He must have been one of those people with the metabolism of a hummingbird.

"Lean towards me," he said as we were finishing up and getting ready to leave.

He dipped his napkin in his water glass and wiped the corner of my mouth. "Something on your mouth," he said.

I smiled. No one had ever done that for me before.

An hour later, after I showed him my apartment and introduced him to Gus, we were kissing. I wasn't too drunk, and so it was beautiful, perfectly choreographed, no fumbling, no falling out of bed, no clothes being ripped or buttons popping off. He took off his clothes and hung them neatly on a chair, then proceeded to remove mine while he stood there in his underwear. He started to fold my shirt and then my pants.

"What are you doing?" I asked.

"Sorry," he said. "I'm sort of a neat freak."

"I'd hate to know what you think about this mess," I said.

He climbed into bed and then proceeded to give me the most satisfying massage I had ever experienced. As my muscles melted into his hands, I kept wanting to do something for him. I wasn't used to being taken care of like this.

Jamie's recent discovery—not to mention my own issues—weighed on my mind as I felt Xander's erection poke through his boxers. But what could I do? Men had penises, and gay men liked to touch other men's penises, and if they couldn't, they might as well just shrivel up and die. I didn't advocate unsafe sex, but a blow job was a blow job. Every action in life came with an attendant risk.

He finally let me give him a massage, which I did clumsily, like a student at a recital with his teacher in the wings. He gave me pointers: "A little more there," "Up a little, that's it," "You got it now!"

Xander motioned for me to lie on my back and started massaging my front. As he went lower, he pulled down my shorts and started rubbing my cock, first gently and then more vigorously. I was going to come; I could feel it. A moment later, I exploded onto my stomach.

It was the first time in four years that I had had an orgasm on a first date.

He was grinning, proud of his handiwork. I jerked him off as well, which seemed like an afterthought instead of the main event. We kissed for a few more minutes, then curled up into each other and fell asleep.

In the morning, I let him take the first shower, and I used the time to examine his clothes. I wanted them to smell like him, but they were smoky, like the bar. I noticed that every item was Polo, right down to his socks.

"So . . . you hate Polo, right?" I teased him as he toweled off.

"I just love his stuff," he said, as if he and Ralph Lauren were personal friends.

There was something slightly disingenuous about him, a boy from the South who had become a Harvard-educated preppy. Maybe it was just the wardrobe that bothered me, the affectation of a lifestyle to which none of us could truly aspire. But in New York, we were all reinventing ourselves every day. How different was that from what I was doing, trying to be a screenwriter? At least Xander had been straightforward about not being a real preppie. He wasn't like Elizabeth, who was my friend one minute and my enemy the next, or Lola, who would promise work to anyone who could help her out.

Even better, I liked him, and he seemed to like me.

Xander and I had brunch together, and he was as charming as he had been the evening before. He gave me his cell phone number, and I gave him my information, all of it, without hesitation.

After we parted ways, I thought about what had happened the night before and this morning. I felt cured, but more important, I had given up control by letting someone else take responsibility for my pleasure. For a life-long masturbator, it felt like infinite possibility.

After I had worked at Eastside Pictures for almost three months, the company was finally hosting a premiere. Dozens of calls a day were made between Ariana's office and ours as we arranged the intricacies of seating charts, press clearances, VIP access, plans for the after-party at Mirror, and a multitude of other details. The film was a sappy romantic comedy about two guys— played, naturally, by straight actors—who meet while training for the Los Angeles AIDS Ride. I had read the screenplay, and I thought as a company we could do better, but it wasn't my place to say anything.

I was allowed to invite three friends, which made this premiere the first time since I had left CityStyle that I was able to bestow work-related perks on other people. I chose Donovan, Jamie, and Xander, whom I was now seriously dating.

In the two weeks since we had met, Xander and I had enjoyed

a boozy dinner at B Bar, had drinks at the scene of the crime, Rocket, and had seen a movie together, which was then followed by more drinks. On several other nights, he called me around eleven, asking to come over. I always let him.

One evening in the second week, we were lying together after sex, sharing a bottle of wine.

"So," I said, rubbing up against his chest, "are we boyfriends?"

I immediately regretted saying it. I should have just let things happen.

And then, just like that, he said, "Sure."

Sometimes it was that simple.

He was the first guy I had ever met who had a greater tolerance for going out than I did. I was usually the one who wanted to stay at a bar until closing time, and now I had become the person who was begging off at 2 A.M., while he wanted to get another round. He was a lush, but lushes love company, so we fit together perfectly. I tried to control the hangover factor by rotating in club sodas, since I knew I would have to be up in the morning for work.

I wanted to see him more during those two weeks, but he often begged exhaustion or said that he had to hang out with a mysterious group of friends that I hadn't met yet. All things considered, though, it was going well, and elevated my status considerably in my friends' eyes. Since we had known each other, I was the first one in the group to go on more than two dates with anyone, save for David and Alejandro, who were practically married and therefore didn't count. I wondered if until now we had effectively all been dating each other, though there was no sex, only friendship and emotional dependency.

Xander was excited about the premiere. He had never been to one before, and since I, having been to one premiere with Donovan, was a virtual expert on the topic, I filled him in on what to expect. The reality was that at Ariana's premiere in the fall, Donovan and I had been seated in the second to last row and had only managed to squeeze our way into the VIP section at the after-party because we spotted Ariana across the rope and she let us in without our names being on the list. Being on the list would have granted us legitimacy, and Ariana wasn't about to do that for two editors at the beleaguered dot-com that happened to be her tenant.

The day of the Eastside premiere, I spent all day at Ariana's office, helping to finalize the seating chart and dividing VIPs from non-VIPs. The VIP area at Mirror could only hold seventy-five people, so the chances were slim that I would be able to slip my friends onto the list. I tried to get us good seats, but the best I could do was the right-hand side, halfway down the aisle. They were decent, considering that we were nobodies in the celebrity-studded universe of Ariana Richards.

I arrived at the theater at six that evening; the film would be screened at seven. Press barricades had been set up, a red carpet had been rolled out, and Ariana and her staff were manning the door. When one of Ariana's assistants saw me, she handed me a walkie-talkie and a clipboard.

"We're missing a staff member, so we need your help," she said. "Photographers will be given fifteen-minute walk-throughs in the lobby and at the party, but then they have to go back outside to arrivals. Don't let them stay longer than that. Nobody likes it if there are too many photographers inside."

I had thought my main job for the evening would be troubleshooting for Cameron, which would consist mainly of fetching him drinks when there wasn't a waitress available. Apparently, he had okayed my deployment with Ariana's team, so I took on this job with a newfound sense of responsibility. Part of me couldn't help thinking, though, *I'm a writer, what am I doing here?*

I felt better when I saw Sonia standing behind a press table handing out kits.

"You've got to see what I wrote about this movie," she whispered to me. "You're going to gag."

My job was more complicated than I thought it would be, because every photographer wanted to get into the theater, especially after bigger celebrities like Gwyneth Paltrow, who was a friend of one of the film's stars, arrived. The photographers kept pestering me, and I had to keep a strict time limit on the ones who were already inside, which often involved grabbing them in mid-shot and pushing them back outside.

Donovan, Jamie, and Xander showed up as I was being has-
sled by an agency photographer. Of course, no flash bulbs went
off for them.

A few moments later, Jordan Gardner arrived, to the great ex-
citement of everyone watching. Her dress looked familiar, and I
realized it was one of my mother's designs. Jordan walked right
by me, clearly not remembering me from our interview or the
night at Flash.

Lola, conversely, was vamping it up for the photographers
when she noticed me near the barricade. She was wearing a
Vivienne Westwood black lace bustier and mini-skirt; her breasts
spilled out like a showgirl's.

"Toby, how *are* you?" she said, giving me a showy air-kiss
that I didn't return. She acted as if I were sure to be devastated
by the termination of our project together, destitute and lonely
on the streets because I was no longer working with the great
Lola Copacabana.

"Fine, Lola, fine. You'd better move along. I think Kim
Cattrall is about to show up." I had no reason to be nice to Lola,
so I wasn't going to be.

Undaunted, she continued sashaying up the red carpet.

It was soon time for the screening to begin, and I had to
round up two remaining photographers who were inside. I found
them just as the lights were going down and hustled them out.
Ariana's people would take over from here.

I went to find my seat, the location of which I had memorized
by now, but I found the row full.

"That's my seat," I whispered to a guy who was sitting next
to Donovan.

"Like hell it is," he said.

"Do you want me to call security?"

"Shut up, the movie's starting," he said.

I was furious, not only that this jerk had taken my seat, but
that my three friends, who had barely even noticed I was there,
had failed to come to my rescue. I walked to the back of the
house, certain there would be something open.

There was nothing. I could sit in the aisle and look like an
idiot, or I could play it cool and pretend that as a staff member

who had already seen the film—even though I hadn't—I wasn't interested in something as pedestrian as watching it again. I opted for the latter.

I went outside to the lobby where several of Ariana's assistants had decamped. Apparently, they were all in the same situation.

"The star brought ten of his friends who hadn't RSVP-ed," one of them said. "We had to let them in, or he threatened not to attend the after-party."

"I'll give you the tape of it," Sonia said. "You can watch it at home."

"Great," I said. "My first working premiere, and I don't even get to see the flick."

"Don't worry about it," Sonia said. "You could write a movie like this in your sleep."

One of Ariana's assistants glared at her, shocked that she had maligned the product.

"Sorry," Sonia said sheepishly.

Outside the after-party, I had the same job as at the theater, which meant I was continually shuttling between the throng of photographers and arrivals outside and the swarm of activity inside. I finally was able to say hello to Jamie, Donovan, and Xander, who gave me a big kiss. They had loved the film, which made me all the more annoyed I had missed it.

"Can we get into the VIP area?" Xander asked. "I just love that leading guy; he's so delish."

"I'll see what I can do," I said.

On my next trip past the entrance to the VIP area, I waved to Ariana.

"Hey, Toby." She smiled at me.

"Can I get stamps for my friends?" I asked. Access to the VIP area was determined for noncelebrities by the presence of a stamp, only visible under black light, that read "Fabulous."

"I can't do it," she said. "I've got too many people in there. It's a fucking zoo."

Now I felt really stupid. I went back to tell the boys they

would have to be content with the open bar in the area for the hoi polloi.

On my way back outside, I ran into Cameron. "How's everything going, Toby? You having a good time?"

I wasn't sure if he was being ironic or if he thought I was so lucky to be there I would have been happy busing tables.

"That guy with your friends, is he your boyfriend? He's really hot."

"Yeah, thanks," I said. It was creepy to have my boss scoping out Xander.

"He looks familiar; I feel like I've seen him somewhere."

"Really, where?" I asked.

"I don't know. I asked him and he didn't think we'd met."

I shrugged, not really sure what to say.

By midnight, we weren't letting any more photographers into the party, so my job was done. I was completely bushed. My shirt was damp with sweat and someone had spilled a drink on my trousers. I couldn't wait to get home and snuggle in bed with Xander. I grabbed the boys and we headed to Cafeteria for a late-night meal. I had forgotten to eat dinner.

"Do you think there will be any more premieres?" Xander asked after we sat down.

"I hope not," I said.

"Toby's become too cool for this kind of stuff," Jamie said.

"No, I haven't," I said. "I just hate being treated like shit."

"Who treated you like shit?" Donovan asked.

"Everyone," I said. "I thought it would be so great to have a stupid clipboard and a walkie-talkie, but instead everyone just pushed me around."

"I'll tell you what was really weird," Donovan said. "Your boss was hitting on me, hard-core. Telling me about his apartment, how I should stop by and see it, giving me his card, telling me to call him."

"And?" I asked. I hoped Donovan would know better.

"I'm not going there," he said. "The guy's a player. Besides, that would be totally weird. I mean, he's your boss."

"I'd do him," Xander said. "He's hot."

"No, he isn't!" I said. "Look, we're not having this conversation, okay?"

We paid the check and Xander and I shared a cab to the East Village. We stopped at my place, and I got out my wallet to pay the fare.

"Actually," he said, "I'm just going to go home tonight. I've got to get up early for work tomorrow. We have a huge, uh, project due, and I—"

"That's fine," I said coolly. "No problem."

I slammed the door with just enough force to keep him wondering.

This was even worse than not getting a seat at the premiere, worse than Cameron hitting on Xander and Donovan, worse than not getting into the VIP area. Xander should have known what I needed was a night with him, a night to be comforted, to be assured I wasn't going to flack for movies for the rest of my life, that I would have a real career, eventually.

I resolved not to call him until he called me.

I spoke with Jamie the next night. We had been talking on the phone regularly since his breakdown. It was late, and I was at home lying on my bed. Gus was perched on the windowsill, anxiously looking at the lightwell.

"I went back to get another test," Jamie said. "I found a doctor I like better."

"Yes?" My heart started beating faster.

"She said the first test could have been a false positive, so she gave me another test, a different kind of test. If that test came up positive, then I would have it for sure. But it didn't: it came up negative."

"That's great!" I said. "You must be so happy."

"Well, not quite. That test gives false negatives. I have to wait at least two more months until I can take the other test again."

"Why don't you just go and take it now?"

"The doctor said the only thing I could do was wait."

"Can't you go to another doctor?"

"No. I don't want my insurance company knowing about

this. I paid for this last visit out of pocket, and in cash. I don't want it on any records."

"Jamie, all that stuff is confidential. You know that."

"They're crazy at Pelham. If they thought I had it, they'd fire me."

"Oh, come on!"

"And there's another thing." I heard him getting choked up on the other end of the line.

"What's that?"

He started to cry. "If I have it, I don't want to know. I want at least two months not to have it."

"Jamie, I'm sure you don't have it!"

"I don't know about that. I talked about it with this new doctor. Did you know that the week after the party, I came down with a terrible fever? I was in bed for two days with the flu and exhausted for a week. They say that happens sometimes right after you get it."

"Maybe, but you had also partied pretty hard and could have caught something else."

"I party all the time and I don't get the flu."

I tried to change the subject. "Why don't you look on the Internet about alternative therapies, what kind of drugs and stuff are out there?"

"You think I have it already, don't you?"

"No, I just think it's better to be informed."

"I can't do that. Have you ever looked at that information? It's so depressing! Weight loss, for example. If I weighed any less, I'd fall through the cracks in the sidewalk! And did you know that people with AIDS can lose their hearing? No, I'm assuming I don't have it. That's the only way I can deal with this."

"Just don't do anything stupid," I said.

"Oh, I'm not allowed to do anything stupid, while you're off fucking with Xander?"

"Fucking safely. There's a difference."

"Yeah, but what do you know about him? Nothing. You met him in a bar. He could be positive."

"You're right," I said. "He could be."

"And the only difference is, you don't know it."

He was torturing me, as if he knew about the condom already, the condom I didn't give him. But there was no way he could know, and I wasn't sure if I should tell him. I knew I would have to eventually, but I wanted to put it off as long as possible.

Xander contacted me at work four days later. He thanked me for the ticket to the premiere, which I appreciated, even though he was four days late. So much for Southern graciousness.

"When can I see you?" I asked, hoping it would be soon.

"Actually, I'm going away this weekend."

"Really, where?" Maybe he was going to visit friends in Boston.

"I'm going down to Florida for a retreat. It's called New Life Directions for Men. You get in touch with yourself through meditation, drum circles, stuff like that."

Drum circles?

"Is it gay?" I asked.

"I don't know," he said. "A friend from work invited me."

Why hadn't he invited me? I would have gone.

I told him to call me when he got back.

I did a Web search for "New Life Directions," and found the institute's site. "New Life Directions for Men is a holistic healing center," it read, and listed the activities and workshops offered. At the bottom, it said, "All activities are clothing optional."

I looked closer at the pictures on the site. The men in the pictures were draped in towels or skimpy loincloths, though I suspected this modesty was for the sake of promotion. I looked closely at one of the photos: there was a guy in the background who was fully naked—

"Are you looking at porn?" Cameron said, suddenly right behind me.

I turned around, blushing. "Actually, I don't know what I'm looking at," I said. "Xander is going on this retreat, and I just found out it's clothing optional."

"I have a friend who went on that," Cameron said. "It's supposed to be one big orgy."

"I thought it was about spiritual awakening," I said.

"Right," Cameron said. "I think it's about awakening your cock."

I conferred with Donovan and Jamie and they agreed.

"I don't know, Toby," Jamie said. "It could be real, or it could be a big fuck fest. I think it's weird, though, that he didn't mention the 'clothing optional' part."

"There's something strange about him," Donovan said. "Are you sure he's the right person for you?"

I was sure Donovan was jealous. He had been unresponsive to me for all these months, choosing random hookups instead, and now that I was dating someone, it annoyed him.

The retreat made me uneasy, but I had faith in Xander. Why would he try to jeopardize our burgeoning relationship? I was a great boyfriend who could offer him perks like movie premieres, we had been having fun together, and we were even having good sex. What more could he want? Why would he want to sleep with anyone else?

I had been monitoring Jamie like a hawk, as I felt like I was responsible for his well-being. Having failed him before, I wasn't going to disappoint him again.

When we went out, he would often beg off early, pleading exhaustion. I thought he was trying to conserve his energy, until I learned he had been going to the Cock, the bar Donovan sometimes frequented, and picking up guys. He even told Donovan he had been hanging out in the backroom, a den of iniquity where men would stand around jerking or sucking, their pants around their ankles, lit only by a single red bulb. It was like something out of the pre-AIDS era, except this was twenty years later, and these men just wanted to forget.

I decided to confront him on Saturday night over drinks at Wonder Bar. It was the weekend that Xander was on his retreat.

"I need to talk to you," I told Jamie.

"Yeah?" he said. He was tipsy, and I knew where he would be headed after this.

"I've heard you've been slutting around, and I, I just feel like I can't let you do that."

"I don't know what you're talking about. Why do you care?"

"Jamie, you know exactly why I care. Besides, what about those other people? Do you want to accidentally give it to someone? Or get infected with something else? I mean, you don't even know if you have it, but what if you do?"

"Toby, it's none of your business. Maybe this is how I'm getting through all this."

"You have so much time. It's not like these are the last two months of your life."

"You don't understand how it is. You'll never be able to understand."

"Please, Jamie," I said. "I'll do anything for you."

"Anything?" He sounded interested.

"You and I can hook up. Safely. We can jerk off together." I couldn't believe I was saying this. It was crazy. There was no way I could follow through. But perhaps it would be my penance for what I had done.

"No," he said. "That wouldn't be right."

Though I was relieved he had said no, I was also embarrassed that I had just been rejected by Jamie.

He paused for a moment and then looked at me. "Why are you talking like this after all these months?"

"I feel like . . . I feel like the whole thing is my fault."

"Your fault? I'm the one who got fucked. It was my stupid decision."

I had to tell him. I didn't know how Jamie would react, but I needed to come clean. I was afraid he would be angry, but that was a risk I would have to take.

I took a deep breath. "There's something you don't know about that night."

"There's a lot I don't know about that night." He stared down into his drink.

"No, I mean, there's something I did—"

He looked at me in confusion.

"Rico asked me for a condom and I didn't give him one," I said. "I didn't want you two to—I didn't know he was going to do it anyway. And in the closet, of all places."

"Don't remind me," he said.

"So are you mad at me? I mean, this has been bugging me for

months. I feel like if you get AIDS—" I realized I was shouting, and I needed to keep it down. "If you get sick, it will be my fault."

"Fuck you, Toby. First you treat me like I'm some charity sex case, then you want me to make you feel better about your role that night?"

"Hey—it's not my fault you didn't use a condom. I just feel bad that I could have provided one and I didn't."

I was annoyed, but I knew he was right. He was the one who was sick, and I was just being selfish, thinking only of how it affected me, whether or not my guilt could be absolved.

"I guess you're right," Jamie said. "I got myself into it. It's not your responsibility to be handing out condoms at your party, at least not at a party in a one-bedroom apartment. I still can't believe it happened. Every time I think about it, I can't believe that was me."

I looked at Jamie as he sat with me in the dim light of the bar. Part of me couldn't believe this was me, either.

Xander was supposed to return from Florida on Sunday night, but I didn't hear from him until Wednesday. I had also started to worry about some of the little hints he had been dropping. He told me he had a group of friends from home, and they were all really close, just like the boys and I were close here in New York. The difference was that whenever they were together, they would all sleep together, swapping beds like a game of sexual musical chairs.

"We do that whenever they come into town," he said, and I wondered whether this practice would be precluded by our being together.

When he finally called me on Wednesday, he said he was booked until Saturday with "friends from out of town." He didn't say if they were the same friends. I wanted to meet them, to assert my presence, but he didn't invite me, and I wasn't going to ask.

On Thursday, Cameron told me he remembered where he had seen Xander. "He works at the Polo store on Madison Avenue. I was shopping there last month. I think he works in linens."

"That's impossible," I said. "He's an architect. He works in Union Square." Did he work in Union Square? I had never seen his office. Whenever I called him on his cell phone during the day, he would say he was at work, and I would imagine him sitting among drafting tables and blueprints.

"No, I'm pretty sure it was him."

"Maybe he was just shopping," I said. "He loves Polo." I knew I was trying to save face with my boss. It was important to me that Cameron thought I had a hot architect boyfriend. It was the one area in my life in which I could be viewed as a success.

On my lunch hour, I took the train up to the Polo store. Housed in the old Rhinelander mansion, it was the perfect example of fabricated WASPiness; it was not hard to imagine Xander working amidst the auction-bought antiques, oil paintings, and Oriental rugs. It was artificial history for people who didn't like the past they had.

I went up to the linens department and hid behind a giant armoire, pretending to examine some throw pillows.

I looked around the corner, and there he was.

There was something so prissy about linens, working with pillow shams and dust ruffles and thread counts. He was talking to a well-known socialite who was buying sheets for her house in the Hamptons. His voice was artificially honey-sweet, the male version of a Southern belle. I imagined he was quite good at what he did.

All the pieces fit together: he had bought his clothes with an employee discount; his impeccable sense of grooming was gleaned from working in a place with so many mirrors.

A Brazilian salesclerk approached me. "Can I help you with something?"

"No," I whispered. "I'm just looking."

He looked at me strangely.

"Sore throat," I said, putting my hand on my Adam's apple.

He scurried away, afraid he might catch something.

After the socialite left with her purchases, Xander began neatly folding up the linens he had been showing her. I wanted to run away, but he looked up and saw me.

I should have said something clever, like, "I need something for a queen," or "Do you have any shams in this department?" but instead all that came out was, "Hi."

"Oh," he said. "Hi."

"So . . ." I said. "Career change?"

"I'm sorry, I should have explained—I never should have told you that—"

"That you weren't an architect?"

"Right," he said. "But you seemed so excited about it, I didn't know how I could let you down."

"And you didn't go to Harvard," I said. This would explain why he had always changed the subject when I brought up his college experience. It had been fine with me, since I rarely felt like talking about my time at college either.

"If I'd gone to Harvard, do you think I'd be working here?"

I frowned. "Why did you lie to me about all that?"

"Would you have dated me if I had told you the truth?"

I thought back to that night at Rocket. "Yes," I said, "I would have. And I would have respected you more, too."

But he had a point. Would I have? A small part of me felt sorry for him, for the fact that he felt he needed to lie about his background.

"Well," I said, "it was nice knowing you."

I headed towards the exit and then turned around. "You know something else? You don't even dress well."

He had an amused look on his face. It was a pathetic exit line, and we both knew it.

I walked down the stairs of the Polo mansion, my chest hot and my legs shaking. I had wanted things to work with Xander, but that wasn't what was making me angry. More than anything, it was that once again, as soon as there was something in my life that made me happy, it was taken away from me.

I met Jamie and Donovan for dinner that night at Odeon. Jamie had picked it because it was close to work and he could expense it. I suspected, too, that it thrilled him to hang out among the neo-yuppie crowd.

Strangely, they weren't surprised about what had happened with Xander.

"There was something weird about him," Jamie said. "I asked him about a few people I knew from Harvard, and he didn't know anyone."

"He had a Harvard key chain," I said, though I knew this meant nothing.

Donovan laughed, which annoyed me. "Any idiot can buy a Harvard key chain," he said. "He's probably been dining out on this story all year!"

"You could have said something to me," I said.

"We wanted to," Donovan said, and I detected a slight sneer in his voice. "You probably didn't know he was cheating on you either, right?"

"We don't know that for sure," Jamie said.

"What?" I could feel my face getting flushed.

"Whenever we went out, he was always grabbing us. He stuck his hand down my pants, he grabbed Jamie's ass."

"I hope you guys told him to stop."

"We did. Actually, we told him if he kept it up, we would have to tell you."

"And kick his ass," Jamie said, though the idea of Jamie kicking anyone's ass was laughable.

"And that night when he told you he had to work? We saw him later at G."

Donovan delivered this last piece of evidence so triumphantly that I wanted to wring his neck. It was as if he was pleased my dating success had turned into a massive, crashing failure.

"Why didn't you tell me about this?" I asked.

"We were going to," Jamie said. "But you seemed so happy with him, we didn't want to ruin it for you. We thought by telling him to keep his hands to himself, he might get the message. He said he wasn't going to do it anymore, but you know how people like that are."

I had believed that Xander was an architect, that he had graduated from Harvard, that he would be faithful to me. I wanted to believe Xander's fantasy so much, I had helped him create it.

My relationship with Xander, if I could even call it a relationship, had lasted a total of three weeks and four days, but it had left me emotionally exhausted. I dragged myself into the office on Friday morning, resolved that I wasn't going to believe just anyone when they told me about their job or credentials. It wasn't even that I wanted someone with an elaborate pedigree. Mostly I just wanted someone who was honest.

Cameron must have noticed that I seemed depressed, because he came into my cubicle right before lunch.

"How are you doing, Toby? You look a little down."

"I'm okay," I said. "Broke up with my boyfriend."

"Really? Did he work at Polo, or was that just my imagination?"

"He did," I said. "He lied to me about it."

Cameron patted my shoulder. "Hey, buddy, don't worry about it. It's happened to all of us. A guy I dated just out of college said he was an advertising exec and turned out to be a waiter."

"Did you dump him when you found out?"

"No, but we ended up breaking up anyway a few weeks later." He looked around my cubicle as if he had never seen it before. "So you've got some pitches, right? I've been thinking about some development people you should meet."

"That would be great," I said, brightening.

"I'll set something up," he said. "We'll get you a deal somewhere."

The possibility excited me, especially since I had recently started writing another screenplay. After the Lola project had been terminated, I looked over the other screenplays I had started in college; each was about fifty pages, plus an outline. In reviewing them, however, I decided they were trite, inconsequential. I wanted to write a story that mattered. I started working on a semiautobiographical story about a young guy who moves to New York after college. I didn't know yet how it was going to end.

11

A few weeks later, Donovan and I were at Hell, a bar in the meat-packing district, when we met a guy who was a twenty-one-year-old industrial design student at Pratt. He would be graduating in May and already had a paid apprenticeship lined up at a firm that designed housewares, the kind sold at the MoMA design shop.

He had definite potential.

"It's nice to meet some normal people here," he said, leaning his lanky frame against the bar. "Last time I was here, this guy came up to me and asked me if I was interested in modeling. I said, 'Sure, why not?' He gave me his card, and it turned out he was a porn producer."

He told us all about his loft around the corner, how his uncle's realty company had offered it to him virtually for free if he could convert it into something livable, how he had spent the summer remodeling it.

Loft Boy invited us to come check it out.

We left the red-walled cave of the bar and walked the block to his place.

Under the street lights, I could see Loft Boy had dark circles under his eyes. I wondered if he had poor circulation.

As we climbed his stairs, I thought about what Loft Boy and Donovan would look like in bed together naked, their blond locks intertwined on the pillow.

The loft was on the second floor of a former meatpacking plant.

"It took forever to get rid of the stench of rotting meat," Loft Boy said. "But forty gallons of paint did the trick."

The space was well lit and airy, with a slim view of the Hudson. Loft Boy went over to his Mac workstation and put on some MP3's. He had his CPU rigged up to a surround-sound system, so the speakers filled the room with a mellow Portishead track. His dog Sebastian, a chunky basset hound, licked our hands appreciatively.

"Let me just take him around the block to pee," Loft Boy said. He poured us two glasses of white wine. "Make yourselves comfortable."

Donovan busied himself by flipping through Loft Boy's CD collection while I looked at a book on industrial design. I noticed his bed was surrounded by scented candles.

I wondered if something was going to happen between the three of us. I still wanted to sleep with Donovan, to prove I could have him, to prove I wasn't only worthy of guys like Xander.

Maybe this just made me a loser. But I was horny, and I didn't care.

Loft Boy came back and I asked him about the candles.

"I like to give massages," he said. "The candles set the mood."

"I want a massage," Donovan said, looking at me out of the corner of his eye.

"Okay," Loft Boy said. "Then take off your shirt and lie down on the bed."

"I want one too," I said. Mainly, I wanted to see Donovan with his shirt off.

"Then you'll both get massages," Loft Boy said.

We both took our shirts off and lay on the bed face down, though I tried to crane my neck so I could check out Donovan. Loft Boy turned the lights down low and lit a few red candles.

He started massaging Donovan's back with oil, and then did mine, with long broad strokes that eased out the tension. After several minutes, I heard him unzip his fly. He took my hand and moved it to his penis. I grabbed onto it, rubbing the skin back and forth. I touched something metallic. Was he pierced?

After we turned around, he leaned over and kissed me and then Donovan.

Was this really happening?

I had been in a threesome one other time, in college. While it visually satisfied every fantasy I had ever had about sex with more than one person, the reality was a big bother: you had to pay attention to two people instead of one, and inevitably, one person was always left out of the action. I didn't want that person to be me.

After we all stripped, I reached over to kiss Donovan, but he pulled away.

"I can't," he said. "It's too weird."

He could see how disappointed I was, though I didn't say anything. Maybe he needed more warming up.

Loft Boy's dick was pierced with a Prince Albert, a ring that dangled lazily over the head of his cock like a silver talisman. Donovan and I looked at it, then at each other's naked bodies. We started laughing.

Donovan suddenly became serious. "We tell no one about this," he said.

Loft Boy started going down on Donovan. When he removed his mouth, I tried to do the same, but again, Donovan said he felt uncomfortable. "You do him," he said, pointing to Loft Boy, "and he can do me."

As I reluctantly went down on Loft Boy, I felt the piercing tickle the back of my throat. It felt like I was about to swallow a wedding band.

I kept looking up at Donovan, watching him as he squirmed in pleasure as Loft Boy blew him. I was getting a kink in my neck from the awkward angle.

Loft Boy took a break from Donovan and lay down next to both of us. I knew I would kick myself if I didn't take this opportunity, so I repositioned myself and began to suck on Donovan. He looked up, realized it was me, and grinned. I could see he was happy, but he didn't want to take responsibility for it happening.

Donovan's body was lithe and toned, though even from this angle, I could see faint traces of stretch marks on his waist. He had lost a lot of weight since college, he had once told me.

It felt good to suck on something that didn't have hardware attached to it.

I lay down next to him and gave him a kiss.

"I've wanted this to happen for a long time," I whispered to him.

"You're so sweet," he said, and kissed me back.

It wasn't the answer I was looking for. I felt a knot rise in my throat.

Loft Boy was now jerking off furiously as Donovan and I lay next to him. The moment had passed. We realized what we were doing, and it seemed ridiculous.

Loft Boy finished, and Donovan and I made half-hearted attempts at getting off, though we eventually gave up. Without Loft Boy's libido to cheer us along, it seemed pointless.

I knew I wanted Donovan, but it couldn't be within the context of friendship.

We were sweaty and slick with massage oil, so Loft Boy offered us his shower. Donovan and I stepped into the large tub together, as naturally as if we were at the gym.

"Can you imagine if our friends saw us now?" he said.

It felt incredibly normal to be standing there naked with him, water running over our bodies. I wanted to remember the moment.

I asked him to kiss me again. Even if it never happened again, I needed something to give me closure.

"I can't," he said.

"Please."

"Toby, I can't. We're friends, okay?"

As I put on my clothes again, I felt angry and unfulfilled. Why did Donovan have to be a tease? Why did he get to decide when we would be intimate and when we wouldn't?

The two of us said goodbye to Loft Boy and walked down to the street.

"I can't believe we just did that," I said. I knew he didn't want to talk about it, but I needed to hear what he thought, if he liked it, if it would happen again.

"It stays between us," Donovan said.

But I wanted to tell the world. I was proud of it, even happy. It meant Donovan found me attractive, that he could be with me if he wanted to. But I knew he would never admit it, that my silence was the price I would have to pay.

We walked up Gansevoort Street in silence, past green dumpsters filled with trash, past the Christmas tree lights dangling outside of Restaurant Florent, past Hell. On the corner, three black trannie hookers were waving down customers. The one closest to us wore a vinyl mini-dress with flames running up it.

"You know you want it, baby!" she catcalled to a passing car. She turned to her companions, flipped her ebony mane. "But ain't nothin' in this life that come for free."

The next day felt surreal. I had finally hooked up with Donovan, but nothing had turned out the way I wanted it to. I was having trouble concentrating as I mechanically went through the day's tasks.

Cameron stopped by my cubicle in the afternoon.

"I've called a few people about you," he said. "We should be able to get you some meetings soon."

"Thanks," I said. "That's really cool of you."

"You know something?" he said. "You and I should really hang out. Ariana always speaks so highly of you."

"That's nice of her." I had no idea how someone I barely knew could speak highly of me, but I found it gratifying nonetheless.

"I feel like I don't really know you that well. Let's try to do something soon, okay?"

"Sure," I said, though I was confused as to his intentions. Surely he wasn't interested in dating me; he had already made that mistake with an assistant. Maybe he really was interested in promoting my career. After all, if I sold a script, it would make him look good. I decided Cameron was on my side after all.

That night, I told Jamie about my experience with Donovan. I had to tell someone. If I kept it to myself, it would feel like it hadn't happened.

Jamie was indifferent. He had just returned from a road show, assisting with presentations in six states in four days, and he was exhausted.

"Don't you have anything to say about this?" I asked.

"Toby, I've got other things to worry about."

I realized how stupid I was being, gleefully announcing last night's hookup after I had told Jamie to abstain from sex. I was a hypocrite. But I also wasn't the one who potentially was HIV positive.

Then again, we were all potentially HIV positive.

The next night, I was meeting all the boys for dinner at an Upper East Side Belgian place that had dark woodwork and walls painted a deep red. Between work, dating Xander, and worrying about Jamie, it had been almost two months since I had seen David, Alejandro, or Brett. I worried that our group was falling apart, that our friendship was part of a time in our lives that would soon be ending.

I noticed Brett looked different. While previously he had been muscular, he now looked artificially pumped. His arms were like ham hocks, with thick veins running along each of them.

"I think he's taking something," Jamie whispered to me.

"What do you mean?"

"Uh, steroids?"

"Shouldn't we tell him to stop?"

"What can we do, Toby? People like him never listen anyway." He paused for a moment and then sneered at me. "It's no worse than shoving white powder up your nose."

I kept my opinions on Brett's drug use to myself after that.

Before David and Alejandro arrived, Jamie told me they had recently decided to make their relationship an open one. I didn't understand. If they had each other, why would they need anyone else? David seemed happy about it, but Alejandro was not pleased. Unlike his usual bouncy self, he sat in the corner of the booth looking sullen.

The other person who was quiet was Donovan. He didn't look at me or speak to me during the entire dinner. A few times I asked him a question, and he pretended not to hear me. When he got up to use the restroom, I followed him.

"What's going on?" I asked. "You haven't spoken to me all night."

"I told you not to tell anyone, Toby, and you went and told Jamie. You might as well have told all of downtown."

"I'm sorry. I'm not very good at keeping secrets. I couldn't hold it in any longer." Suddenly, my guilt turned to anger. "But why does this get to be your secret? It happened to me as much as it happened to you!"

"People say enough things about me," Donovan said. "I don't need them gossiping about one more thing."

"You know something?" I said. "I think you have an inflated sense of your own importance."

I knew people could say the same thing about me, but it felt good to tell it to Donovan.

I went back to the table. My cheeks were hot.

"Are you okay?" Brett asked.

"I'm fine," I said. "Too much red wine."

At the end of the meal, I went to the restroom again. Alejandro was already inside, washing his hands. He was wearing a long-sleeved designer shirt, one with slashes down the sides. As he stood at the sink, his wrists were exposed, and I noticed several red marks on them.

"Jandro, what happened to your wrists?" I asked.

He quickly pulled down his sleeves so I couldn't see them. "Oh, that. It's nothing."

"Come on, it's not nothing. It looks like you were tied up or something—"

I realized what it was, and he knew it.

"David likes to mess around, you know, in bed, and sometimes it gets a little, what's the word . . . ?" He fixed his perfectly styled coif in the mirror in an attempt to distract me.

"Rough? Like with rope?"

"Yeah. Sometimes with these leather straps he has."

"Do you like it? Why do you let him do it?"

He turned away from the mirror, towards me.

"I don't like it," he said. "But if I don't do it, David will leave me."

I shook my head sadly. I would never put up with someone treating me like that.

"It's simple, Toby. Don't you understand? I don't want to be alone."

*   *   *

Everyone had different commitments after dinner—David and Alejandro to have sex, Brett to meet some college friends downtown, Donovan to avoid me—so Jamie and I went to his place. It was rare to have a night when we weren't running around like crazy.

I was glad to be visiting Jamie's apartment under less stressful circumstances than the last time I was here. I sank into his couch.

Jamie went to check his messages on his beat-up answering machine. For someone who always had the latest technology, he was too cheap to get voice mail.

The first message was from Donovan.

"He must have left it right before dinner," Jamie said.

He turned up the volume and went over to the kitchen table to sort through his mail.

"Hey, Jamie, it's me," said Donovan on the tape. "Uh, listen, about the whole thing with Toby, I don't know how it happened. It was a huge mistake, I just—"

Jamie ran over to the machine and pressed STOP. I jumped up and tried to press PLAY.

"You've got to let me hear it," I said. "I need to know why he's acting this way."

"Okay," Jamie said. I knew part of him wanted me to hear the message.

The tape continued: "I didn't realize what was happening, and I'm sort of disgusted by it now. Anyway, I guess I'll see you at dinner."

Disgusted?

"He was disgusted?" I said. "He certainly enjoyed it while it was happening."

"Toby, don't take it personally. Sometimes he says things that—"

"Don't take it personally? He just said I was disgusting. The guy I'm in love with said I was disgusting."

"Toby, you're not in love with Donovan. You're in love with the idea of Donovan. There's a difference. Donovan as a person is a pain in the ass. You've created this whole fantasy about him, just like you did with Xander and—"

I wanted him to shut up, because I knew he was right.

"I don't care," I said. "That little bitch! How could he say something like that? I'm calling him."

I got out my cell phone and started scrolling through memory.

"No, you're not!" Jamie said. He grabbed the phone from me and ran into his bedroom.

I tackled him on the bed and took my phone back.

"You can't let him know you heard the message," Jamie said. "He'll kill me."

"This isn't about you," I said, placing the call.

I reached Donovan's voice mail: "Hey, it's D. You know what to do."

"It's Toby." Suddenly I didn't know what to tell him. "You can forget about being friends," I finally said. "Next time you want to talk shit about someone, don't do it on an answering machine."

I hung up.

"Brilliant," Jamie said. "I'm sure he'll hang on every word."

I didn't hear from Donovan for the entire next day. Every time I picked up Cameron's phone, I was sure it would be him. We usually spoke regularly, so now that we were in a fight, wouldn't he rush to resolve things?

That evening, Ariana's firm was hosting a launch for a new fragrance to be held, predictably, at Mirror. Since a group dinner with Donovan and the boys was not an option, I accepted Cameron's invitation to go with him that night.

We stayed late at the office, grabbed a bite to eat on the way, and arrived at Mirror around 9 P.M. The fragrance was called Harem, so the club was decked out in an *Arabian Nights* theme that Ariana had orchestrated: potted palms, enormous silk throw pillows, gold tablecloths, candles, and incense. The club's many mirrors had been draped in filmy, shimmering fabric. Ariana had hired a handful of club kids dressed in harem outfits for the event, and some of the guests had taken part in the theme as well, but it was mostly a suits crowd of fragrance buyers and fashion professionals. Jordan Gardner, who was attending as a favor to Ariana, made the biggest splash of all when she arrived in a pair of gold harem pants and a midriff-baring top. The photographers snapped away, certain they would be able to sell a photo of an Arabian Jordan to any of the top newspapers and magazines.

The club had decided an orange-infused martini spiced with cinnamon had a vaguely Middle Eastern flavor to it, and the crowd—which was composed of people who wouldn't know, anyway—seemed to agree. I tried the specialty drink, but decided to switch over to vodka cranberries. I wanted to forget about everything that had happened, even if it meant being whisked away to an incense-clouded world of fragrance buyers for an evening.

I ran into Cameron in the restroom and he offered me some coke, which I accepted. I didn't care anymore about what was right or wrong, what was appropriate or not. I just wanted to escape.

After doing several bumps in the toilet stall, I felt more alert, more focused. Things were right with the world. I was supposed to be at this party; I was supposed to be hanging out with these people.

Cameron and I ran into Jordan outside the restroom. She had a new film coming out the following week, a thriller co-starring the hunk on the cover of this month's *Vanity Fair*.

"Hey, I know you!" she said to me, pointing wildly. She was clearly fucked up. "Your mother lent me that, that dress. I got a lot of press out of that dress!" She threw her head back and laughed. "Someone spilled soy sauce on it, though, so it was ruined!"

My mother hadn't told me Jordan had trashed her dress.

Cameron led me to the VIP area, where Ariana was standing with one of her employees. She gave me a suspicious look and then forced a smile.

"They're fine," she said. The rope was drawn open.

Cameron motioned for me to sit next to him, and he started chattering on about how important I was to him, and how he could never survive without me. All I could think was, *So this is what it's like to hang out with Cameron.* He kept putting his hand on my knee and looking at me with puppy dog eyes.

He slipped me the vial and I went back to the restroom. I would keep this high going all night if I had to. On my way back out, I had the urge to call Donovan on my cell phone, but I resisted. He had to call me.

The party was wrapping up, and Ariana was free to go. Jordan was now sitting with us. We had been chatting about her latest film, and I wanted the conversation to continue. She wasn't terribly bright, but she had access to a world that I didn't, and I was curious about it.

"Are you coming with us to Flash?" Ariana asked Cameron. "We've got my car. Jordan's going to drive."

"Why are you driving?" I asked Jordan.

"Ariana hates driving," Jordan said. "But she knows I love her car. I never get to drive in New York."

"That's cool of her," I said.

Jordan looked at me like I was an idiot. "I don't pay her ten thousand dollars a month for nothing."

"Let's go," Cameron said.

Jordan turned to him. "Listen, love, do you have any more—"

"Sure," Cameron said. He handed her the vial.

"Be right back," she said, and headed towards the restroom.

Ariana had to take care of some last-minute details, so she gave Cameron her keys, and the two of us stepped out onto Eighth Avenue. Though it had started raining, a large crowd was gathered on the sidewalk, since the launch party was over and the club was now open to the public. Ariana's car, a black BMW convertible, was parked in one of four spots in the club's loading zone. Cameron and I squeezed into the back seat and waited for Jordan, who finally came stumbling out of the club, escorted under a large umbrella by one of Ariana's assistants. She got into the driver's seat.

The club's bouncer motioned for her to roll down her window. He was a big beefy guy wearing a black T-shirt with the Mirror logo on it. I noticed a scar running from his left cheek to his lip.

"Miss," he said, "you can't park here."

"We're waiting for someone," Jordan said. I could tell she was in the mood for a fight.

"Your car's been parked here all night in the loading zone, and we've been nice enough to let you—"

"We're waiting for Ariana Richards. I assume you're not so stupid that you don't know who she is?"

"I don't care if you're waiting for the fucking Pope. You can't park here."

"Do you know who I am?"

"Yeah, I do."

"Who am I?"

The bouncer crossed his arms. "Who are you? Another bimbo actress who thinks she can get whatever she wants. And I'm telling you to move."

Jordan's eyebrows arched up in anger.

Ariana was now standing next to the bouncer.

"Come on, Jordan, we're going to be late," Ariana said.

"Fucking Guido," Jordan slurred to the bouncer, before rolling up her window.

The bouncer walked behind us and attempted to clear a small group of clubgoers away from the loading zone. Ariana got in the front passenger seat.

"He's right behind you. You ought to give him a little tap," laughed Cameron.

Jordan had the car in neutral, but she was revving the engine.

"Jordan, what are you doing?" Ariana said. She was starting to panic.

"I'm going to do just what Cameron said. Bloody bastard."

I couldn't believe what I was hearing. I looked at Ariana, but could read nothing from her expression.

The car accelerated in reverse, skidding on the wet pavement. Cameron and I looked through the back windshield to see the car hurtling toward the bouncer and the crowd of people.

With the force of a carnival roller coaster whose operator has fallen asleep at the brake, the car hit the group of people, smashing their bodies against a van parked behind us. There was an enormous *Crunch! Crash! Thud!* as my body slammed against the backseat and my head struck the back windshield, which had cracked but was still intact. Pressed up against it was a screaming mélange of bodies, a wriggling, slippery mess of flesh and blood and hair and clothing.

I winced as I realized that the crunch I had heard was the car breaking people's bones.

Ariana had started crying. "What the hell are you doing? What the hell did you do?" she screamed at Jordan.

"I don't know—I didn't mean to—"

Cameron sat next to me, his head in his hands, as he chanted, "Oh shit, oh shit, oh shit," like a mantra.

The car was still in reverse, and it was pinning the crowd against the van. My stomach turned as I saw how close we were to the injured. I grabbed Jordan's shoulders, trying to shake her back into consciousness.

"Put it in drive!" I shouted. "Put the car in drive!"

Jordan was too stunned to do anything. Ariana put the car in drive and it lurched forward. The people spilled out behind us. The back windshield was splattered with blood. I felt dizzy and couldn't see straight. Jordan opened her door and tumbled out, barely able to stand on her heels. She stood there, held up by Ariana's assistant, and looked at the mayhem she had created, unable to speak.

Cameron, Ariana, and I got out and moved away from the car.

Dozens of people were now crowding the sidewalk and it became impossible to separate the injured from the merely curious. Every other person was on his or her cell phone, calling 911, reporting the news to friends, calling information for private ambulance services to bring help to the scene faster.

My heart was pounding and I was grinding my teeth.

Within ten minutes, six ambulances had arrived and paramedics were frantically engaged in triage. Most of the people who had been hit were lying near the curb or leaned against the back of the van. Blood flowed from their wounds, pooling on the asphalt before being washed away by the rain. Two young women were surrounded by the contents of a spilled purse; someone said it had come open moments before the crash and they had been collecting its contents. One had her hand over her right eye; her face was covered in blood. The other woman's arm was sheared all the way to the bone; a friend had fashioned her a sling from her shirt. The friend squatted on the sidewalk wearing only a soaked black bra, comforting the crying and wounded women.

People were fighting over who got to go first in the ambulances, and several people had to double up. For every injured person, there were two or three others who were equally if not more hysterical about their friend's injury.

I was suddenly more sober than I'd been all night.

Two squad cars arrived, and officers started taking statements from witnesses.

Ariana was on her cell phone talking to her lawyer and barking orders to Jordan, Cameron, and me. She was in high crisis mode.

"We're going inside the club," she said.

She pulled us all through a side door down the street from the main entrance.

"Why?" I asked.

"Just do it, okay?"

Ariana led us into the club's offices, in the basement near the restrooms, and shut the door. The four of us stood together in a circle, soaking wet from the rain.

"I think we're okay to talk here," she said, making sure no one else was around. "Jordan, can you act sober?"

"Sure," Jordan said.

"No, I mean, seriously, you cannot let on that you've been drinking or doing anything else tonight. The police are going to ask you what happened. You will not, under any circumstances, take a Breathalyzer test. My lawyer will meet us at the station and he'll take care of everything else. You got all this?"

"I think so." She took out a pocket mirror and started applying lipstick, preparing for the role of a lifetime.

"They're going to be nice to you because of who you are. Just charm them, you know how to do that, right?"

Jordan nodded.

"Okay, now we all need to have the same story." She took a

deep breath. "What happened is Jordan's foot slipped on the gas pedal. She was about to pull out and she thought the car was in drive. It was wet, and we spun out of control. Those heels you're wearing? Have you ever driven in heels?"

"Sure," Jordan said.

"Well, we're saying you haven't, okay? You weren't familiar with the car, because it was my car and I was letting you drive."

"Because Jordan loves driving foreign cars," Cameron said.

"That's right," Ariana said. "You were excited to drive my car."

Cameron looked at me. "Toby, you're cool with this?"

Though he phrased it as a question, it was clearly a command. There was only one way I could answer.

"Yeah," I said. "Sure."

It was all happening so quickly. I knew what was going on, but I didn't know how to react. There was no precedent in my life for what to do when my boss's publicist asks me to lie to the police.

"Jordan, do you have any drugs in your purse?" Ariana asked.

Jordan rifled through her tiny handbag and pulled out the vial. "Sure. You want some?"

"No, you need to get rid of that!" Ariana was getting frustrated. "Give it to Toby. He'll flush it."

Jordan handed me the vial of cocaine.

"Do I have anything on my . . ." I motioned to the spot on my upper lip below my nostrils.

"You're clean," Ariana said, as if it were the least of her concerns, which it was.

I went into the restroom. The attendant seemed oblivious to what had happened. I locked myself in a stall. I briefly, stupidly considered doing some more of the coke, but then decided to flush the entire vial. I washed my face at the sink, left a dollar tip, and grabbed some mints to mask my party breath.

Upstairs, Cameron and Ariana were standing together on the sidewalk as the police questioned Jordan. She looked ridiculous standing in the rain in her harem pants.

Several reporters had arrived on the scene, including a TV crew.

"No press, no interviews," Ariana said to them.

Several photographers kept snapping. I turned my head away.

An officer motioned towards me. "Are you Toby? Where have you been?"

"I was in the restroom."

"Don't worry, officer," Ariana said. "He's not going anywhere."

The other officer came back to talk to us. "We're going to need to take you all down to the station for questioning."

They're going to know I've done drugs, I thought to myself. They're going to be able to tell. I didn't know if I was more worried over lying about Jordan or getting in trouble myself. That was all I needed, to get busted for cocaine possession.

Ariana and I were put in one squad car, and Cameron and Jordan were in the other. Ariana held my wet hand like a big sister. Over and over again, she kept whispering to me, "It's going to be okay."

For a moment, I believed her.

They took us to the local precinct, the Tenth, on Twentieth Street. The four of us were separated and I waited alone in a dingy interrogation room for twenty minutes.

Detective Ron Shiro, a middle-aged officer, interviewed me. Under the light, his skin looked gray and pockmarked. Behind him was a large mirror; I was sure there were people on the other side watching us.

I told the detective the story that Ariana had instructed us to. As he made notes on his pad, I had the feeling he didn't believe anything I was saying. I told him I didn't know Jordan well, but she didn't seem like the kind of person who would do something like this on purpose.

He smirked at me. Perhaps it was best if I didn't editorialize.

As I told him my story, I looked him straight in the eye. I remembered reading somewhere that a liar was someone who averted his eyes. When I realized my eyes probably looked bloodshot under the fluorescent light, I stopped staring so hard.

"Had you been drinking at all?" he asked.

"Sure," I said. "I had a few drinks."

"Were you hurt in the accident?"

"I hit my head," I told him, "but I think I'm okay. It's just a bump."

"You should go to the hospital and get that checked out," he said.

"Really, I'm fine," I said. The last thing I wanted to do was to spend time in a hospital tonight.

"It's for your own good: just get yourself checked out. We'll have a squad car take you there."

I finally agreed. I didn't want to seem like I was avoiding anything.

"And Toby," he said, handing me a card, "if you think of anything else—anything at all—give me a call. I know it all happened really fast, and there may be things you're forgetting. If you remember anything else, even the smallest detail, give me a call."

I shook his hand and was released from the station. Ariana, Cameron, and Jordan were nowhere in sight. Maybe they had left this party early, too.

I was escorted to a squad car outside. As it pulled away from the station, its sirens started blaring.

"Could you not—could you not put those on?" I shouted through the partition.

"Don't you want to get there faster?" the officer said.

"I don't care how long it takes," I said. "They're just, they're just really hurting my head."

The officer switched them off.

I was dropped off at the nearest hospital and examined for head injuries and whiplash. The doctor and nurses said I seemed fine, though I was told to limit strenuous exercise for the next day or two and not drink alcohol or take aspirin or pain killers. I was to call them if I experienced anything unusual.

"You were lucky," the nurse said. "You could have had a concussion."

"Will I have any memory loss?" I asked. I was hoping I would. I wanted to forget the whole thing.

"It's a possibility," she said. "But we've seen much worse.

Some of those people who were hit? They're going to be here for a long time."

I felt terrible. I was worrying about a small bump on my head, and there were people who had surely suffered broken bones and worse.

I was supposed to have someone wake me every hour and ask me where I was, who I was and who they were, and check if my movements were unusual or clumsy. I lied and told them I had a roommate who would take care of it.

I was released just after 4 A.M. and took a cab home. The rain had stopped, but the streets still smelled wet.

12

At 8 A.M., my phone started ringing. I pulled it out of the wall and let all my calls go to voice mail.

I finally woke at eleven, bounding out of bed to run to the bathroom and throw up. My skin felt tight and dry; every nerve ending was screaming for water. I looked in the mirror to find my face had broken out in three places.

When I checked my messages, I discovered I had sixteen, mostly from the press. I had thought my number was unlisted.

I got into the office at noon. Everyone was sympathetic and inquired repeatedly about my well-being. Cameron invited me into his office. He told me I could take as much time off as I needed, that it was understandable if the shock continued to affect me.

"I feel awful that you were part of this, Toby," he said. "You wouldn't have been at that party if you weren't working for me."

He lit a cigarette and exhaled a plume of smoke. Business as usual.

"It's not your fault," I said. "Ariana invited me to ride with you guys."

"I know," he said, "but I still feel responsible." As he said the words, he was distracted by something on his desk. When he looked up, he seemed almost surprised that I was still standing there.

I asked him what had happened to Jordan. I could see he was about to choose his words carefully.

"Jordan was released on bail this morning. The car was impounded. It's all procedure, you know. It was just such a terrible accident. Jordan is so torn up about it."

He spoke to me as if I were an outsider, as if I hadn't been in the car alongside him. If he believed his story long enough, he might think it was the truth.

Cameron spent most of the day talking on the phone with the door shut. I was tempted to patch myself in on his calls, but I restrained myself.

At three, Cameron said he was going out to a late lunch with his mother.

The story had already shown up on some of the online versions of the local papers, and I realized it would be all over the print editions tomorrow. Jamie called me just before four.

"I just heard about the accident from my secretary. Were you really there?"

I told him I was.

He asked what happened.

"It's complicated," I said. "Let's have dinner tonight, okay? You, me, and Donovan."

"Are you talking to Donovan?"

"Not yet," I said. "But I need to."

I realized I should let my parents know I was okay, in case the news reached them in San Francisco. I called home and left a voice mail that I hoped would make sense.

I went out for a long lunch, as Cameron had suggested. When I returned, there were several more messages: one from Sonia and three more from reporters. Apparently, it was now common knowledge where I worked.

I wrote down the messages, but didn't return any of the calls. I knew if I called Sonia back, she would start asking me questions I didn't want to answer.

I told Cameron about the calls.

"I've been getting them, too," he said. "Don't return any, okay? From now on, Eric is going to screen everything for you. He'll take mine, too. It's too difficult not to talk once you've got a reporter on the phone. This will make things easier on both of us."

Now I knew what it would be like to have an assistant. The lack of control made me feel like I was in jail.

One call that was put through was from Ariana.

"Hi," I said. "Did you want to talk to Cameron?"

"No," she said. "I wanted to find out how you're doing."

"I'm fine," I said. "A little tired, but fine. I didn't get to leave the hospital until four."

"Yeah, they kept us all really late, too," she said. "Look, if you need anything—anything at all—just give me a call, okay?"

"Thanks," I said. "I appreciate it."

Just before I left that evening, Cameron came into my cubicle.

"I know it may not be the right time to tell you this, but I just spoke with a development person at Miramax about your work. She sounded really interested. I thought maybe the three of us could have lunch in the next few weeks. I know you've been working hard on your writing, and believe me, it hasn't gone unnoticed."

"That sounds great," I said. Maybe, just maybe, this would be a situation I could turn to my advantage.

That night, I made plans to meet Jamie and Donovan at a quiet bistro in Chelsea. Donovan was sitting alone at the bar when I arrived. He got up and gave me a hug.

"I'm so glad you're okay," he said.

"Can we deal with what happened between us?" I asked.

"Yeah, I—"

"Me first," I said, interrupting him. "I'm sorry I told Jamie. It was inappropriate."

"Look, the whole thing was just stupid. I mean, it wasn't stupid that it happened, but I shouldn't have freaked out. I'm sorry about that. When I said I was disgusted, I didn't mean about you. I just would have preferred it hadn't happened in the way it did."

"I had wanted it for a long time, but I guess you didn't feel the same way."

"Toby, I wanted it too. I wouldn't have done it if I didn't. It's just that we're friends. We know too much about each other."

Why was it that for some people, intimacy meant death for relationships?

I accepted his apology, but I knew things would never be the same between us.

After Jamie arrived, we sat down at a banquette. I ordered a cheeseburger. I needed comfort food.

"So are you going to tell us what happened?" Jamie asked.

I knew I wasn't supposed to be drinking, but I had ordered a glass of red wine to keep me calm. I took a sip.

"The whole thing was an accident," I said. "Jordan's foot slipped and she didn't know she was in reverse."

"How bizarre," Jamie said.

"Why didn't she stop the car?" Donovan asked.

"I don't know," I said. "It all happened so quickly."

"Did you have to talk to the police?" Jamie asked. "Was that weird?"

I nodded. "It was okay."

"Will you have to testify in court?"

"Probably."

"Do you have a lawyer representing you?"

"No. Why do I need a lawyer?"

"You should have one. For protection."

"I can't afford a lawyer."

"I know someone good," Jamie said. "I'll email you a number tomorrow."

The way the two of them were talking about testifying in court and having a lawyer made me think they didn't believe me. But I knew I couldn't tell them the truth.

We finished the meal. My stomach was starting to hurt.

"Do you want to come out with us?" Jamie asked. "We're going to Starlight."

"I'm not feeling well," I said. "I should rest tonight."

I took a cab home. As I patiently endured the Friday night traffic, my stomach started to turn. As the cheeseburger settled in my gut, I realized I hadn't gone to the bathroom in more than twenty-four hours.

When the cab got to my apartment, I stumbled out, holding my stomach and hoping it wouldn't let loose before I got to my apartment. I had only reached the second floor when I couldn't hold it any longer.

After I cleaned myself up in my bathroom, washed out my boxers, and took a shower, I felt like I had let go of something emotionally as well. Maybe things would sort themselves out. Maybe I would wake up in the morning and find none of it had really happened.

On Saturday morning, I walked to a local newsstand. "Jordan Gardner Smashes Up," screamed the cover of the *Post,* with pictures of Jordan and the wrecked car. The story was also featured in a double-page spread in the *Daily News* and reported in the Metro section of the *Times*.

According to the articles, all of the victims had extensive scrapes and bruises. Since the point of impact was below the waist, many had suffered broken legs, and one young woman's pelvis had been shattered. Few of the breaks were clean ones; nearly everyone needed reconstructive surgery that would require lengthy rehabilitation. Of the two women I saw sitting together on the ground, one had lost vision in her right eye and the other had broken an arm. They had both been pushed against the van's bumper by the mass of bodies.

In all three articles, I was named as the fourth passenger in the car. There were no quotes from Jordan, Ariana, or Cameron, only observations from onlookers at the scene. Witnesses were angry Jordan hadn't been handcuffed, and that she and the car's passengers had "mysteriously disappeared" right after the crash, only to emerge ten minutes later to speak with police. "She thinks because she's a celebrity, she can get away with this," one victim said in the *Times* article. "Well, she can't."

Incredible details were being thrown around, like the fact that Jordan could face 104 years in prison if convicted on all eleven felony counts; among them were first- and second-degree assault, first-degree reckless endangerment, and driving under the influence of drugs or alcohol, though there was no hard evidence to support the last allegation, since Ariana's lawyer had made sure Jordan was not given a Breathalyzer test. As a further complication, Jordan had never bothered to get a U.S. driver's license after moving to the States. She had been released after posting $20,000 bail; the judge set a court date for the beginning of July.

In an attempt to gather evidence, the police had tried to interview employees of the club as well as members of Ariana's staff, but an informal gag order (that, the articles noted, could be construed as an obstruction of justice) had been slapped on all of them by their employers. Significantly, a witness had noted to reporters that there were no brake lights visible on the car as it raced toward the group.

My phone continued to ring over the weekend, so I pulled it out of the wall again, only plugging it back in occasionally to make calls. One of the messages was from Jordan, making sure I was okay. Another was from Sherry Merrill, who had read about the accident in the LA papers. I left a message at her house to say I was fine.

I couldn't sleep all weekend. I didn't enjoy hanging out with my friends on Saturday night, because everyone wanted me to talk about it, and I had to keep telling the same lies over and over again.

On Monday morning, I arrived at the office and greeted the main Eastside Pictures receptionist. She looked at me glumly.

Cameron called me into his office before I had a chance to check my email. Once again, he shut the door.

"First of all, how are you holding up? I've been worried about you."

"I'm fine," I lied.

"There's something you should know," he said. "The girl who lost vision in one eye? She died yesterday morning in the hospital from internal bleeding."

I sank into a chair.

"I don't believe this," I said.

"You realize this makes the charges against Jordan extremely serious," Cameron said. "She could face life in prison for this."

"I know that," I said.

"It's very important that we all stick with the same story."

Why was he telling me this? Did he think I was going to go to the cops?

"Of course, Jordan will pay for the girl's funeral," he said.

"Like that's going to make it better?" I said.

"Toby," he said sharply, "it's not going to make it better. But there are things one does in this kind of situation, things that are appropriate."

"I guess there are," I said.

I left, closing the door behind me.

I checked the news. Stacey Davis was a twenty-four-year-old junior market editor at a fragrance industry trade magazine. She had only recently moved into the city, where she had lived with three roommates in Yorkville. Jordan had already issued a statement expressing her regret and offering to pay for the girl's funeral. "We don't want her money," the girl's mother told reporters. "She can't buy her way out of this."

In a strange way, I felt sorry for Jordan. I knew what it was like to be accused of something. The difference was that Jordan was guilty.

That morning, as I was responding to my email, Cameron came in with a page from *Daily Variety*.

"Did you see this?" he asked. "Lola Copacabana just sold her life story for a hundred thousand dollars."

"I was supposed to be part of that project," I said. "But her agents had someone else they wanted to work with."

"You know, this transsexual stuff is really hot right now. People are fascinated by it." He showed me the article. "How far did you get on her story?" he asked.

"I finished it," I said. "I was just about to send it to her when she cut me out of the deal."

"You and I should talk about this more." He motioned me into his office and shut the door.

"Do you think you could revise the screenplay, take out anything specifically about her life—fictionalize it all, basically—and then show it to me?"

Maybe all my work on Lola's story wouldn't go to waste.

"Sure," I said. "I mean, we would have to make sure we weren't stealing anything from her. But I could change things around. She doesn't have to be a nightclub performer. She could be a fashion designer or a hairdresser or something."

"We'll clear it all with legal ahead of time to make sure there are no problems." He looked out the window, musing for a moment. "I think a real woman should play her, though, don't you think? That would be more bankable."

Before I could say anything, he stood up and shook my hand in a gesture of mock formality. "You, my friend, have your first screenwriting gig."

I was grateful for it, mainly because I thought it would take my mind off things. Fictionalizing Lola's life, though it would be more work, could be absorbing. By lunchtime, I had already come up with elaborate scenarios about her life as a child, her sex change, and her eventual move to New York. It was refreshing not to be bound to the truth.

I got another voice mail from Sonia before I left for the evening. Without even thinking, I deleted it.

On Tuesday morning, Cameron asked me if I'd like to join him at B Bar that night. He held up a copy of *Time Out*.

"Lola's supposed to be performing. I thought it would be fun to check it out. You, me, Ariana, Jordan, a few other people. You know, distract us a bit."

I agreed to meet them that evening in the back room.

Later in the afternoon, there was a black envelope on my desk addressed to me. It was an invitation, for me and a guest, to the premiere of Jordan's new thriller, to be held at the Ziegfeld with an after-party at Flash. As this was a time of crisis, Ariana wasn't about to deviate from the formula.

Inside the invitation was a note from Jordan: "Toby, I hope you can make it to my premiere. Love, Jordan." It felt like a six-year-old's invitation to her birthday party.

I decided I would bring Jamie. Donovan wasn't going to get off that easily after our fight.

It felt like I was accepting a bribe, but I figured I was free to accept whatever perks came my way.

I looked at the note again and realized the handwriting was familiar.

It wasn't Jordan's. It was Ariana's.

*   *   *

I met Cameron in the back room of B Bar that evening. It was the same Tuesday night party I had attended with Jamie and the boys eight months ago, the same blend of pseudo and real celebrities, downtown freaks, and slaves to fashion. But this time, instead of staring at Cameron Cole from a booth over, I had been invited to hang out with him and his friends.

Jamie had called me earlier to say he and the boys were going to Wonder Bar, but I declined his invitation to join them. I didn't tell him where I was going to be.

As I checked out the crowd at B Bar, I wondered if I might run into Subway Boy. According to that bar rag, he had come here at least once on a Tuesday night.

Cameron was sitting in a vinyl booth with Ariana, Jordan, and a few other friends of his. One was an underwear model whose supine torso was plastered across every bus in the city and had just made the *Out* 100; another was a young actor-writer-director who had been nominated for an Oscar two years ago. Everyone was drinking champagne and smoking cigarettes.

Two bodyguards stood next to the booth, watching over Jordan.

Cameron introduced me to everyone and I sat down next to the actor. As a glass of champagne was poured for me, I was unable to think of anything clever to say. I had seen the actor's films, but I didn't want to seem like a fan. I realized I needed to relax. They invited you here, I reminded myself. You're one of them now.

"I want to make a toast to Jordan," Ariana said. "We all know her premiere is going to be a big success tomorrow night. I'm proud of you, J."

We all raised our glasses as Ariana gave Jordan a kiss on the cheek.

"What's the occasion?" said a thin man in a dark suit.

Everyone looked up. It was a famous fashion designer whom I recognized from numerous party pages.

"Jordan's premiere," Ariana said, as she got up to give the designer an air-kiss. "Tomorrow night. You'll be there, right?"

"Do you know my assistant, Toby Griffin?" Cameron asked him.

"I do now," he said, shaking my hand and giving me a wink. "Ariana, make sure he gets an invitation to the benefit next month." He smiled at everyone. "I've got to get back to David's table. You kids have fun tonight."

He disappeared into the crowd.

"Was he talking about David Geffen?" I asked.

"Yeah, he comes here every once in a while," Cameron said.

"I'll put you on the comp list for that benefit," Ariana said to me. "It's a huge celebrity AIDS thing."

Out of the crowd appeared a party photographer.

Ariana jumped up to give him a big hug and a kiss.

"Let me get a shot of all of you," he said.

We all slid close together in the booth.

His camera flashed several times.

He pulled out a notebook and handed it to Ariana. "Can you write down all the names for me?" He looked at me and smiled. "I don't think I know you."

Cameron introduced me. "Toby's a screenwriter," he said, and the photographer nodded.

Through the crowd, I saw Jamie and Donovan. Compared to my glittery companions, they looked young, inexperienced. Jamie saw me and dragged Donovan over to the table.

"Hey there," I said.

Jamie looked at my companions and then back at me, confused.

"This is my friend Jamie," I said to everyone. "And this is Donovan."

Everyone at the table smiled weakly.

"How ya doing?" Cameron said.

"We'll be sitting over there," Jamie said, motioning to a table in the corner.

"I'll catch up with you later," I said, and they made their way into the crowd.

"God, your friend Donovan is so hot," Cameron said, and the underwear model agreed.

My stomach turned.

The music changed from lounge to classic disco. Lola mounted a platform above us and started dancing. She was wearing a black vinyl catsuit.

"She is so outrageous! I love it!" Jordan said.

"She dresses like that all the time," Ariana said.

"You taking notes?" Cameron said, giving me a friendly pinch under the table.

Another transsexual go-go dancer climbed onto a platform at the opposite end of the room. Her look was early eighties punk, mohawk and all. She had painted a red lightning bolt across her face, the exact color of fresh blood.

The tabloids continued to devour news about the accident. The club's bouncer gave an interview about the fight he had gotten into with Jordan; the headline in the *Daily News* read "F***ing Guido!" In response, the National Italian-American Foundation was urging a consumer boycott of all of Jordan's films. In a statement released by her lawyers, Jordan denied having made the slur. A spokesperson for the group said if Jordan didn't apologize for her actions, and specifically for her ethnically motivated insult, the boycott would be broadened to include not just Jordan's movies but all films released by her current studio.

The lawsuits had also started coming in. Jordan was being sued for a total of $123 million, including $50 million by Stacey Davis's parents and $32 million by the bouncer. All of the suits charged intentionality in the accident; several asserted that Jordan was drunk or high at the time. Additional lawsuits had been lobbed at Ariana, her company, the nightclub, the City of New York, and BMW.

For the most part, Jordan was unable to leave her Gramercy Park apartment, as photographers were camped outside it around the clock. Bodyguards accompanied her during her few forays out, one for a meeting at Ariana's office, one on Tuesday evening to B Bar, and one to get her hair cut in preparation for her premiere on Wednesday night. Even for Jordan, Frédéric Fekkai was not making house calls.

*   *   *

On Wednesday morning, there was a report on Page Six about Jordan's premiere. "Publicity Machine Barrels On," the headline read. Currently, almost all of Ariana's clients were sticking with her, the article said, and major celebrity attendees were expected tonight. Celebrities banded together in times of crisis, since they had all been there before. Monica Lewinsky, the article noted, was a definite yes.

Because of the controversial nature of the premiere, Jamie had been apprehensive about accepting the invitation, but ultimately his love for gossip got the best of him. I picked him up at his office on Wall Street in a car Cameron had ordered for me.

The scene at the Ziegfeld Theater was a madhouse. Because of the accident, there were twice as many photographers on the red carpet as usual. In addition to the Italian-American group, a coalition of nightlife workers was striking to protest Jordan's behavior towards the bouncer. Police barricades were keeping the protesters on one side of the red carpet, while the press was sequestered on the other side. I later found out that Lola had been confused about whether to attend the premiere or to show solidarity with the bouncers and doormen who let her in free everywhere in the city. She ultimately decided to hang out with them and then slip into the screening at the last possible moment.

When our car arrived, the driver opened our door and Jamie and I stepped out. "They're fine," said a woman with a headset, and we were waved onto the red carpet.

"Toby!" a photographer shouted, and I turned around.

A flashbulb exploded in my face.

"Toby, one of you alone!"

A dozen more flashes went off as Jamie stood there, stunned like a bunny.

"Come on!" I said to him, grabbing his hand.

Near the entrance were several local television reporters, plus crews from E! and *Entertainment Tonight*.

"Toby, do you have anything to say about the recent accident?" a reporter shouted as she waved a mic in my face.

"Was it really an accident?" another said.

"No comment," I said, waving them all away.

I had always wanted to say that. I just wished it didn't have to be in this context.

I pulled Jamie farther up the red carpet and through the theater's double doors. Once inside, we were safe.

Ariana was on her way out. "Toby, I'm so glad you could come!" she said.

"We just got mauled by photographers."

"Oh, my God, I'm so sorry! We should have had an escort for you. I promise it won't happen again. It's fine in here; we're not letting in any walk-throughs."

Jamie and I took two glasses of champagne and found our seats, fifth-row center. The theater was filling up, but the seats next to us remained empty. That figures, I thought. We're like the plague to these people: no money, no connections, no power.

Just as the lights were going down, there was a commotion at the back of the theater. Everyone turned around as Jordan entered with her co-star. She walked down the aisle and stopped at our row. The two of them slid in.

I stood up to greet her. She was wearing a low-cut black dress and her eyes were ringed with kohl.

She gave me a hug and a kiss, as if we were old friends. The combination of her makeup and perfume smelled like plastic.

I felt like all eyes were on us as we sat down.

"I don't believe you," Jamie said to me.

After the movie ended, Ariana came rushing down the aisle. "Toby, there are some people I want you to meet."

She introduced me to the film's producer and to Jordan's co-star. "Toby is a fabulous up-and-coming screenwriter," she said. "You really should read his work."

The producer looked at me suspiciously. "Are you repped by anyone?"

"Sherry Merrill," I said.

"Sherry and I go way back," he said. "Have her give me a call. Nice to see you."

I ran into Sonia in the lobby. "Have you been hiding from me?" she said.

"No!" I said. "Where have you been?"

"Mostly telling reporters we have no comment on the accident. Are you coming to the party?"

"I don't know. Those reporters were pretty scary."

"Come with me," she said, dragging us away from the crowd.

The three of us escaped through the rear of the theater. We found ourselves on the next block over, free from the crowd. Sonia hailed a cab.

"Why haven't you returned my phone calls?" she asked after we had piled in. "I've left you several messages."

"I've been busy."

"Toby, don't fuck with me. I know something's going on."

Jamie looked at me suspiciously.

"Nothing's going on!" I said. "Things have just been crazy."

"I'll take you to lunch. Tomorrow. Balthazar."

"Are you joking?" Even on her PR salary, Sonia never shelled out for expensive meals.

"I got promoted yesterday. Ariana gave me an expense account."

"Okay," I said. "Tomorrow. But for now, let's just try to enjoy ourselves."

This was something my mother used to say when my father and I were arguing at the dinner table. It seemed like ages ago.

Sonia also knew of a back entrance to Flash, so we were able to bypass the throngs of reporters and photographers who had followed the crowd to the club.

"This place still sucks," I said, remembering my review.

"I know," she said. "But don't quote me on that."

"Don't have anyone to quote you for," I said. "I'm just a film industry whore."

"You should be freelancing," she said.

"So should you."

She sighed. "I need to wait until all this crap dies down."

Ariana beckoned to me from the VIP area. She seemed a little tipsy.

"Someday," she said, "you're going to have a premiere just like this one."

"I can't wait," I said.

"Jordan just had the most brilliant idea. You know she hasn't been giving interviews since the . . . you know."

"Crash?"

"Right. But she'd like to give one to you. This could be major. I can call someone at *Entertainment Weekly* who will print it."

"I don't know," I said.

"Toby, this is the chance of a lifetime! She's not giving interviews to anyone else!"

I knew this interview would be a big one, far bigger than the profile of Jordan I had written in December. But there was no way I could do it. It had "conflict of interest" written all over it.

"I'm going to have to pass," I said. "But how about someone else? Do you have any other interesting clients?"

"Let's see. How about Miles Bradshaw?" The director rarely gave interviews. When he did, it was only to top-notch publications: *Vanity Fair, Rolling Stone, Playboy.*

"It's a deal," I said.

The next morning, the *Post* uncovered some more dirt on Jordan. The reason she didn't have a U.S. driver's license, they revealed, was that she had crashed into a tree while driving drunk after a house party in London. "Gardner a Double Fender Bender," read the headline. There was a picture of Jordan drinking a Cosmopolitan.

Cameron was out the entire morning, so I was free to attend to my own business, not that it made a difference anymore. Ever since the accident, he had been treating me like a partner. He didn't ask me to make his protein shakes, he placed his own calls, and I even saw him trying to figure out the copy machine. I was becoming obsolete. I worked on the Lola screenplay for most of the morning.

At one, I met Sonia at Balthazar, where she had already tucked into half a bottle of Pellegrino water.

"Order whatever you want," she said. "According to my expense report, this is lunch with a client."

I wasn't very hungry, so I ordered a salad.

Sonia had chosen a banquette in a back corner of the restaurant. It wasn't busy, so we were surrounded by empty tables.

"So are you finally going to tell me what's going on?"

I had avoided this meeting, this conversation, all week. I didn't know if I could lie to her. Sonia could identify a liar at three o'clock in the morning while on a drinking binge, especially if it was someone she knew.

But maybe I didn't have to lie. I could tell her the truth, and she could advise me on what I should do.

"Okay," I said. "You'll be the only person who knows about this, and you can't breathe a word of it to anyone. This could fuck up a lot of people's lives, including mine, if it got out."

I told her exactly what happened.

She listened, silently shaking her head at my tale.

"The whole thing doesn't surprise me," she said. "It was too unbelievable that it was an accident. You don't just back into a crowd at that speed without hitting the brakes unless you're really trying to hurt someone."

"I know," I said. "I wish someone would come to that conclusion without my help."

Our food arrived.

"I suppose it would be wishful thinking that Jordan might confess," Sonia mused before taking a bite of her salad.

"Yeah, right," I scoffed.

"What you need is a good lawyer."

"Jamie gave me a number."

"Call him. Make sure you didn't commit perjury. You didn't take an oath, did you?"

I said I didn't.

"Good. So in your testimony, they can't get you for that. But you should still have a lawyer to work all that out."

"I can't give testimony," I said. "I'll be a social pariah. Ariana will never speak to me again, I'll get fired from my job. Things are finally starting to happen for me. Cameron is setting up meetings, he's asked me to write a screenplay. People are paying attention to me instead of treating me like some kid."

"Toby, people will pay attention to you. You're extremely talented. But sometimes you've got to wait your turn. It's bullshit that this culture has decided you have to sell a screenplay at twenty-two, write a novel by twenty-five, and win a Pulitzer before thirty. You've got your entire life ahead of you to do all that stuff."

"I just feel that as soon as something good comes along, I get it taken away from me."

"Toby, that's not true. You've got to consider the more important issue here. Someone died. People are still in the hospital because of what she did."

"It's so easy for you to make these pronouncements," I said. "This doesn't affect you or your job. I mean, will you quit working for Ariana? You don't want to be working for someone who played a part in all this, do you?"

"No," she said, "I don't. I will need to quit, that's true. But let's worry about that when the time comes, okay?"

"Right," I said, sitting back in the banquette. "When the time comes."

"Kiddo, you're not getting something here. There's a bigger issue. Bigger than you or your career."

"What's that?"

"The point, Toby, is that I know you're better than all this. You're above getting sucked in by them, sucked into their world. I know you're going to succeed, but you're going to do it on your own terms, not theirs."

"But what if people find out I was doing coke with Jordan and Cameron?"

"Toby, in the grand scheme of things, you could be shooting up and no one would care. So you did a few lines. It's not the same as killing someone."

When I got back to the office, I knocked on Cameron's door.

He motioned for me to close the door behind me and take a seat. My legs were shaking. I hoped he wouldn't notice.

I told Cameron I thought we should tell the police what really happened. "It's not right that all those people were hurt, that someone was killed, and she gets away with it."

"Toby, she's not getting away with anything. Jordan is going to have years of legal trouble ahead of her."

"I think we should tell them exactly what happened, exactly what we saw and heard."

"We tell them her foot slipped and the car went out of control. That's what I saw."

"Cameron, you know that's not what happened." I remembered he had joked that she should "give the bouncer a little tap." He didn't want to be seen as an accessory.

"You're going to tell them what happened, right down to your doing blow in the men's room?"

"You were doing it too," I said.

Cameron got up from his desk and started pacing around the room.

"Toby, I'm not making claims about people driving under the influence. If you tell the truth, Jordan's lawyer will cross-examine the shit out of you and declare you an unreliable witness. Everyone will think you're a druggie."

"I am not a druggie," I said, though now I felt like the one who was lying. But I wasn't. I was a recreational user. I knew, though, that the recreation had to stop.

"That's not what her lawyers are going to say," he said, smirking. "Actions have consequences, Toby."

He sat on the edge of his desk, looming over me.

I wanted to kill him.

"Look," I said, "I don't want to get Jordan in trouble, either. But it's a matter of right and wrong."

"What's right, Toby," Cameron said, patting me on the back, "is to keep the whole thing to yourself. Believe me, it's for the best."

An assistant from Ariana's office called to say they had scheduled the Miles Bradshaw interview for the following week. Bradshaw was currently in the middle of writing his next film, so it was a hot story. He had also just separated from his wife of fifteen years.

"We've been pitching it to a few key places. Editors at both *Rolling Stone* and *The New Yorker* are interested."

"I think *The New Yorker* would be a better place for it," I said, trying to sound casual.

"We'll see what we can do," she said.

This was fabulous, having someone do my bidding like this. This was what it was like to work inside the publicity machine.

That evening, I met Donovan and Jamie for drinks in the meatpacking district. Donovan had picked one of those new places without a sign outside, and he had failed to give me the exact street address, so I had some trouble finding it.

Two cell phone conversations later, I arrived at the dark, clandestine lounge. Donovan ordered me a drink.

"Let's talk about your birthday," Donovan said to me.

"May seventh, right?" Jamie said.

"So how are we celebrating?"

"I don't want to do anything," I said. "Not with everything going on right now."

"Bullshit. Of course you're doing something," Donovan said. "Besides, I know Brett, Alejandro, and David are really concerned about you. They hardly ever see you anymore."

"I haven't been in a very social mood lately."

"Didn't you say you wanted to have a dinner party?" Jamie asked.

"That was several months ago. That was before all this happened."

"We'll arrange everything," Donovan said. "Just give us a guest list of all your friends, and we'll take care of it. Does the Saturday before the seventh sound good?"

"Fine," I said. "Whatever."

On Friday, I skimmed over Page Six, as Cameron had instructed me to do every morning. There was a blind item near the bottom of the page: "Which screen bombshell denies she was on drugs during a recent accident but was actually high as a kite? Sources say she was seen entering and exiting the restroom numerous times that evening and was doing more than just powdering her nose."

As I started my daily routine, I prayed Cameron wouldn't see the item.

At quarter past ten, he called me into his office, waving the *Post* in front of me.

"Have you been talking to anyone?" he asked.

"What do you mean?" I said.

"Look at this. How did they know about this? Did one of your friends call Richard Johnson?"

"My friends don't even know what happened," I said. "It could have been anyone. A waiter, other people at the party . . ."

His face softened. "I guess you're right. Hey, I'm sorry. It was stupid of me to call you in like this."

I was convinced Sonia had told someone. Was she trying to force me to tell? Whatever I ended up doing, I wanted it to be my decision.

I instant-messaged the link to Sonia, adding, "What do you make of this?"

She immediately shot back a reply. "It wasn't me," she wrote. "I swear."

That night, I had dinner with Jamie and Donovan. They had also seen the blind item.

"Is it true?" Donovan said.

"I don't know," I lied. "I couldn't tell if she was high or not."

"Oh, come on," Jamie said. "You must have been able to tell."

"Seriously," I said, "I couldn't tell."

After dinner, as we stepped out onto the sidewalk, the decision about whether to talk weighed heavily on my mind. It was like being in the closet again, except this time I had the option of staying there.

13

Ariana had started sending party invitations directly to my apartment, a sign that she now regarded me as an individual, not just as Cameron's assistant. Three more invitations had arrived since Wednesday: one to a film premiere, another to a club opening, a third to a private dinner for a fashion designer.

I should have been excited, but instead I wanted to flee. I wanted to leave the city. How far would I have to go in order to avoid testifying?

On Sunday, I went for a walk through Washington Square. The sun was blazing, and the park was packed with college students. I imagined that life for them was so much more clear, so much less complicated. There were fewer tough decisions to be made. But I knew I wasn't in college anymore.

By keeping quiet, I could have everything I had ever wanted: connections, contacts, a writing career. But it felt like fraud, like I was as bad as Jordan herself, foot on the gas pedal of that car.

I needed to come back to center, back to some point of certainty. I bought a copy of the weekend *Post* at a newsstand and started flipping through it. One of the lead stories was the memorial service for Stacey Davis, the girl who had been killed in the accident. I had avoided all mention of her and her family until now. There was a picture of her parents and a recent photograph of her. Nearby was Jordan's mug shot from the night she had been arrested. I looked back and forth between the photos, and realized there was only one right thing to do. I had been so foolish. There was no decision that had to be made.

* * *

On Monday morning, I called in sick and then went to the police station. The waiting room at the Tenth Precinct was crowded. I wondered if I should have consulted a lawyer first. I still had the number Jamie had given me, scribbled on a piece of paper in my wallet.

A large female cop announced my name and I was led to Detective Shiro's office. He was sitting at his desk and looked like he was wearing the same rumpled clothes from the last time I had seen him.

"I'm glad you decided to stop by. Can I get you some coffee?"

I passed on the offer, since I was jittery already.

"So you got some new information for us?" He pulled out his notebook.

After taking a deep breath, I told him I knew Jordan was drunk and high and I recounted what I could of the conversation in the car. I told him Ariana had asked me to lie about what happened.

He listened intently, and took copious notes.

When I finished, he asked me if I would be willing to tell everything in sworn testimony.

"Yes," I said. "But I have a question—I know you're going to think I'm an idiot—but do I need a lawyer for this? I mean, I know I didn't do anything wrong, but—"

He chuckled. "Yes, you should have a lawyer. You should have had one from the beginning. Nobody told you that? Your friend Miss Richards seems to have had her lawyer on this case before they were done loading the bodies. Your other buddies have them, too."

"They're not my buddies," I said. "I work for one of them, and the other two, I mean, I'm not even their friend. But they're all rich. They can afford lawyers."

"I think you can well afford a lawyer."

"Why? What do you know about me?"

"More than you'd think," he said.

When I left the station, I was so relieved he hadn't asked me if I was on drugs that I almost forgot what I had just done.

I phoned my mother in San Francisco. She would know what to do.

"Call your friend's lawyer," she said.

"What about the cost?"

"Don't worry, we'll pay."

My fears were momentarily assuaged. It would be good to have someone on my side who knew what he was doing.

I was able to get a last-minute appointment at 5 P.M. that day with Clifford Bronstein. His office was in an anonymous building on Park Avenue South that housed lawyers, accountants, and insurance agents.

Clearly, Clifford Bronstein had done well for himself. He looked tan and healthy; his office was all plate glass and chrome. When he shook my hand, I noticed his manicure.

Jamie had told me that Bronstein was one of Manhattan's savviest criminal attorneys. I hated that word, *criminal*.

"Your friend Jamie told me about the case and mentioned you might be calling," he said. "His father and I play tennis together."

I wanted to get right to the point. I told him my side of the story, including the part about the coke.

When I had finished, he examined me closely for a moment.

"Did the police ask you about whether you were under the influence of drugs?" he finally said.

"No, and I didn't mention it to them. I said I'd had a few drinks."

"You know this actress—Miss Gardner—her lawyer will ask you that. He'll claim it could contaminate your testimony."

"I understand," I said. "But can I be charged for it?"

He leaned back in his leather chair. "We'll get you immunity for your testimony. This head injury you had—Jamie mentioned it—that may play into this. But you'll have to come clean about everything."

"What do you mean?"

"Well, for example, how much were you carrying for Miss Gardner?"

"I don't know. Less than a gram. I wasn't carrying it. Ariana just asked me to flush it down the toilet."

"You can't be charged for it, since there's no actual evidence. You can really only be charged for possession, and it sounds like the drugs weren't technically yours. Now, you're sure it was only cocaine, right? It wasn't crack?"

"God, no." What kind of person did he think I was?

"The penalties for crack are much higher."

"You won't have to worry about that," I said.

"And you've never sold coke or carried it for someone else?"

"Carried it?"

"Carried it across borders, transported large amounts?"

"No, of course not."

There was a pause between us.

"Everyone will know," I said.

"Yes," he said, "everyone will know. In terms of this case, I wouldn't worry about it. The jury will be much more focused on whether Miss Gardner was doing drugs. Since she's a celebrity, they're going to let her hang. Besides, the other two—Ariana and Cameron, is it?—they will certainly face charges for witness tampering. That's a much more serious offense."

A line kept running through my head: *Actions have consequences.* I hated it when people like Cameron were right.

"What about my job?" I asked. "If my boss finds out about this, he'll fire me."

"He can't fire you," he said. "The only thing you can do to get out of that job is quit."

When I left the apartment the next morning, there were five photographers, three television crews, and four reporters camped out on my front steps.

I froze and they snapped. After about five seconds, I realized I had to keep moving.

They kept bombarding me with questions.

"On the advice of my lawyer, I can't comment on the case," I said to all of them. Saying I had retained a lawyer seemed like an admission of guilt.

I considered the consequences of giving testimony, something I had tried to avoid thinking about in the last twenty-four hours. Jordan could go to jail. Ariana and Cameron would face criminal charges. Everything I had built up over the past eight months would go to hell. I would have to start over.

But this is the right thing, I kept telling myself. You're doing the right thing.

I wasn't looking forward to going to work that morning, though I knew Cameron couldn't fire me, at least not without the prospect of a huge lawsuit. As much as I dreaded being around him, I knew that I could take as much time as I wanted to find a new job.

On my way to the office, I saw the *Post* had run a banner headline across the top of the front page: "Backseat Witness Tells All." The picture that ran was from the night Jamie, Donovan, and I were at Flash with Jordan. The small photo next to the banner was a close-up of Jordan and me; inside the paper was the full photo, including Jamie and Donovan. I cringed when I saw their smiling faces.

The story on page three was largely regurgitated information from the past week. The press had no idea what I had told; they only knew I had told something.

The headline alone was enough for Cameron.

"You've got some explaining to do!" he screamed at me. "This is what you do on your day off? Didn't I tell you not to talk to the police or reporters?"

I said nothing.

"What did you say to them?" he asked.

"I can't tell you that," I said. "My lawyer said I shouldn't say anything."

"You can forget about writing the Lola screenplay," he said. "Someone with your lack of experience never should have been working on that project anyway."

"Whatever, Cameron," I said, turning back to my computer as if he didn't exist.

"You know, Toby, sometimes you drive me fucking crazy." He turned around, went into his office, and shut the door.

I could tell he had no idea what to do. He knew he couldn't fire me, and yelling at me wasn't going to do any good, either. As much as I hated being in the same office as Cameron, I wanted to leave on my own terms. Quitting at this stage would be admitting defeat.

Later that morning, I started browsing the online job listings. I restricted my search to film and media, but found only listings for assistants in finance, human resources, business development—none of the things I wanted to do.

Jamie called me as soon as he read the news.

"I'll explain everything," I said. "Dinner tonight?"

I met Donovan and him at a dim sum place in Chinatown. They were already sitting down when I arrived.

Jamie didn't waste any time in quizzing me about what was going on.

I told them the entire story.

Jamie leaned forward when I finished. "Look, we're glad you told the truth about what happened, but why did you lie to us?"

"There's no way you can understand the pressure I was under," I said, squirming in my seat. "Ariana has so many contacts; she controls everything. And now that I'm on Cameron's shit list, I may never live to see one of my screenplays produced."

"I know how it is," Donovan said. "Sometimes the time just isn't right to tell the truth about things."

"I can't believe you went to all that trouble to protect those bastards," Jamie said, shaking his head.

"They were all I had."

"Hey!" Jamie said. "You have us."

I knew he was staring at me, but I couldn't meet his gaze.

Cameron was an expert at the art of subtle war. My workload tripled from what it had been before the accident. Tasks Cameron had been handling himself for the past week were foisted on me, and everything needed to be done immediately, today. Once again, I had to take care of Cameron's personal needs, from fetching his lunch and making his protein shakes to picking up his dry cleaning and returning his DVDs. Every half hour I thought to myself, *I have to quit, I have to quit.* But quitting would be giving up, letting Cameron be the bully. I needed the paycheck, and I needed to stay in the business, at least until I found something else. If I quit, he would win.

The day after Cameron's blow-up, I stocked up on protein powder for him, enough to last several months. That evening, though, I replaced his containers of Metabolic Support Formula with the Super Weight Gain Formula that Jamie used, keeping the lower-calorie powder for myself. With each shake, Cameron would now be getting twice as many calories and four times as many grams of carbohydrates. It was sure to wreak havoc on his waistline.

Reporters kept hounding me over the phone, but I gave no interviews, so all the articles resorted to speculation. The photographers had stopped stalking me, so the press kept running file photos as there were new developments in the case.

On Wednesday, I slipped out for lunch and, armed with notebook and tape recorder, took the train uptown for my interview with Miles Bradshaw. I knew Cameron would be upset if I was gone for long, but it wasn't every day I was offered an interview I could sell anywhere in town. There was a chance Ariana had cancelled the appointment, but there was an equal chance she had forgotten. Once I had conducted the interview, it wouldn't matter whether or not it was sanctioned by the director's publicist. It would be mine.

Bradshaw lived in a beautiful pre-war co-op on Central Park West. After I was let up by his doorman, his assistant greeted me and took me to his study. The director was in his late forties, though even with his beard, he looked younger. Talking with him was like hanging out during office hours with a friendly college professor. I was surprised Ariana had a client who was so down to earth.

The interview was going swimmingly, and Bradshaw seemed charmed by my youth and extensive knowledge of his films. Halfway through, his assistant came in and whispered something to him.

He turned to me. "Apparently, my publicist wants this interview to be cut short. Does this have anything to do with that accident a few weeks ago?"

"It has everything to do with it," I said.

He turned to his assistant. "You tell Ariana I'll give whatever interviews I damn well please."

I grinned as his assistant scurried back to her office. The guy had balls.

"Never let anyone tell you how to do things if you think you know better," he growled. "That's the only way you can ever get anything done in this lifetime that's of real worth."

The following day, I was getting back to my desk with a stack of freshly copied scripts when I ran into Margaret.

"Toby, can you pick up lunch for us? I'll have a tuna on seven-grain and Cameron will have the creamed spinach. And two iced teas."

"Creamed spinach?" I asked. "He never orders that. He must have meant steamed spinach."

"I thought I heard him say 'creamed,'" she said, "but you would know better."

Surely Margaret had misunderstood him; he would never order something so fattening. I picked up the food for the two of them, opting for steamed spinach for Cameron.

I left the food in his office and went to make the rest of the copies. Just as I was returning with a second stack of scripts to bind, I heard Cameron yelling.

"What the fuck is this?" He was standing in the doorway of his office. "I ask you for creamed spinach and you bring me this shit?"

He lobbed the open take-out container at my desk, splattering my keyboard with wet strands of spinach. Margaret and several other staff members stared in horror at the mess Cameron had created.

I knew he was trying to get me to quit, so I decided to piss him off even more.

"Sorry about that," I said. "I'll go get that creamed spinach for you. But Cameron, food fights in the office?"

The rest of the office snickered at Cameron as he stood in the doorway like a guilty child.

Just as I was about to leave the office that evening, my phone rang. I answered it, trying not to sound too dejected.

"Toby? Sherry," Sherry Merrill said, with a familiarity that would indicate we spoke every day.

"I just got off the phone with my contact at a studio I sent *Breeders* to. They were extremely excited about it. They think it has real potential, real punch. When I mentioned how old you were, they were rolling on the floor."

"Is that a good thing?"

"That's a great thing! They were thrilled someone so young had written such a clever comedy."

"Comedy?"

"I was going to mention that to you. They're seeing it not as a serious film but as more satirical, more camp. Sort of like a gay *Barbarella*."

A gay *Barbarella*? I had tried to write a serious societal commentary, and I had ended up with a drag queen in a zero-gravity striptease.

It had been so long since I'd sent it out, I couldn't even remember if *Breeders* had the potential to be campy. I decided it didn't matter. If *Breeders* was going to be my introduction to the business, then so be it. I'd have more serious stories to tell in the future.

"There's something else," Sherry continued. "In addition to taking out an option on *Breeders,* they're interested in considering you for another project." I heard her shuffling through her notes. "When I told them about your history, they said they had been looking for something on young gay life set in New York. Do you have anything like that?"

Only the last eight months of my life. "I have something I've started on," I said.

"Good. Start getting a pitch prepared. But Toby—"

"Yeah?"

"You've got to remember something. This business is always changing, and they could feel differently about your work next week. So don't get your hopes up before anything's certain."

"I understand." I took a deep breath. "So where do we go from here?"

"Let me follow up on it in a few days. They need to show your work to some more people, come to some sort of decision. I'll keep you posted."

Finally, I thought. The studio was like a handsome guy who

walks into a party just at that moment when you think all hope is lost. It was one more chance.

That evening, Donovan and I went out to dinner, just the two of us, at a new tapas place in the West Village.

When I arrived, he was sitting in a dark corner. He poured me a glass of sangria and I lit a cigarette.

He looked extremely tan.

"Did you go away for the weekend?" I asked. "You got some sun."

"Nope," he said. "Tanning booth."

That figures, I thought.

I was starving and anxious to place our order.

"There's something I need to tell you," he said. "I feel awful it's taken so long to get this out."

"Oh, my God," I said. "You tested positive."

"No, it's not that!" he said. "I'm negative."

"Then what?"

"You know how Elizabeth and I slept together?"

"Yeah?"

"Well, she lied about being on the pill."

"And?"

"She's pregnant."

Just at that moment, the waiter came to take our order. I had lost my appetite, so I waved him away.

I turned to Donovan, stunned. "Is she going to have the baby?" I finally asked.

He sat back in his chair and sighed. "She wants to have it. I wasn't crazy about the idea at first, but I've sort of warmed up to it. I mean, it's not how I imagined my life would turn out, but I feel it's a responsibility I have to accept."

"Are you sure you're the father?" I asked. "You know, I wouldn't trust her about that. She was with that guy Chad for a while."

I lit another cigarette and poured myself more sangria.

"We're sure," he said. "We had a paternity test done."

"When did you find out about this?"

"She told me about a month ago. She had papers drawn up that say I won't be financially responsible for the child."

"And will you ever get to see the kid?"

"She included something about that, too."

"I don't believe this," I said.

I didn't know if I was more upset that Donovan was going to be a dad, or that Elizabeth hadn't picked me to father her child. But it was absurd for both of them to be doing this at such a young age. The whole thing made me sick.

"She's been calling me," he said. "She wants me to stop talking to you, but I told her that was ridiculous. You're one of my best friends. Besides, you brought us together. She should be grateful."

"I'm not sure that was a good thing," I said.

"Look on the bright side," Donovan said, raising his glass. "Maybe he'll be gay like us."

The next morning, Cameron beckoned to me from his office. "There he is!" he said as I came in. "There's the man! Come into my office. We need to talk."

In the past few weeks, those words—"We need to talk"—had never meant anything good, so I was suspicious.

"I got a call from a friend last night," he said. "You've probably heard, but your script is very hot."

"Who told you that?" I said. How did word travel so fast about these things?

"It doesn't matter. I'd love to see a copy of it."

"I gave you a copy when I first started working here."

"I think I lost it. Can you make me another copy?"

I stood there for a moment, looking out his window at his view of the Hudson. I glanced around his office, at the pictures I had hung, the filing cabinets I had organized, the piles I had sorted through.

I realized that for the first time, Cameron needed me more than I needed him.

"I could make you a copy," I said. "But I'm not going to, because I'm quitting."

He sat there dumbfounded, as if I had thrown hot coffee across his desk or told him he was ugly. Cameron wasn't used to people saying no to him.

I turned around and walked out of his office for the last time.

* * *

I called Sonia and asked her to meet me for a drink. We chose Fez, because it was close to both our apartments.

We ordered drinks, and I told her what had happened.

"I can't believe you quit!" she said, sipping her martini. "That takes a lot of balls. I'm proud of you."

"I'm completely screwed now. I'm unemployed; I won't be able to get a recommendation from Cameron—"

"I've got an idea," she said. "Just leave everything to me."

It was 7 P.M. and I was already on my second vodka cranberry. In the dark Casbah-themed lounge, it could have been midnight.

"I hope you know what you're doing," I said.

After paying the check, Sonia and I stumbled out into the warm light of Lafayette Street. It wouldn't get dark for another hour or so, but all I wanted was to go home and sleep.

For my birthday dinner the next evening, Donovan had picked Lucky Strike, the French bistro on Grand Street that was a perennial favorite with the Eurotrash crowd. He made a fashionably late nine-thirty reservation for our group of twenty.

I was supposed to meet him at his apartment in the West Village beforehand. Jamie, David, and Alejandro were already there when I arrived.

"We have something for you," Donovan said, after giving me a hug.

The two of them handed me a box from Gucci, and I opened it.

It was a baby blue short-sleeved shirt in my size.

"Wear it tonight," Donovan said. "You'll look hot."

"We thought it might cheer you up," Jamie said.

"You guys bought this at Gucci?" I said, amazed.

"No," Alejandro said. "I made it."

"Turn it around," David said.

I looked at the back. My name was spelled out in cursive script, studded with Swarovski crystals.

"It's perfect," I said. It was like a bowling shirt designed by a Studio 54-bound club kid, but I loved it.

I changed into it—it hugged my torso perfectly—and I had to admit I looked good.

The five of us took two cabs to the restaurant. Soon everyone else started to arrive, including Brett, Sonia, and several other friends from high school and college I hadn't seen in ages. The boys had also invited a number of cute guys I didn't know as well to round out the group. The male to female ratio was about four to one, and all the males except two were gay, but the girls didn't seem to mind. I realized how this had become my world in the past eight months. As far as my social life went, straight people had been rendered a silent minority.

I looked around at the group gathering: Sonia, the writer-turned-flack; Jamie, who was potentially positive; Donovan, who was about to be a father; David and Alejandro, whose relationship had become physically dangerous; Brett, whose consumption of protein shakes and designer supplements bordered on an eating disorder. These are my friends, I thought.

Twenty-three suddenly seemed very old to me. I was no longer close to twenty-one, which felt like the cusp of adulthood, and I wasn't twenty-two, which meant I could no longer pose as a college student, or even as someone who had recently graduated. Twenty-three meant my life had started, and I was already in the thick of it. I had been living in New York for more than six months, and I had no boyfriend, was recently unemployed, would have to testify at a criminal trial, and hadn't sold my screenplay. Weren't Matt and Ben twenty-three when they sold *Good Will Hunting?*

I wondered if birthdays would be like this from now on. I wondered if they would always remind me time was slipping away. I was beginning to understand why some people avoided them altogether. Looking at my friends, I realized I was in danger of turning into a jaded queen before I had fully experienced my gay adolescence. I was determined not to become old before my time.

A few other people straggled in and we all sat down. As we were looking at our menus, one more guest arrived and took the last empty seat. He was wearing a white Lacoste polo and khakis; he looked like he had just come from a game of tennis or a sailing meet.

"Who's that?" I asked Donovan.

"Who?" he said.

"That guy sitting over there, next to Alejandro."

"Andrew? You don't recognize him?"

"Oh, my—" I slapped my hand over my mouth.

It was Subway Boy. He had cut his beautiful long hair, but it was still undoubtedly him.

"How did you find him?" I whispered to Donovan.

"Brett finally located him through a friend."

"Did he go to NYU?"

"I think he went to Brown." Donovan went back to looking at his menu.

I was so excited that I kept tapping my foot frantically under the table.

"Just relax," Donovan said. "Relax and enjoy what's to come."

A perverse thought hit me: Subway Boy is a hustler and the boys paid him to show up.

"How did you convince him to come?" I asked Donovan.

"He wanted to. He's excited to meet you."

Excited to meet me? That possibility had never crossed my mind.

I tried to stay relaxed during the meal. I was trapped between the table and the wall, so it wasn't easy for me to circulate among my guests. When the time came between courses to slip out, I made my way over to where Andrew was sitting.

"I'm Toby," I said to him.

"I figured that." He smiled, revealing the slightest gap between his two front teeth. It was cute.

We chatted for a bit. He had graduated from Brown almost two years ago, though we were the same age, and was now an assistant editor of science fiction and fantasy books at a well-known publishing house.

I told him about my screenplay. I made it sound like there was a virtual bidding war going on.

"Do you have a day job?"

"I quit yesterday," I said.

"What are you going to do?"

"I don't know," I said. "Write, I guess." I must sound like an idiot, I thought.

"You look really familiar. Did I see your picture in *New York* magazine this week?" he asked, referring to the photo from my recent night at B Bar.

The main course was about to be served, so I mumbled something about being in the papers lately, and scurried back to my seat. It wasn't the first time someone had pulled me aside in the past two weeks, though most of the time I told them they must be thinking of someone else. I had spent all this time in New York wanting to be acknowledged for who I was, and now I was being recognized as a person I didn't want to be.

My birthday cake arrived glowing with candles, and everyone sang. I felt like I was eight years old again. I closed my eyes to make a wish.

I wish Andrew would be my boyfriend. And also for lots of fame and success. And to get out of the Gardner trial alive.

I must have closed my eyes for an eternity, as everyone was looking at me expectantly when I finally blew out the candles.

"He's a good blower," Donovan said, and I blushed.

The cake was cut. Jamie ate three pieces, knowing he wouldn't gain a pound, and Brett took a piece, ate one bite, and then covered the rest with salt so he wouldn't eat any more.

I ate a few bites, and then stopped.

You don't have to be good, a voice said to me.

But I want to be good, I said.

You don't have to be, the voice said.

I finished my cake. But I wanted to be good. I wanted to be good for Andrew's sake, if not for my own. He was good, I could tell he was, sitting at the end of the table all in white.

Splitting a check nineteen ways is never easy, but on the night of my party, it was accomplished with remarkable grace and efficiency. Before I knew it, we were out on the street smoking.

Someone offered Andrew a cigarette.

"I don't smoke," he said.

I tried to hide my burning cigarette behind my back, taking furtive puffs when Andrew wasn't looking.

It was decided by group consensus that we should all go to Blow Pop, a bar in the East Village that featured a talent contest on Saturday night.

I got in a cab with Andrew, Donovan, and Alejandro. It wasn't until the cab started moving that I realized how loaded I was. Donovan had kept ordering me flavored martinis, which, though not a favorite drink of mine, I had been sucking down during dinner.

The radio in the cab was tuned to an oldies station. The sounds of Petula Clark singing "Downtown" drifted towards the backseat:

When you're alone and life is making you lonely,
You can always go Downtown.
When you've got worries, all the noise and the hurry
Seems to help, I know, Downtown.
Just listen to the music of the traffic in the city.
Linger on the sidewalk where the neon signs are pretty.
How can you lose?

The lights are much brighter there.
You can forget all your troubles, forget all your cares.
So go Downtown.
Things'll be great when you're Downtown.
No finer place, for sure.
Downtown: everything's waiting for you.

"I love this song," Donovan said, but I barely heard him. For the first time since I had met him, it was as if he didn't exist.

"Have you been to Blow Pop before?" I asked Andrew, who was sitting on the other side of me.

"No," he said. "I don't really go out much."

"I saw a picture of you in a bar rag," Donovan said.

I laughed, as if I hadn't seen the photo.

"Oh, that?" he said. "Honestly, that was one of the few times I've been out. That, and . . . what was it called? I went to this really crazy party right before Halloween."

"The Naked Halloween Party?" I offered.

"Right," he said. "I mean, I wasn't naked or anything."

"I know," I said.

He looked at me askance.

"I think I saw you there." I smiled. "So you're a homebody?"

"No, I like going out," he said. "Just not as much as you guys. I'm usually really tired when I get home from work. Sometimes I have to bring manuscripts home to read."

I pictured the two of us cuddled up in bed, me reading a screenplay, him reading the latest science fiction manuscript. And then I thought, *Don't jump to conclusions. Take things one step at a time.*

"Well, I've been to Blow Pop," I said. I looked at him seductively. "But I'm always up for it again."

Actually, I was worried about whether he would like it. Since it had opened in January, Blow Pop hadn't been known for the most savory of entertainments. Tonight's talent contest was called Hustle; the acts vied for the play money given to each patron as he entered. The performer with the most play money at the end of the night won $200. As a general rule, the raunchier the act, the greater chance it had of winning. The club had seen everything, from male strippers straight from the boroughs who took everything off, to drag queens demonstrating their deep throat technique on a dildo, to eighteen-year-olds jerking off into the crowd. The club had been shut down several weeks ago after a drag queen lip-synching "It's Raining Men" had concluded her act by lifting her skirt and spraying the crowd with a champagne enema. The thought of it made me cringe.

I suddenly felt this was not an appropriate place to bring Andrew.

"Why don't we go somewhere else?" I suggested. "It's always so sweaty and crowded in there."

"It'll be fun," Donovan said. "Besides, you know how hot the boys are."

"That's what I've heard," Andrew said, as I felt a pang of jealousy. "I've always wanted to see this place."

With any luck, I thought, the performance will be tame tonight.

The cab driver overshot Blow Pop by a block. I grabbed Andrew's hand and we ran down Avenue A together, leaving Donovan and Alejandro behind. Now that I had him alone, we were able to chatter on endlessly. I had the strange feeling I was asking him the same questions over and over again.

We paid the five dollar cover and went in. Everything was painted black; the walls were decorated with cheap gilt mirrors surrounded by smatterings of glitter. It reeked of alcohol and men. I stumbled over to the bar, as I wanted to fortify myself further. Andrew stayed behind with Donovan.

The performance started on a little platform in the back, and I saw that it was Lola performing her pussy-money trick.

When I found Andrew, he was standing with Donovan and talking. They were laughing like old friends.

I've blown it, I thought. He likes Donovan more than me.

But then Donovan went off to talk to some other people, and the two of us were together again.

I asked Andrew if he wanted to sit down. I thought it might steady me a bit. God, I was shit-canned. Why did I have to be this way on the night when I met him?

"Donovan says you used to work with that, uh, person performing."

"She was around the office," I said. "But we never really hung out or anything." I didn't want Andrew to think I was friends with someone like Lola.

We talked for a moment more, and then my tongue was in his mouth. The world around me didn't matter anymore. People could be looking, all my friends could be watching, and I didn't care. It was just the two of us.

After what was probably only a minute, I pulled away to take a breath. I also wanted the room to stop spinning.

He smiled. "I never do this."

"Me neither," I said. "Well . . ."

He punched me playfully. "I bet you do this all the time."

"No, really I don't. At least not like this." I paused. "You live in Manhattan, right?"

"Riverdale," he said.

"Where?" It sounded like it might be in Westchester.

"It's in the Bronx," he said. "About forty minutes away on Metro North, or an hour by subway."

The only thing I knew about the Bronx was that it was where you went when your car was impounded.

"It's a nice area. Very quiet. Lots of old Jewish couples."

"Do you want to go to my place?" I slurred into his ear. It didn't seem like a sleazy question. It seemed natural, the next step.

He looked panic-stricken. "I don't think that's a good idea," he said.

"Why not?"

"I think we should wait."

I will be grateful for this later, I thought to myself.

We exchanged phone numbers and promised to call each other the next day. He left and I sat on the bench alone for a moment, stunned.

Donovan and Brett joined me. "Where did Andrew go?"

"He left," I said.

"Are you going to hang out with us and cruise?" Brett asked.

"No," I said, clutching Andrew's card. "There's no point."

14

I woke up the next morning feeling like pigeons had picked at my brain. I glanced at my bedside table, where I had put Andrew's business card. He had written his home phone number on the back. Was 11 A.M. too early to call?

I decided to wait. I went back to sleep, woke up at one, and ran some errands. When I got back, there was a message on my machine.

"Hi, uh, Toby, it's Andrew, from last night? Happy birthday again. Was last night your real birthday? I can't remember. Anyway, um, it would be good to see you again, like, soon." He left his work, home, and cell numbers, even though I already had them. I loved that his message was awkward and fumbling.

I called him back and we agreed to meet on Monday evening at a small Moroccan restaurant on Thirteenth Street.

Brett called me that night. "Don't sleep with Andrew on your first date," he advised. "He's pretty new to all this, so you don't want to scare him off. And don't drink too much. He drinks, but he's not a drinker, if you know what I mean. You don't want him to think you're a—"

"A lush?" I said.

"Right." I wasn't even offended. Brett was just trying to be helpful. "And don't smoke," he continued. "Andrew hates smoking. His mother's a smoker, and he's trying to get her to quit."

I wondered if it was time for me to quit as well.

*   *   *

I was determined to make a better impression on Monday than I had on Saturday. I cleaned my apartment, throwing out my pornography and hiding the books on transsexualism I had used to research the Lola screenplay. I scrubbed Gus's litter box and aired out the apartment of smoke and sex and sin. I took long baths on Sunday and Monday, went to the gym, gave myself an at-home facial, moisturized constantly, and applied four sets of teeth-whitening strips. Andrew and I were the same age, but he was so beautiful that I was sure he would notice every imperfection.

I did everything to hide the way I felt: like damaged goods.

It was warm on Monday evening. When I arrived at the restaurant, Andrew was already standing near the entrance. He was wearing glasses, tortoise shell frames that made him look studious and intellectual. From his tousled hair and wrinkled khakis, it was clear he had just come from work.

I greeted him, leaning forward to give him a kiss on the cheek, but he seemed stiff about it, embarrassed.

We sat down in the dark dining room amidst tapestries and throw pillows. There was Moroccan music playing and the owner's children were playing hide-and-go-seek among the tables.

"It adds to the ambiance," Andrew said, shrugging. He asked if I had enjoyed my birthday party.

"Sure," I said. "But that wasn't my actual birthday."

"When is your actual birthday?"

I paused. "Tonight," I said, blushing.

"I'm flattered," he said.

"I spent so much time thinking about that dinner, I didn't make any plans for tonight," I explained. "But I guess it worked out perfectly."

Andrew filled me in on everything I had heard and forgotten on Saturday night. He had grown up outside Boston and had gone to boarding school at Andover. By loading up on classes, he had managed to skip a grade and finish in three years. He had gone to Brown, where he had been an English major, writing a thesis entitled "Political Influence in Science Fiction and Fantasy." After taking internships each summer with various publishers in New York, he had been offered his current editorial job when he graduated. I felt proud of his achievements, even though I barely knew him. Maybe it was because he was shy about it, almost ashamed at his precociousness.

"When did you come out?" I asked him.

"I don't know if you could really call it coming out," he said. "After sophomore year of college, I guess. But my parents don't know yet."

I had always considered a guy's gay adult life to begin after he got over the inevitable task of coming out to his parents. By this estimation, he was still a teenager.

Andrew was turning out to be a very different person than I had imagined Subway Boy to be.

"How about you?" he asked.

"I told my parents after I started my freshman year of college," I said.

"How did that go?"

"It was fine," I lied. "They were pretty much okay with it."

We ordered our entrees and split a bottle of red wine between us; I promised myself I would make this bottle last, that I wouldn't drink more than two glasses. When our food arrived, we both dug in, grateful for the momentary lapse in conversation. It wasn't that I didn't have a lot to ask him; it was just that first dates were such hard work.

"Did you have any hobbies as a kid?" he asked after a few minutes.

"I don't know," I said. "I liked to read a lot."

"I had three listed in my elementary school yearbook: bonsai trees, comic books, and model railroading."

It was nerdy, but I found it charming. Most guys would have answered, "Not really," or, "I liked to hang out at the mall."

I imagined his apartment: bonsai trees in the living room, stacks of comics in the bedroom, and a giant model railroad set running between them.

We split the bill after drinking mint tea and sharing a filo pastry. I was dying for a cigarette, but I knew I couldn't have one, not if I wanted this to work.

As we stepped out onto the sidewalk, I suddenly felt like the city was a new place, a place I had never been before.

"What do your parents do?" Andrew asked me as we walked east.

"My dad's in venture capital and my mother's a fashion designer."

"Really?" He frowned. "I don't know much about fashion."

"That's okay," I said. "Most real people don't."

We came to an intersection and crossed.

"How did you lose your job?" he asked when we got to the other side.

I told him about the accident, in the vaguest terms I could.

"I read about that," he said. "I was waiting for you to say something."

I realized how strange the situation must seem to an outsider.

"You don't think it's weird?" I asked.

"You seem like a good guy," he said, "and I'm sure you're doing the right thing."

I was instantly relieved.

We were approaching the East Village, so I decided to face the inevitable.

I asked him if he wanted to see my place, and he said yes.

We walked east on Thirteenth Street and then down Second Avenue. I steered him away from Avenue A so we wouldn't have to pass Blow Pop. I didn't want him to think of me as that person, the Toby who stayed out all night and propositioned boys he had just met.

As we walked, I thought about what I was doing. Andrew wasn't the slickest guy I'd ever met, but I liked that. In order to be with him, I was going to have to shape up. How much was I willing to give up of myself, of my former life?

"I'd been meaning to tell you—I have to go out of town tomorrow," he said. "To a science fiction convention in San Francisco. A total geek fest." I had a vision of him running into my parents in the city, though I knew that would be unlikely. "I get back on Friday, though I might be able to change my flight so I can see you sooner."

"There's no hurry," I said. I didn't want him to know I would be eagerly awaiting his return, that the sooner he came back, the better.

We arrived at Seventh Street and he followed me upstairs. From the hallway, I could hear Gus crying.

"I love cats," he said. "I want one, but I'm hardly ever home."

I unlocked the door and Andrew immediately got down on the floor and started petting Gus. "Good kitty," he said. "Good girl."

"He's a boy," I said. "This is an all-male establishment."

We sat together on my tiny couch. He let me run my fingers through his hair.

"Have you read any good books lately?" he asked.

This is stupid, I thought. Either he was incredibly nervous or was an expert on stalling techniques. I would have to make the first move.

I pulled him towards me and kissed him, first strongly, to make sure he was really mine, then a little more lightly. He tasted like spices and red wine.

"Do you want to go into the bedroom?" I asked, and he followed me.

We lay down on my bed, which, thankfully, I had made before I left that evening.

It was the best make-out session I had ever had. We rolled around for almost ten minutes and then I lay my head on his chest after kissing him lightly on the nose. I wanted him badly, but I knew we should wait. I was becoming a prude before my own eyes. I decided chastity was the new sluttiness.

I got up to go to the bathroom, where I discovered that Gus had puked his dinner onto the floor. I cleaned it up quickly so Andrew wouldn't notice.

I lay down next to him on the bed again.

"I would love to, you know . . ." I said. "But it probably isn't a good idea."

"Yeah," he said. "I should get going."

We kissed for several more minutes. We couldn't get enough of each other.

Eventually, he got up. "You have my numbers," he said. "I'll be back Friday." He paused. "There's something you should know about this trip." He stood by the door.

I took in a quick breath. Even Gus sat near the door, listening expectantly.

"I'm interviewing with a publisher that wants me to move out to San Francisco."

"Are you looking for a new job?" I asked. He had his hand on the doorknob, was ready to leave.

"Not really," he said. "But it's always good to interview, you know, to see what's out there."

I nodded dumbly.

He opened the door and then turned around. "If I get offered something, I'll just have to tell them I need to bring my new boyfriend with me."

I was so taken aback that I just gave him another kiss on the lips and shut the door behind him.

Boyfriend? Already? Was he more clueless than I was? Did I have the upper hand without knowing it?

I grabbed a cigarette from the pack in my desk drawer and lit up. I needed to process this information. I sent an email to Jamie, Donovan, and Brett.

"He is already referring to us as a couple," I wrote. "I think this is a good sign."

My phone at home remained unplugged, so whenever I checked my messages, there was a slew from various reporters. On Clifford Bronstein's instructions, I didn't return any of the calls.

On Wednesday, I was at home when I got a call from Jamie on my cell.

"Have you seen the *Observer* today?" he asked. "There's a big story about you. Check the Transom section."

My palms were clammy as I looked up the paper online. The Transom was a column that reported on Manhattan media and entertainment gossip. The article was the first item of several.

THE SPINACH HITS THE FAN

Employees of whiz kid gay producer Cameron Cole have described his office as alternately "hectic" and "laid-back," but never as downright hostile. The tide of opinion changed, however, last Friday morning, when Mr. Cole's assistant, Toby Griffin, quit "under duress," an anonymous source said.

Mr. Griffin, a twenty-three-year-old aspiring screenwriter, was a passenger in the automobile driven by actress Jordan Gardner that hit eight people, injuring seven and killing one. Mr. Cole and Ms. Gardner's publicist Ariana Richards were the other two passengers in the car. The extensively chronicled incident occurred on April 19 outside the nightclub Mirror.

Mr. Cole and Ms. Richards reportedly told Mr. Griffin not to reveal any information to police beyond the initial testimony he gave on the night of the accident. Rumors have abounded that Ms. Gardner was under the influence of drugs and alcohol that evening.

Mr. Griffin decided to break free of his boss's informal gag order on April 30, when he reportedly gave testimony to Detective Ronald Shiro of Manhattan's Tenth Precinct. The contents of that testimony have not been released, but insiders say Mr. Griffin revealed Ms. Gardner was indeed under the influence of drugs and alcohol, evidence that would severely increase the penalties she faces for the current charges of involuntary manslaughter, first- and second-degree assault, and reckless endangerment, among others.

If Mr. Cole and Ms. Richards did try to prevent Mr. Griffin from giving evidence, they could both be guilty of witness tampering and obstruction of justice. Insiders have speculated that Mr. Griffin will most likely be given immunity on the count of giving false evidence in exchange for his testimony.

After the *New York Post* and other local papers revealed Mr. Griffin had been witnessed giving evidence, Mr. Cole reportedly became nasty towards his assistant.

In addition to tripling Mr. Griffin's workload, Mr. Cole apparently threw a container of steamed spinach at Mr. Griffin's desk in an effort to reprimand him for bringing him his spinach steamed, as he usually takes it, as opposed to creamed, as he wanted it that day. The next day, Mr. Griffin quit working for Mr. Cole.

Though Mr. Cole's office denies the incident ever took place, a call to the Organic Delights deli in Tribeca revealed that steamed spinach is indeed Mr. Cole's vegetable of choice.

"I'm not worried about Toby. He's an incredibly talented writer, and I know he'll find something," said Mr. Griffin's Beverly Hills agent, Sherry Merrill. "Cream always rises to the top."

As long as it's not in spinach.

—*Eli Kostenbaum*

I called Sonia on her cell phone. "Who is this Eli Kostenbaum?"

"Just a friend from college," she said. "He loved the scoop."

"The story makes me look like an idiot."

"No, it doesn't! You're a hero. It's great. I think he spun it really well."

Spun it. Sonia had been spending too much time working in PR.

"What are you doing with that Bradshaw interview?" she asked.

"I don't know," I said. "I know this sounds crazy, but I'd like to sit on it for a little bit. It would be just like Ariana to call every editor she knows and tell them not to take it."

"I could sell it for you," Sonia said. "But suit yourself."

"Are you at the office now?" I asked.

"Nope," she said. "I quit."

"I hope you didn't do that on my behalf."

"I needed to get out of there," she said. "I needed to stop being so afraid."

"Another defector from the downtown bullshit machine. I'm proud of you."

"I'm not out of the business entirely," she said.

"What do you mean?"

"I've decided to start doing some PR consulting, freelance, with a little event planning on the side."

"How are you going to do that?"

"It'll be easy," she said. "I've got Ariana's client list."

For the rest of the week, I was floating over the memory of my date with Andrew. We emailed back and forth several times.

"I am surrounded by guys who consider a wild night out to be a discussion of *Star Trek* reruns over pizza and Coke," he wrote. "I can't wait to see you."

He signed his name ANDREW, all caps.

As happy as I was, I had to face that I was still unemployed. I had left a message with Sherry's office to check on the status of my screenplay, but hadn't heard back. I started preparing my resume to send out.

On Friday morning, Andrew wrote me another email from the airport. "I think I'm going to be exhausted tonight. Can we do something tomorrow?"

I was dying to see him, but I left him a voice mail saying Saturday would be fine. I had never waited so long to sleep with someone.

I suddenly had the fear he wasn't really gay, or was squeamish about actual sex. There were some guys who had so little experience that they were afraid of sex. Maybe I would have to survive several months of clothes-on makeout sessions before we were comfortable with each other. I wasn't sure I could wait. For me, sex sealed a relationship, made it permanent. I had to remind myself that it also had the potential to drive people apart, to give either person a reason not to see the other again.

We made plans to meet at Flea Market in the East Village. I arrived a little early this time and fortified myself with a glass of red wine as I let my eyes wander over the bric-a-brac decorating the walls. I was determined to relax. We would sleep together or we wouldn't, and either way, it would be fine. He wasn't going anywhere, I reminded myself.

When he arrived, he kissed me squarely on the lips. We sat down and he ordered a gin and tonic.

"Glad to be rid of the science fiction geeks?" I said.

"Hey, I'm one myself, you know!"

"No, you're not," I said. "At least, you don't look like one."

"That's true. I feel like a freak at these things because I look like I don't belong there. I don't wear ripped jeans and *X-Files* T-shirts."

We ordered our food and a bottle of Merlot. I splurged and got steak frites, extra rare.

"How did the job interview go?" I was hoping it was a bust, but I wanted to appear enthusiastic.

"It was fine. But I'm not going anywhere. All the publishers outside of New York are so small. I'm much better off where I am now."

I smiled. It was the answer I wanted to hear.

"You haven't told me about your parents yet," I said.

"There's not much to tell," he said. "They're boring, they live in the suburbs."

"Well, what does your dad do?"

"He sells life insurance."

"And your mom?"

"Takes care of me and my little brother and my dad. Worries about us."

"She must do something else."

"I don't know. Plays bridge. She works at the vet ten hours a week."

I nodded. I was having trouble relating. My parents considered games like bridge a waste of time and hadn't set foot in a vet's office since I was twelve years old and our cat was put down.

"You know," Andrew said, "I was a little scared of meeting you."

"Why's that?" I grinned.

"Brett said—he said a lot of great things about you—but he sort of made you out to be this party boy. I mean, he is, too, so I guess I—"

"It's okay," I said. "I understand."

"It was funny, the first night when we met, you couldn't seem to remember anything I told you. I think you asked me where I grew up three separate times."

"Too many martinis," I said.

"But you just seemed so comfortable with, you know—"

"Being gay?"

"Yeah, that. I mean, I've only had three boyfriends, two at college and one several summers ago in New York."

"Who was the guy in New York?"

"It was nobody. Just someone I met through friends."

"I don't know," I said. "I think you have it pretty good. You're not jaded, you're not over it all already. I mean, the more you're out, the more shit you see. It's not always a good thing."

"What do you mean?"

I wasn't sure how to phrase this properly. "I feel like some of my friends have made somewhat questionable sexual choices."

And so have I, I thought as soon as I said it.

I could tell he wanted to know more.

"I mean, you know Donovan got a girl pregnant, right?"

"He mentioned something about that. He said she was a friend and he donated the sperm—"

"It was an accident," I said. "They slept together without protection."

"That figures," he said.

"What do you mean?"

"I don't know," he said. "Donovan just seems like a flake."

"And Ja—a friend of mine—might be HIV positive."

"Jesus, really? That shit scares me to death."

"I know," I said. "It scares us all."

Our salads arrived. Without having noticed it, I was already on my third glass of wine. I was feeling a buzz and wanted to have a cigarette. People around us were smoking, but I didn't want to do it at the table. I waited until we had finished our salads.

"Listen," I said, "I'm dying for a cigarette. Do you mind if I just step outside for a moment? I know it's rude, but—I'm sorry."

"It's fine," he said. "Go ahead."

I made my way through the crowded restaurant and stood

outside. As I looked at the passing crowds on Avenue A—the skate rats, the Rastafarians, the neo-punks, the goth kids—I felt like I was bringing an outsider onto my home turf. I may not have fitted in either, but I was certainly more at home than Andrew would ever be.

Just as I was stubbing out my cigarette, I swore I saw Goth Boy walking toward the restaurant. I ducked back inside and navigated my way back through the maze of tables to where we were sitting. I knew I could no longer leave these traces of my past around the city, around the country. It was too risky.

"Feel better?" he said.

"Much." I sat down and placed my napkin back in my lap. "So you haven't dated anyone since you've been out of college?" I asked.

"One person," he said. "But she was a girl."

Shit, I thought, he's bisexual.

"I thought I would try it once. You know, just to see if I was really gay. I had never dated a girl before."

I knew it, I knew it.

"And what happened?"

"We dated for a few weeks. But there was nothing between us."

"Where did you meet her?"

"We worked together. We're still friends. I finally told her I'm, you know—"

"429?" I said. I was almost certain he wouldn't get the reference.

"Yeah, right," he said, smiling that he understood. He took a sip of wine. "Anyway, it was a disaster. She had these weird food allergies. Ordering in a restaurant with her was a nightmare."

"Did you ever, you know, sleep with her?"

"All we ever did was kiss. I had her over to my apartment a few times, and I would always get scared and end the evening."

I was relieved nothing had happened, though I wondered what kind of person could lie to himself like that. What kind of person would hope so desperately that he could be straight?

"You're sure you're gay now?" I said.

"Oh, yeah," he said. "One hundred percent."

*   *   *

After dinner, we walked the few short blocks to my apartment. I lit another cigarette on the way. "Could you not smoke that?" he asked. "I hate the taste of, you know, ashtray mouth."

I stubbed it out, though I was annoyed. Maybe I would have to quit.

"I can brush my teeth when we get home," I said. "Of course, that's not—" I stopped myself. I remembered it wasn't safe to brush your teeth before sex, since it led to the possibility of bleeding gums.

"Not what?"

"Oh, nothing." I didn't want him to think I was at risk, that I had to worry about things like that.

We went right to the bedroom this time and started making out. He lifted his arms up over his head, and I pulled off his shirt. His body was taut but not overly worked out; he had mentioned that he swam each day, a habit he had continued after being on the Brown swim team. Like Donovan, he had almost no chest hair.

We continued kissing as my shirt and pants came off. I was planning on attacking his pants, too, when he lightly pinned me down on the bed. To my surprise, he started kissing my chest, following the trail of hair down past my navel, removing my boxers, and working his tongue over me.

Well, I thought, at least now I know he's really gay.

After about five minutes, he lay down on the bed and slid off his pants. His white shorts gleamed in the dark of the bedroom. I kissed his stomach and breathed in his clean laundry detergent smell as I slid off his boxers.

He groaned as I went down on him.

I wanted to swallow him. I had never done it before, but now I was sure I wanted nothing more. I wanted that feeling of having him in my mouth, him under my control and me under his.

I kept going, even when he tried to wave me off. Eventually, his body started to shake and his leg muscles grew tense.

He continued to groan as he climaxed into my mouth. I didn't gag. I swallowed every bit of it.

I have done this for no one else, I thought, but I will do this for you.

Why did I do it?

Because I was sure he was safe.

Because I didn't care if he was safe.

Because I wanted to own him.

After he finished, he gave me an impish grin.

"You're doing that look again," he said. "You kept doing it in the cab the night I met you."

"What look?"

"You know, the 'Bad Toby' look."

"You mean the 'come hither' look?" I was known to do it when I was drunk or feeling flirty.

"Yeah, the look that says, 'Come do something bad with me.' "

"When I was little," I told him, "I had two teddy bears. One was debonair and wore black tie; the other was scraggly and rough and had devil horns and a little cape."

"And which one are you?"

"I'm both," I said. "But I'm trying to be good."

We chatted for a little while longer, and then Andrew went down on me again. Afterwards, we took a shower together, and I let my body fold into his. I ran my hands over every part of him as the water rinsed us—his smooth ass, his sinewy shoulders, the fuzz on the nape of his neck.

After drying each other off, we fell asleep in each other's arms. It was midnight on a Saturday, and there was nowhere else in the world I wanted to be.

We woke up around 9 A.M. Andrew's hair was a blond tangle and we both had dog breath. I gave his morning erection a tug.

He yawned and then kissed me. "It's nice to wake up like this, isn't it?"

"Maybe you should try it more often."

"I don't know about that," he said. "I never sleep naked."

I wanted to loll around and cuddle, but he jumped in the shower almost immediately.

It was going to take some doing to get him to relax. It would be a project, an agenda.

I remembered I was supposed to have brunch with Donovan and the boys in the West Village, so I invited Andrew to come along.

We arrived at Paris Commune a little after eleven. Jamie and Brett were waiting on the sidewalk. It felt good to be up this early on a Sunday, to be energetic and not hung over.

"Where's Donovan?" I asked.

"Not here yet," Jamie said. He eyed Andrew suspiciously.

Brett winked at me. "Did you two have a good date?"

"We went to Flea Market," I said, avoiding the question.

Donovan, Alejandro, and David all arrived at once and we were led to a table inside. Donovan had just returned from California, where he had visited the pregnant Elizabeth.

"So what was it like?" David asked him after we had all ordered. My former friend's pregnancy was the last thing I wanted to think about. It was exactly the type of event that would hold a curious fascination for David. He had always said his fantasy was to get Alejandro pregnant.

"She's okay," Donovan said. "A bit moody. It's so incredible! She has this *thing* growing inside her." He waved his arms around to illustrate the point. "She let me feel her stomach and it's kicking. It's *kicking.*"

With this last statement, he knocked over his glass of iced tea. It fell to the floor and smashed, spilling tea and ice and broken glass everywhere.

Everyone laughed as Donovan reddened. A waiter rushed over to clean up the mess.

Andrew rolled his eyes at me.

I looked at Donovan across the table and then I looked at Andrew. I realized how foolish I was to have ever been so enamored of Donovan. He was an idiot. He would be saddled with this responsibility, this emotional burden, for the rest of his life, and he didn't even understand what it meant. I was no longer attracted to him, nor did I envy him.

Why had I been so obsessed? Was it because he was someone I couldn't have, someone I saw every day, but who remained unattainable?

Had Jamie been right? Was I not so much in love with Donovan as I was in love with the idea of Donovan?

All I knew now was that the reality of Donovan made me sick.

"What's she going to name the baby?" Alejandro asked after the glass had been cleaned up.

"If it's a girl, she'll be named Tina."

"And if it's a boy?" Jamie asked.

Donovan paused. "You guys are going to think this is weird, but . . . she likes the name Toby. If it's a boy, he'll be named Toby."

"How bizarre," I said, frowning.

"Come on, Toby, the two of you will be friends again," Donovan said. "I'll make sure she comes around."

"Don't waste your breath," I said. After everything that had happened, I realized that I didn't need people like Elizabeth in my life. It was her right not to want to be friends with me, but that didn't mean I had to forgive her when she changed her mind.

After brunch, we all stepped outside. It felt warm, like summer, even though it was only May.

"Let's get cupcakes at Magnolia," Donovan said.

We walked to the bakery down the street and checked out the selection. Andrew and I split one with vanilla frosting.

There was a cute guy working behind the counter. He wore a bandanna and an artfully ripped T-shirt, and he had a nose ring.

"He's totally my type," Donovan said after we had stepped outside again.

"Why don't you ask Cupcake Boy for his number?" I said. "Maybe you can get him pregnant, too."

By now, the party invitations had stopped coming and the word from a former co-worker of Sonia's was that Ariana was furious about the situation. Two more account execs had quit after Sonia, and several studios had pulled their premieres because of the testimony I would be giving.

Amidst the chaos, auditors had examined the ARPR books and discovered that Sunny, Ariana's office manager, had stolen over

$30,000 in cash via a company ATM card. There were rumors that between Ariana's mounting legal costs and her dwindling client roster, she might be forced to close shop or merge with a competitor. Sonia, conversely, had already signed three new clients, including Miles Bradshaw, in her new role as a PR consultant.

To make matters worse for Cameron and Ariana, legal experts were saying they were sure to face individual charges of obstruction of justice, conspiracy, and witness tampering.

Furthermore, Donovan said he had seen Cameron out at a club and he was "looking a little puffy."

On Monday, I started getting calls back about the resumes I had sent out. Several of the companies I had targeted were contacts I had made through working for Cameron; others were editorial contacts of Sonia's. Most places said they weren't hiring currently, or to try again in September. I had put my cell number on my resume so people could reach me directly. I answered one of those calls on Tuesday afternoon, from an assistant at another production company.

"We would love to hire you, Toby," she said, "but there's too much controversy surrounding you right now with the trial and everything. Wait until everything calms down a bit, and then give us a call."

I started to wonder if I would ever have a career in the film business.

As I was sitting in my apartment sorting through my email, I realized the accident could be the end of my story, the defining moment. The semiautobiographical screenplay I wanted to pitch to the studio—and that had been lying dormant on my desk for two months—needed a turning point in the main character's life. I could capitalize on what happened that way; I did own all the rights to my story, after all. But it was a long-term plan, something that could pay off in two or three years, not anything that could help me now.

I had enough money saved to take me to the end of July. After that, I would need to find something permanent.

Andrew and I continued to see each other. It was starting to become a pattern: we would go to dinner, grab a drink at a suitably nonsmoky bar, and then go home. Since I had not worked a full day in an office, I would watch Andrew as he fell asleep and then go into the living room to do some writing or read a novel. Around one in the morning, I would slide into bed next to his bundled-up body clad in pajamas, underwear, and socks. I would watch his quiet breathing until I fell asleep myself, spooned against the curve of his back.

When we woke up together on Saturday morning, he was surprisingly relaxed in bed. He didn't jump in the shower immediately as he had before.

"I was wondering . . ." he started. "Do you want to . . . you know . . ."

"Do I want to what?"

"Try out, um . . ."

"Try out what?" I really didn't know what he was talking about.

"You know, sex."

"Haven't we been having sex?"

"No, I mean . . ."

"Oh, that," I said.

"Yeah," he said, "that."

"Sure," I said. "I mean, it's been awhile since I've done it, but sure."

I went to the bathroom and checked on my box of condoms. I hadn't used any of my own in so long, I was worried they might have expired. The print on the box said they were safe until June, just a few weeks away.

"So, uh, how do you do this?" Andrew asked when I returned.

"You've never put on a condom before?" I asked.

"No," he said.

I smiled and gave him a kiss.

"I'm just going to have to show you everything, aren't I?" I said, grinning.

Some people would have been annoyed, but I approached my assignment with a newfound sense of purpose.

When it was over, he looked euphoric.

"Wow," he said. "So that's what it's like."

"You know something?" I said, nuzzling his neck. "You were my birthday present."

"Oh yeah?" he said.

"And I love my birthday present."

"I love you too," he said.

15

Dating Andrew had a number of side benefits. I had no desire to do drugs anymore, and I knew he wouldn't approve if I did. I was smoking and drinking less. My skin cleared up, and I was even enjoying going to the gym.

That he cared for me made me feel younger, gave me cleanliness and sanctity. Every night I was with him, I was purged of my sins. I felt able to start anew.

Just as my romantic life was falling into place, my career seemed shakier than ever. I had left Sherry another message, but hadn't heard back. I was getting annoyed, but I knew I would have to wait it out.

The following Wednesday, I got a call on my cell phone.

"Is this Toby?" someone said. "This is Maura Goldberg from the *Observer*. I got your number from Sonia. Did you get my other messages?"

I remembered a few recent calls from the *Observer*, but I had deleted them, as I had with all the others from the press.

"I'm not supposed to give any interviews," I said.

"This isn't about an interview," she said. "This is about a job."

Maura Goldberg was the film editor at the *Observer*, and she needed someone to help her with a new listings section.

"I read the article about you that Eli wrote. Between you and me, I'm not crazy about Ariana, and I'm not so big on Cameron, either."

"Really?"

"Trust me, you have so many people on your side for what you've done. Anyway, I want to help you, but most importantly, I'm interested because I've heard you're good. You'd be able to pitch pieces to people around the office. The pay isn't much, but I think you'd enjoy the job."

"When do you need someone?"

"We're not launching the section until September, but we would need you to help design the format and create dummies ahead of time. Why don't you and I plan to meet in a few weeks? You can show me your clips."

I said that sounded good.

"Oh, and Toby, don't stress about it. Sonia and I go way back, and I trust her judgment."

I remembered something, and I realized it couldn't wait until we met in person.

"I was wondering: would you be interested in a recent interview I did with Miles Bradshaw?"

I received a call from from Sherry's office on Friday. Her assistant said they hadn't heard anything from the studio yet.

On Friday evening, Andrew picked me up in his car. It was a beat-up old Cherokee, the kind my San Francisco friends used to drive in high school. He was taking me to see his apartment for the first time.

I told Andrew about the call from Sherry's office.

"It'll happen," he said. "You just have to be patient. Your screenplay is good; they're going to want to meet with you."

"How do you know if it's good?"

He looked sheepish. "You had a few copies lying around the apartment. I snagged one and read it at work."

"You don't think it's silly?"

"Sure, it's silly, but that's why I like it. I mean, *Star Wars* is pretty goofy when you think about it, right? Besides, it's the other project they're interested in that's much more exciting."

We were on the West Side Highway now, heading up toward the Bronx.

"Where are we eating dinner?" I asked.

"We're making it," he said. "I went shopping last night."

"Making dinner?" I said. "You mean, like cooking our own food?"

"Sure," he said. "I do it all the time."

"I haven't used my own oven since I moved in. Donovan used it once, but it was a disaster."

Andrew lived in a white box of an apartment, outfitted with Ikea furniture and mismatched leftovers from his childhood. Some of the walls were decorated with black and white photographs taken by the girl he had dated for several months. I made a note to myself that I would have to do something about them.

That evening, Andrew and I cooked dinner while sharing a bottle of white wine. We made pasta with fresh pesto and grated parmesan, steamed asparagus, and spinach salad with pears, goat cheese, and walnuts. I was impressed with the care he put into preparing the meal.

When we finished, we sat together. I wanted more wine, but I settled for water. I remembered what Brett said about not drinking too much.

"I worry," Andrew said, "that this isn't exciting enough for you."

"What do you mean? This is great."

"You're used to the clubs and bars and everything, and I can't really give you that. I just hate all the smoke and the noise."

"That's fine," I said. "I'm tired of all that stuff anyway."

Andrew had rented a few DVDs for us to choose from, so we picked one and got settled on his couch.

"There's something I want to tell you," I said.

"What's that?"

"My coming out wasn't as easy as I said it was. Actually, it was horrible. I've never told anyone about it."

"What happened?"

I told him the entire story as we sat together. I felt like Andrew might be the first person who would understand, who would accept me even if he knew these truths. The telling—the mere act of releasing the story inside me—made me feel better, started to heal the wound that had been open for so long.

"I'm so sorry you had to go through all that," he said when I had finished.

"You don't think I'm a freak?"

"Of course not," he said. "You're just . . . well, you might be a little overly dramatic at times, but I still like you."

What he thought about it, whether he accepted me or not, shouldn't have mattered, but in that moment, it meant everything.

Andrew had a solitary twin bed, the kind I had slept on as a child. He offered it to me to sleep in that night, and took for himself a small roll-away cot that he kept in the closet. The cot sat several inches lower than the bed, even when they were put side by side. We fell asleep that night holding hands.

In the morning, I looked around his apartment while he was in the shower. On his coffee table, next to a stack of comic books, there was a photo album. I opened it up. It was filled with pictures of his parents, friends from boarding school, parties with co-workers. Then I saw a familiar face. There was a picture of him with Donovan at a bar. They had their arms around each other and were grinning deliriously.

I flipped through the album looking for more photos of them together, but found only the one. What did this mean? Had he and Donovan been friends? Or worse, had they dated? How could I not have known about this? I didn't want to be with someone who had lied to me. There was no way I was going to let myself get into another Xander situation.

I bolted to the bedroom and threw my stuff in my bag.

As I was zipping it up, I heard the shower turn off. A moment later, Andrew emerged from the bathroom in a towel.

"Where are you going?"

"I just, I have to get going," I said.

"Toby, what's going on?"

He followed me into the living room, where I pointed to the photo. "Is this Donovan?"

He blushed and looked away. "I'm sorry. I was meaning to tell you."

"Tell me what?"

"The guy I dated, several summers ago? It was Donovan."

"Why didn't you tell me this earlier? Why didn't he tell me?"

"I don't know. I guess we were embarrassed. It was only for a few weeks. It ended badly, and I didn't want it to get in the way of our being together."

I sank down on the couch.

"I don't understand. Why didn't Donovan give me your number earlier? Had you guys been in touch?"

"We hadn't. I thought he would have mentioned it to you, and then when he didn't . . . well, I guess we both just chickened out."

"Have you guys talked about this? Or are you pretending it never happened?"

"We don't talk about it," he said.

"How did it end?" I asked.

"He cheated on me," Andrew said, shrugging.

How could anyone cheat on Andrew? He was so beautiful and vulnerable, standing in the doorway to his bedroom, only a towel around his waist.

Andrew came over and sat down next to me, putting his hand on my shoulder.

"Is this why you've dated so few people? Because you got dumped by Donovan?"

"I didn't want to get hurt," he said.

"Neither do I. But I guess I just keep throwing myself out there."

As we sat there, him rubbing my back, I decided it wasn't fair of me to expect Andrew to be pure. I wasn't, after all. I realized that I needed to stop imposing my own ideas on what the relationship should be. Even in the short time we had been together, I knew that he loved me, and I loved him back. That was all that mattered.

Still, that day, I called Donovan to ask about it.

"You knew I liked him," I said. "Why didn't you say anything?"

"I wasn't sure it was the same guy, and then it seemed weird, just going up to him saying, 'Hi, I know it didn't work out between us, but I have a friend who wants to meet you.' "

"He said you cheated on him. Why did you do that?"

"I don't know, Toby. Do we have to talk about this? It's in the past." He sighed. "You know, honestly, I don't know why I do half the things I do."

It had been more than six months since Jamie's experience at the crash party. I had been bugging him to get tested for weeks, but he kept putting it off. Finally, he did it, and we both eagerly awaited the results. I had a feeling, though, that I knew what they were going to be.

A week after he got tested, he called me.

"Can you meet me for coffee?" he asked.

"Sure. Can you tell me what the outcome is, though?"

"I'd rather not do it over the phone," he said. A lump started to form in my stomach.

"Just tell me if it's good or bad."

"It's good."

"You mean, you're negative?"

"Just meet me at the Starbucks on Spring Street. I'll explain."

Oh, God, I thought. It's something complicated, like he's positive, but his T-cell count is good.

I took the train down to Soho. Jamie was waiting for me at a table near the back.

"Do you want to get something?" he asked.

"No, just tell me what's going on!"

Why was he stalling like this?

"I'm negative."

"What?" I leaned forward. "You're joking, right?"

"No, I'm serious. I don't have it. Remember how I told you about the false positive and the false negative? Well, this test gives true negatives."

"Jamie, that's great!" I said. I leaned forward to give him a hug.

"Come on, don't make a scene," he said.

I relaxed for a moment. Strangely, though, I felt a twinge of disappointment. Had I wanted Jamie to be positive? Would that somehow make my situation seem less precarious? Suddenly, with Jamie out of danger, I felt like I was the one who was in trouble.

"Now I'm the only one who's screwed."

"What do you mean?" Jamie asked.

"The trial. Having to testify. Having to put my life on display."

"But you're not that person anymore," Jamie said. "You don't party as much. And you're about to sell a screenplay. The person who's on trial is Jordan, not you. You're going to be fine."

"I don't know," I said. "I feel so vulnerable."

"I'll go with you."

"Go where?"

"I'll come to the trial with you. I'll be there for you at the courthouse. I mean, you don't have anyone else to go with you, do you?"

"You're right," I said. "I don't have anyone." I couldn't ask Andrew to come; I knew work was too important to him. Besides, I didn't want my former life bleeding into our relationship.

I took a sip of Jamie's soy latte. "But you can't just take off from work, can you?"

"I have vacation days," Jamie said. "I think this is more important than a vacation."

I took Jamie's hand and kissed it.

He squirmed.

"I love you," I said. "I don't deserve to be your friend."

"I love you, too," he said.

We paused for a moment, looking out at the mid-afternoon shoppers strolling by the window.

"There's something else I wanted to tell you about," Jamie continued. "It's only been a week, but I met this guy online—"

I leaned forward, happy for him.

"And the crazy thing is, he's a temp in word processing at Pelham! He's really cute, and I think he likes me."

I grinned.

"I wanted to ask your advice. Do you think it's too early to invite him to stay with me for a weekend in the Hamptons?"

A few days later, there was a message on my voice mail from Sherry. I called her and was put through immediately.

"I've got good news," she said. "We've got a meeting set up. Can you be in LA next week? The studio will book you a ticket and get you a room at the Standard."

I was thrilled. I knew nothing might come of it, but at the very least, it felt like slow, steady progress.

A few days before I left for Los Angeles, I spent the night at Andrew's. He had bought a new bed at Ikea, so we would have plenty of room.

As usual, he went to bed early, and I stayed up reading. As I thought about being with Andrew, I realized we were fast approaching our six-week anniversary. Unlike my previous relationships, I knew we would stay together. Things weren't perfect and I didn't know if they would last forever, but he made me happy, the happiest I'd been since I moved to New York.

Before heading to bed that evening, I looked down from Andrew's apartment building onto the Bronx, over the Harlem River, past Columbia's football field, towards the city. The glittering lights of downtown looked like they were on another planet as they tumbled in the moonlit fog, beckoning, calling, daring me to come closer.

The day before I left for Los Angeles, my mother was in the city for a meeting, so I made a date with her for afternoon tea at Fred's, the restaurant at Barneys. In this retail emporium, amidst shoppers taking late lunches, she looked less like my mother and more like the fashion doyenne she was.

We ordered tea and sandwiches, and I showed her the article from the *Observer*.

"This really happened to you? With the spinach?" she asked after reading the article. "Unbelievable. These people are beastly. I can't believe I lent a dress to that woman."

"That was my fault," I said.

"You had no way of knowing. At least we got some good press out of it."

"I should have told the police the truth in the beginning," I said. "Such an obvious thing."

"Why didn't you?"

My face grew flushed. "You won't be mad if I tell you this?"

"Of course not."

I explained about Jordan and Cameron and the coke. When I was finished, my mother examined me closely.

"I don't understand this country when it comes to drugs," she said after looking away.

"You're not mad?"

"Toby, you're an adult. You can make your own decisions. You don't need me anymore to tell you what's right or wrong."

I still wanted someone to tell me what was right and what was wrong. But I knew there wasn't anyone in my life who could do that for me.

"The important thing is, you set the situation right again. I'm very proud of you for that. And we know this lawyer is qualified. I had your father look into it."

I smiled. When it came to the important things, my mother rarely failed me.

"Let's talk about something more positive. What about the screenplay? So they're flying you out to LA . . ."

"We'll have a big meeting with the studio, and then a few general meetings that Sherry's set up with other industry people."

"I had no idea you were doing so well," she said. "Your father and I are very proud of you."

"He is?"

"Of course he is. He's always been proud of you."

It had never occurred to me that he was actually on my side. I had always thought of him as someone who was challenging me, someone who was daring me to fail.

"But I wish you would tell us more often about what's going on."

"I guess I just didn't want to tell you about this until something real happened. This feels like I'm getting further than I have in the past."

"You know how many orders I got after my first fashion show?"

She had told me this story before, but I liked it.

"One, right?"

"One order, from Bendel's. Five hundred dollars. It was barely enough to keep the company running for a week. But it was something."

The tea arrived and we were both poured cups.

"I remember my first year in New York," she said. "After I broke up with Henry, I had no money, and I had to work in a dress shop when I wasn't in class. You know what I ate for dinner every night? Steamed vegetables and rice. I used to go on dates just so I could have a good meal. I wore dresses from the shop and then put them back on the rack."

"I can't imagine you not having money," I said.

"Well, imagine it. As they say, not a pretty sight."

"I just feel like so much has happened since I've been here."

"What else?"

I told her about Elizabeth and Donovan and the baby, and I explained what had happened to Jamie and how it would have been my fault if he had been positive. I knew she wouldn't want to hear Jamie's story, that anything AIDS-related was her least favorite topic in the world. But I had to tell her. I was done with keeping secrets. This was my life, and I wanted to talk about it.

"I'm so sorry," she said when I had finished. "No one should have to experience something like that."

She stroked my hand softly. I remembered the last time she had done that. It was when she and my father had met me in the school infirmary in the first two weeks of my freshman year of college. And I remembered I was that same person: I was no different from that Toby who was tired and afraid and wanted to kill himself because it seemed easier than facing the reality of his life. I was that same boy who had gotten himself in trouble. It had happened to me, and I couldn't run away from it any longer.

And I thought, despite everything, how far I had come.

"You should also know I'm with someone new," I said. "I didn't want to tell you because you hate everyone I date."

"Toby, I don't hate everyone you date. I just . . . I just haven't taken a liking to any of them yet."

That was putting it mildly.

"This one is different," I said. "He's wonderful and sweet and he loves me."

"I'm sure he's lovely," she said, and I had the feeling she really meant it, or at least she was going to try.

As I looked at her, I realized my parents were no less confused than I was, that it was unfair of me to expect them to be any better at raising a son than I was at being one.

After she paid the check, we got up and she gave me a hug. I pushed my face into her hair, afraid I was going to cry. I knew, though, that my mother didn't believe in wallowing, so we left the restaurant and walked through the main lobby together, past gloves and handbags, scarves and cosmetics.

The two of us stood together on the sidewalk, in front of a glorious display of hats, and it was warm, and there was that blooming spring smell mixed with taxicab exhaust in the air.

We said goodbye, and I headed downtown once again.

THE TROUBLE BOY

TOM DOLBY

ABOUT THIS GUIDE

The suggested questions are intended to enhance your group's
reading of Tom Dolby's *The Trouble Boy*

DISCUSSION QUESTIONS

1. Toby Griffin is a character that readers have alternately compared to Holden
   Caulfied in *Catcher in the Rye*, Bridget Jones in *Bridget Jones' Diary*, Carrie
   Bradshaw in *Sex and the City*, and the nameless narrator of *Bright Lights,
   Big City*. How is Toby similar to or different from these characters?

2. It could be said that Toby is often delusional about achieving fame and success in New York. What are Toby's delusions about succeeding as a screenwriter? Are they realistic ambitions for a young person to have, ambitions
   that can motivate him to greater heights, or do they threaten to destroy
   him?

3. Some of the characters in *The Trouble Boy* don't have proper names; they
   are referred to as Subway Boy, Goth Boy, Decorator Guy, Real World Guy, or
   Army Guy. Why does the narrator refer to some characters with proper
   names and others with nicknames? Is there a pattern there? What signifi-
   cance does the title of the novel have in light of these nicknames?

4. *The Trouble Boy* is not a "coming out novel," and yet the third chapter
   portrays an important coming out episode in Toby's life. What other types
   of coming out does Toby have to do throughout the course of the novel?

5. The third chapter of the novel is told in the third person. Why do you think
   the author chose to tell this part of Toby's backstory in this way?

6. Some of the sexual encounters in the book are portrayed in a way that is
   very graphic, and others, especially toward the end of the novel, are merely
   hinted at. Why do you think the author decided to portray the sex life of a
   twenty-two-year-old like this? Is there a pattern to the portrayal of sexual

encounters in the book? How do Toby's issues with antidepressants and his libido play into this?

7. One of Toby's character traits is that he doesn't realize that he often treats others as poorly as people treat him. Is his behavior justified? Is it a harsh fact of gay urban life (or even urban life in general) that there will always be some sort of "pecking order"?

8. How do the car crash and potential for criminal prosecution function in the novel? If they had not occurred, would Toby have found redemption in some other way? How do you think his habits will change as he goes on with his life? What would you have done if you were placed in the same situation?

9. Toby clearly has issues with drugs and alcohol, and yet the author never forces him to make any hard decisions about his substance use and abuse. Does Toby "hit bottom" in other ways? Did you want Toby to address his issues with substances directly, or did you feel it was implied that he would clean up his act?

10. One of the great fears Toby has during the novel is that of contracting HIV. How does his fear manifest throughout the novel? Why is it that when confronted with his friend Jamie's dilemma, his reaction is first compassion, then prejudice? Is Toby's judgment of those with HIV insensitive, or is it simply a defense mechanism against something that he fears?

11. The novel interweaves a number of social issues through the plot: alcohol and drug abuse, male eating disorders, safer sex, pregnancy, and HIV/AIDS. In many instances, Toby judges his friends for making choices to which he himself is not immune. Is it unfair of Toby to judge his friends? Is he judging them as a substitute for judging himself?

12. Toby often says and does things that aren't nice or compassionate. While he is not always a nice character, is he sympathetic? What are the ways in which you can or can't sympathize with Toby?

13. While Toby ultimately finds love with Andrew, one of the most intimate relationships in the book is the friendship between Toby and Jamie. How is this portrayed in the last scene between Toby and Jamie? Is it possible that while Andrew becomes Toby's boyfriend, the real love affair of the book is between Toby and Jamie?

14. In the final scene in the novel, Toby has tea with his mother, and tells her about what has been happening in his life. How does this scene conclude the novel? What are the ways in which Toby wants to please his parents, or gain their love and acceptance?

15. *The Trouble Boy* is a novel in which many of the characters are gay, and yet it deals with issues that pertain to many readers, gay and straight, male and female. Would you classify the book as "gay literature"? How important are such classifications to you before you read a novel?